A.R Kimberlin is a born romantic. Living in the Midlands, with her husband, Mark, a gorgeous Brummie backpacker she met in Cyprus over thirty years ago, and her beautiful daughter, Em. She loves to people-watch, read and write and get lost in romance and drama novels, whilst drinking a large spiced rum.

This book is dedicated to the most amazing woman I know, my lovely mum.

A.R Kimberlin

ALL FOR LOVE...

AUSTIN MACAULEY PUBLISHERS™

LONDON ★ CAMBRIDGE ★ NEW YORK ★ SHARJAH

A CIP catalogue record for this title is available from the British Library.

ISBN 9781398452961 (Paperback)
ISBN 9781398452978 (ePub e-book)

www.austinmacauley.com

First Published 2022
Austin Macauley Publishers Ltd®
1 Canada Square
Canary Wharf
London
E14 5AA

A huge thank you to Mark, Em and Jack for all of your support. To all of my family, friends and my besties. Thank you to Austin Macauley for having faith in my work and publishing my first novel.

Chapter 1

Ava sat on the edge of the wooden arbour, her eyes gently closed against the late afternoon sun. As she wiggled her toes in the soft, powdery white sand, she tried to ignore the stabbing pain in her side and the pounding headache that seemed to be getting worse. She contemplated the events of the last two weeks and wondered how everything could go so dreadfully wrong? Just when she thought all in her life was going well, really well, it all falls apart.

She let out a long sigh and slowly opened her heavy eyes to reveal the tropical paradise before her. The idyllic beach was lined with gently swaying palm trees, their leaves just catching the gentle ocean breeze. The stunning aqua marine waters softly lapped the soft, white sand of the shore. It truly was the most beautiful place she had ever seen.

She looked down at her torn, blood-stained dress and cringed at the thought of how much it had cost. It was now in tatters, like her life. She shook her head slowly, trying to ignore the pounding pain and gazed at her discarded Manolo's, embedded in the sand, to the right of her feet. The sun was starting to lower in the clear blue sky, meaning the relentless heat of the day was subduing slightly. Although nestled under a white satin covered shade, she was still catching the sun and she knew she couldn't sit here much longer. She turned slowly, ignoring the spasm of pain that shot through her ribs. She took in the damage behind her.

The overturned altar table, the shells, which had scattered and shattered across the floor. The stunning flowers, now in pieces, their petals strewn all over the decking, spilling on to the surrounding sand. Behind the arbour, were the rows upon rows of empty seats, all except the front right-hand row.

There, looking as if they had been dragged through a hedge backwards, were her family. The people who had been on this journey with her, in the hopes of a happy ending. There was now no hope, it was all over. There, underneath the expansive, crisp, white canopy, they at least had some protection from the sun's strong rays. Ava gazed at these four individuals, who apart from her little sister Kit and Lou's younger brother Dan, were the most important people in her life.

Rachel sat in the nearest seat to the aisle, fast asleep and gently snoring. As bridesmaids, they all wore different styles of teal chiffon gowns. Each bespoke and tailored for their individual shape and character. Rachel's was long, flowing and off the shoulder. She loved the feminine look and had felt incredible wearing it. Rachel's head was resting on Lou's shoulder. Although much curvier than Rachel, Lou wore a strapless, tight-fitting, ankle-length dress, with a large daring split up the front left leg. She was swigging out of a large bottle of champagne, painstakingly decorated with small, hand painted white flowers. Lou had liberated it from the ice bucket, which was now lying amongst the wreckage, on the floor of the arbour. On top of what she had already drunk today, Ava was amazed to see her friend still conscious.

Next to Lou, was the doll like frame of Bella. Her halter necked, fitted dress showing off her petite frame perfectly. The lower part of the dress consisted of layer, upon layer of graded teal petticoats, creating a princess effect skirt. A huge diamante flower adorned the left-hand side of her tiny waist. Bella had zoned out of the drama and was sitting sideways on the chair. Her skirt ruffled and bunched up on her lap, exposing her legs. One of them strapped up in heavy black support, that covered her ankle, up to just above her knee, both resting over Jez's lap. Ava realised that Bella had been crying as dark streaks ran down her perfectly made-up cheeks, revealing the red, blotchy skin that lay beneath. A black wobbly line was making its way down from her left eyebrow, running into her eye and clashing with her eye makeup, making her look like a rather sad panda. Even after all that had happened today, Jez looked like he was modelling for an Armani fashion shoot. He sat laid back on the chair, with his long arms spreading wide across the seats either side of him. His midnight blue, navy tux still immaculate and the only difference from when she had last looked at him, was that he had taken off his jacket and undone his bow tie, letting it fall either side of the unbuttoned crisp white shirt. His scorching gaze was directed squarely at Ava, they locked eyes and she knew he had been watching her like a hawk, whilst she had sat and tried to regain her dignity. She knew she had to move; however, her head was throbbing and the pain in her ribs was escalating. She turned away from Jez to face the stunning shoreline again. Still mortified at the events that had transpired earlier that day and wondering how it had it all so gone so wrong.

Chapter 2

As the battered sea plane finally made its bumpy landing on the sparkling topaz ocean, the chatter in the tiny sweltering cabin grew louder. Although tired and overheated, Ava was smiling and relaxed as she nudged him awake. Jez had sat next to her, domineering the space in the cramped seats. He had fallen asleep before take-off, completely missing the fifty-minute journey and the spectacular scenery that this flight had allowed. Ava had actually enjoyed the sea plane, although it was the last part of a very long journey and a little claustrophobic and noisy, the views had been spectacular.

A small desk fan, secured in the corner of the cabin, with red, plastic cable ties, simply blew around the hot air, its whirring noise adding to the din of the plane engine. Everyone was sweating and uncomfortable, however their spirits were high. This was an incredible opportunity for them all to spend time together and celebrate, in such a beautiful environment.

Ava had looked out of her small window in awe, marvelling at every deserted island they had flown over and admiring the amazing blues and turquoises of the crystal-clear waters below. Jez rubbed his face with his hands, his eyes opening slowly, squinting as the rays of sun streaked though the cabin, onto his handsome face. Even after twenty-four hours of travelling, he still managed to look like a film star. His dark brown hair still perfectly coiffured, his stubbled jawline made him look even hotter than usual, his mouth twisting into a wry smile as he spoke, "I slept the whole flight?" he questioned.

Ava nodded and grinned, "Great company you were!" she said teasing him.

He stretched his arm around Ava's shoulders and squeezed her even closer to him.

"For god's sake, can we get off this tin can? I need a wee and I'm sweating like a pig on heat!" a loud, female voice came from the seats behind and both Ava and Jez looked at one another and laughed.

"It's not funny you two, I'm busting," the strong voice retorted.

Ms Louise Hunter, or Lou to her close friends, of which there were very few, was not happy. This had been the worst part of the long fun-filled journey for her.

"Lou, we haven't even been flying for an hour yet, surely even you can cross your legs for that long?" Jez smirked as he spoke, receiving a loud slap around the side of his head, for his cheek.

The seaplane was now bobbing gently towards a long, wooden-decked pier. At the end of the pier, was a row of cushioned benches, underneath a large, white sail canopy, presumably for the loading and unloading of the sea plane.

"An hour is a long time for Lou," Rachel piped up from a few seats behind.

"Rach!" a little voice scolded; Bella had sat quietly for the short flight.

She was fighting the overwhelming urge to sleep, as she didn't want to miss a second of this spectacular journey. Being the quiet one in the group, she didn't usually get involved with the banter and teasing, however a rather large Bacardi and coke on the last flight had slightly increased her bravery. The usual mouse-like, tea-total Bella Ricci, had grown some confidence with the help of her liquid courage, which she could still feel swilling around her system.

"Well, if I'd have known there were no toilets, I'd have opted for the speed boat," a grumpy Lou argued.

Like the others she was exhausted from the long journey, but also miffed that there was absolutely no eye candy on this flight.

"There are no toilets on a speed boat either" countered Rachel with a huge grin on her face.

She loved winding Lou up. Everyone was laughing now, even the bare foot pilots, who were busy flicking switches and pulling levers in the tiny cockpit that was visible from the cabin. Lou had already tried it on with the main pilot whilst boarding. He was a thirty something Australian and Lou had decided his tanned, fit body would do. However, much to her chagrin he had turned her advances down, something she was not used too. Her curvy body and strong independent nature, meant she was never without a man. Lou had the most beautiful, smooth, caramel skin and could have easily been a plus size model. Instead, she ran a PR company with a rod of iron and spent her evenings and weekends with any man she chose. She had hooked up with a fellow traveller at Manchester airport and was nearly kicked out of the airport lounge for inappropriate behaviour. It was only because the timid female manager was literally swooning over Jez and his smouldering smile, that she didn't call the airport security. On the flight to Dubai,

Lou had hit it off with a handsome air steward. They had both disappeared for a good thirty minutes behind the privacy curtain that usually indicated the stewards were on a break during a long flight.

Upon her return, a flustered looking Lou had loudly informed the rest of the first-class cabin, that "Not all male cabin crew are gay!"

A few passengers had tittered, finding her funny. Bella was mortified and had hid herself under her blanket. The other passengers, including members of their group, gave Lou disapproving looks. You could hear some of the weary travellers' tutting, every time she left her seat to preclude another alcoholic beverage, not having the patience to wait for it to be offered.

Ava and Jez had pretended to be gripped by an inflight film, so they didn't have to get involved. In Dubai airport, Bella had quietly had words with Lou, telling her that she needed to slow down on the gin, which she had been knocking back since arriving at Manchester airport. She also tried to dissuade her from hooking up with strange men, however, as usual, Lou did exactly what she wanted.

Dan, Lou's younger brother had completely given up lecturing her years ago, as Lou was strong willed and fiercely independent and never listened to a word he said anyway. He had also inherited the youthful, good looking, 'Hunter' genes. His skin tone was slightly lighter than Lou's, his luxurious, caramel complexion would soon darken under the tropical sunshine and although not as loud and outgoing as his boisterous sister, his laid back, easy come, easy go nature, was a pleasure to be around. He used to get embarrassed about his sister's shenanigans, but now he just accepted that she was a boozy, sex addict and nothing would ever stop her. He loved and adored his sister and the rest of his little family who were on this journey with him and was just looking forward to the next three weeks of no work, lots of sunshine and possibly, dare he say it, a little romance.

Rachel had enjoyed the long flights, being able to watch films, completely uninterrupted. Finding the latest albums that she listened to on her entertainment system in her exclusive pod, she had relaxed in style, sipping cocktails and listening to music from her favourite singers and bands. This was sheer heaven. No hassle, no stress, just peace, quiet and relaxation. The huge comfortable seats were amazing, she could actually lie flat if she chose to do so and it would not inconvenience the person behind, as the pod area was so spacious. This was really the only way to travel, she thought to herself as Adele's smooth voice, sang into her posh head set, the sound just incredible. She had been on lots of holidays to Europe, travelling economy class, or cattle class, as her husband called it. This, however, was seriously out of this world and was she going to make the most of every second, as there would be no way she could ever afford to do this again.

She had felt so guilty, waving off her family at the airport. Her two daughters crying at the fact they wouldn't be seeing their mum for a whole three weeks, not wanting to end their last hug with her. Her husband squeezing her tightly and kissing her forcefully, with such love and appreciation, it had almost made her turn round and go straight home. Instead, she had put a brave face on it, knowing that this was a chance in a lifetime, she really wanted to be part of this wonderful occasion and spend some quality time with her extended family. After a mini meltdown in the toilets of the designer airport lounge, Ava had hugged her tightly and given her a glass of prosecco, which she downed in one. After that she had calmed down, knowing her family could cope without her for the next few weeks. Her work would still be there on her return and she was going to make sure she had a bloody good time.

Bella had been in the pod next to her; her seat lowered into the lying position. She had snuggled under a soft fleece blanket, fast asleep for most of the long flights. Bella had worked both night and day to get the dresses completed up to her ridiculously high standards. She had a few bits to finish off, but as an elite couturier, she had created four commissioned bridesmaid dresses and one wedding dress, that she was proud to say were the best she had ever made. The hours of sweat, toil and worry she had put in, had left her completely exhausted. An avid reader, she had saved Ava's latest novel to read on the journey, however, after the excitement and nerves of her first ever take off had worn off, she had realised how tired she was and decided to take a nap. Her face had been a picture as she clung on to Rachel's hand, during the planes rally down the runway. She felt completely light headed as the wheels had left the ground and the huge plane had somehow managed to climb high into the cloudy grey skies, soon leaving the sprawling city of Manchester below.

Rachel smiled and stroked her friend's shoulder, trying to reassure her. She felt a little motherly towards Bella and was glad she too was getting a well-deserved rest.

Dan had his designer headphones on, nodding his head to the beats of his latest mix. An up-and-coming DJ, he was more than excited that he had been asked to perform at this special event, although he did find it unnerving when the plane hit any turbulence. His precious records were safely stowed in the hold, but he was still anxious that they wouldn't survive the long journey unscathed.

There were only sixteen seats in the sea plane cabin and the pilots were literally in front of Ava and Jez, there was no separate cockpit and space was extremely limited. Their little group had been the only one travelling to the island today, so they had boarded the sea plane with no issues and in high spirits at Male airport. Their cases had been placed in the back of the plane and spilled over to some of the seats. Ava could now understand why there were such strict baggage restrictions to be adhered to and why each item of luggage had been deftly weighed before loading. God knows how Lou managed to get three weeks of clothes and toiletries into one twenty-kilogram case. She liked to dress well and had expensive taste, so pretty much everything she owned had a designer label, even down to the Louis Vuitton luggage.

Rachel had also brought along Louis Vuitton luggage, but hers was a knock off from her last holiday to Spain. She had heard so much about Lou's designer cases that she had decided to buy her own, just to wind her up. As Lou's face had been literally stuck to another human's at the check-in desk, she hadn't yet seen Rachel's posh luggage, but boy were the whole group looking forward to the moment that she noticed it.

A cooling breeze blew through the cabin as the young assistant (also bare foot) opened the side door of the cabin and leapt out onto the sea planes floats, in order to secure it to the pier. They had finally arrived in paradise.

Reethi Loabi was a Maldivian island, surrounded by crystal clear waters of a lagoon and a magnificent array of marine life. Its name, roughly translated, meant 'beautiful love'. The island was incredibly exclusive and usually occupied by affluent couples celebrating their weddings and honey moons, or wealthy, older couples who had achieved years of wedded bliss, deciding to make it to a once in a lifetime, special wedding anniversary. Celebrities also stayed here as it was so remote and blissfully peaceful. At around one hundred and twenty acres, it boasted six restaurants, two spas, beach bars, a nightclub, casino, and several intimate dining areas. It was a place for the rich and famous to hang out in opulent luxury. However, this was the first time ever that the whole island had been booked for one special, lavish, tropical wedding.

After a few minutes, their group was asked to alight the cabin, which was easier said than done. The first part of the jetty was actually a float, so with the seaplane and the jetty both moving in different directions with the waves, it took a time to navigate them. After their sea legs adjusted and their backs and arms had been stretched out, the group chatted happily whilst walking in the glorious sunshine, along the large wooden pier. Taking in the stunning beaches on either side, the group were delighted to find at least ten members of staff lined up against a thatched structure, housing huge comfy chairs and a well-stocked bar. They were dressed in long white tunics and dark green cumber bands and began to clap their hands and sing, as the weary travellers approached. Each guest was gracefully bestowed a beautiful lei of flowers, gently placed over their heads. The staff wore genuine welcoming smiles and were immaculately turned out. The last member of staff in the line was carrying a large tray of orange and yellow cocktails, garnished with exotic flowers and classy silver expandable straws. Everyone gratefully accepted the delicious concoction, even Bella took one. This was only out of politeness, as she was aware that drinking could be the start of a dangerous habit.

As the weary travellers each took a large comfortable seat, they were introduced to the island's manager, Amir. He was a kind looking, elderly gentleman, with clipped, white hair and a twinkle in his eye. He wore a white suit, a matching white waistcoat and a dark green bow tie. As he made his way around the group, he firmly shook the men's hands and gallantly took the ladies hands and planted a soft kiss on each. As he welcomed his important guests, he advised that they were some of the first of the wedding guests to arrive and that over the next two weeks, the island would be greeting a full complement of guests and staff.

Ava swallowed slightly at the "staff" comment, as she tried not to worry about being the lowly working-class guests. The wedding party comprised mostly of ultra-wealthy people, who had their own paid staff to do their every bidding, from personal hairdressers to security teams. They were simply in another world from her and her little family. She shuddered at the thought of security teams roving around, it seemed pretty pointless, as they were on an island in the middle of nowhere.

As she sipped her delicious cocktail and felt the cool liquid slip down her throat, she gazed out at the glorious ocean view, the white powdery beach, surrounded by gently swaying palms and the soft lapping of the ocean waves as they ebbed and flowed onto the sand.

Amir was informing the group of the island's amenities, which of course were all complimentary. Ava closed her eyes briefly and breathed in the warm ocean air. This place was truly idyllic. Jez nudged her and she opened her eyes wide and blinked a few times. Jez's hand had rested on her shoulder as his long finger gently traced the line of her neck. She smiled at him and then in turn to each one of these amazing people, who were about to share this adventure with her and make some incredible memories.

After the brief welcome talk, Amir indicated to his staff that the new guests were ready to be shown to their rooms, with a simple nod of his head. Seven gentlemen identically dressed in the white tunic and dark green sash, surged forward and collected the hand luggage, from the small wooden tables in front of the guests. Each beckoned a traveller and Ava noted the young man escorting her, had the name Abdul, displayed on a shiny badge on the left of his chest.

"Thank you, Abdul," she said gratefully, as she was now wanting nothing more than a shower and a change of clothes.

Abdul smiled broadly and gestured with his hand, for Ava to follow him.

"At least we are all in the same area," Bella sounded a little nervous.

Rachel grabbed her hand and whispered kindly, "We are in heaven; you have nothing to be frightened of."

"I still need a wee," moaned Lou and with the sound of laughter taking over the hushed sounds of the waves, the group made their way to their accommodation for the next three weeks.

The group were spread between three large electric-buggies that gently navigated their way past thatched buildings and tropical gardens. After a five minute pootle along a sand flattened path, the three buggies slowed down to a stop. There was a gap in the tropical foliage and a small wooden sign, with the words 'Water Villas' intricately carved out. They "trekked through the jungle" as Lou had not so discreetly put it, in reality, a two-minute walk down a sandy path, lined with tropical trees and bushes.

At the end of the winding path was an opening, revealing another magnificently stunning beach. This one had a wooden path across it, leading onto a long-curved jetty, which protruded out into the sea. Following the curved jetty led them to the impressive-looking water villas. The group all stopped walking and gawped at the villas.

"There must be some mistake," said Rachel politely, "we should be in garden villas."

The older member of staff spoke up, "As you are a very special party ma'am, your rooms were upgraded, we will be taking very special care of you all ma'am."

He gestured towards the start of the jetty. The group erupted into excited chatter, nearly all of them delighted with this news. They made their way onto the wooden decked path, which carried them across the deserted beach. The decking led them directly onto the beginning of the jetty, which itself was raised on stilts, stretching out into the ocean.

As they reached this point, Ava stopped dead in her tracks. To the right of where she stood, there was a small step on to the sandy, inviting beach. Jez turned as if sensing her fear and walked back to where she was frozen to the spot. Abdul and Jez's escort stayed back at a respectful distance. Jez stood in front of her, put both hands on her warm cheeks and adjusted her view from the ocean to his face. He stared intently into her eyes.

"You are safe…you are with me," he said seriously, "we really need to conquer this fear Ava. This is a dream vacation."

Ava's face crunched up in disgust at the use of the word 'vacation' and Jez grinned. Being a jet setting super model, he had travelled the world and picked up words and phrases as he went.

"You mean holiday," she smiled weakly and again her gaze drifted to the jetty.

Her fear of the ocean was huge, her fear of sharks even greater. *Come on get a grip*, she scolded herself and tried to focus on the fact she had been upgraded out of kindness and should be grateful. Letting out a deep breath she looked back at his gorgeous face.

"I will hold your hand the whole way." Jez consoled her and grabbing her hand, pulled her gently, but forcibly towards the start of the jetty, with Abdul and his colleague walking quickly on ahead.

Jez was very gentlemanly and directed Abdul to show Ava to her room first, so that he could remain by her side, tightly gripping her hand. She didn't know if it was the weariness of travelling, lack of sleep or the number of drinks she had consumed during the last few hours, but she felt as if the decking was moving beneath her feet. Her water villa was one of the last rooms on the extensive curve. Each villa was widely spaced apart, with the curve of the deck, allowing every room an isolated, private area with a glorious, uninterrupted view of the ocean.

Jez followed Abdul through the door of what was going to be Ava's home for the next three weeks. She squeezed his hand tightly as they entered, the air conditioning an instant relief to the intense heat of the midday sun. They both stood speechless, gawping at the view that lay before them.

The villa was a colossal, octagon shaped construction. Consisting of different shades of wood, it was incredible to think it was standing on stilts, in the middle of the sea. On entering the room, your eyes were drawn to the enormous, sliding-glass walls, that gave the occupier an unobstructed view of the stunning ocean vista. It was amazing and even with a shiver of dread that sharks may be swimming around underneath her room, Ava had to agree this was the most stunning sight she had ever seen.

"Wow," said Jez.

"This is awesome!" he whistled and walked over to the doors, dragging Ava behind him.

"Your case is here ma'am." Abdul gestured to the right-hand side of the massive room, where there were ginormous dark wood double wardrobes and a case stand where Ava's silver suitcase had been neatly placed.

"There are jackets and umbrellas in the wardrobe ma'am and your refreshments, towels and bedding is replaced daily. If you need anything at all please dial zero for the water villa's reception," he pointed to a phone sitting on a small table along with a bouquet of beautiful flowers. "We can help twenty-four hours, day or night." He finished with a nod.

Ava broke free of Jez's grip and went to retrieve her purse to give Abdul a tip.

As if knowing this was the plan, Abdul held his hands up and shook his head. "No tipping is permitted ma'am; it is all taken care of ma'am."

Abdul nodded again and went to the door where Jez's escort was waiting patiently.

Suddenly Jez's arms embraced her from behind as he gave her a big squeeze before kissing the top of her head.

"Right then," he said brightly letting her go and walking to the front door. "Shower, then bar!" he smiled his killer megawatt smile, that every woman swooned over and Ava couldn't help returning it.

"Later tater," he said with a wink and closed the door.

"We are actually here!" she whispered to herself as she turned back to the wall of glass, standing in awe and gazing at the devastatingly impressive ocean view.

Chapter 3

Standing in the cool of the air-conditioned room, rejuvenated her tired limbs. The aches and pains of the long journey here and the sweat box of the sea plane, were all soon forgotten and she just stood in the room, gazing at the stunning scene laid out before her.

Time stood still and it seemed like an age before Ava could tear herself away from the spectacular panoramic ocean view. It was quite relaxing watching the surf breaking on the coral reef, off in the distance. Ava could see the tropical coloured fish, darting about in the crystal-clear turquoise waters below. There were large pockets of clear sand banks amongst the swaying kelp, fish scuttling around, beneath the gentle waves below.

Behind the expansive glass walls, stood a large private decking area, enclosed by a rustic wooden rail. To the left of the outside deck, sat a table and chairs, to the right a huge day bed, with a dark green padded mattress and soft, cotton cushions. Neatly rolled matching towels lay at the end of the bed, all of which was shaded by a large white canopy. Also, under this welcome shaded area, a box-like side table and a luscious green leaved, tropical plant, sat in a massive terracotta pot. Ava smiled as she knew she would be spending a lot of time on that bed, as she had work to complete. She would have to put aside time each day and dedicate it to getting some chapters completed. After all, she had a deadline to meet. This had nothing to do with her publishers, they were delighted with her work and as her novels were always handed in early, they had never put any pressure on her for strict completion dates. She was their highest earning author and the publishing company knew they were lucky to have her.

She approached the huge glass wall and finding a small latch, clicked it open. The glass wall slid effortlessly to the side, opening up the private decking area. Taking a deep breath, she bravely stepped out.

Steps led down to a smaller decking area, with two large padded sun loungers, the same dark green fluffy towels rolled and perched neatly at the foot of each bed. Another set of steps presumably led down to the water below. Ava shuddered; *I won't be going down those* she thought. She turned to admire her unusual accommodation, stepping back inside, she closed the huge glass wall smoothly.

This villa really was incredibly luxurious and she felt like a complete fraud being here. Ava was well travelled, however this island, this place, was simply spell binding. Stunning exotic blooms were dotted around the room and the floral scent was simply divine. The humungous wooden four poster bed, looked fit for a princess, with sheer white netting delicately tied at each corner. Above the bed was a large dark wood ceiling fan, which was gently whirring round. The air con was obviously working well, as her whole body had cooled down, the second she had stepped back inside.

Beautifully carved bedside tables stood on either side of the magnificent bed, one holding a sophisticated looking digital clock and docking station. In the corner, there was a large, well-stocked, glass-doored, fridge. Ava made her way over and whilst retrieving a can of pop, she was delighted to find a number of chocolate bars, along with red, white and rose wine, beers, spirits and selection of soft drinks. With a huge, satisfied smile she decided she would definitely have a glass or two of red wine and a chocolate bar later. On the other side of the bed was a huge comfortable looking settee, two chairs and a large glass coffee table with scattered seashells and a beautiful glass bowl filled with stunning white flowers. She walked over to the table and picked up and examined each shell carefully. For someone scared of the ocean, well actually… sharks, Ava was fascinated with shells. Her favourite past time on holidays, was beach combing for shells, which she would clean and take home with her.

Once she had finished admiring each shell on the table, she made her way past the wardrobe and her unopened case, to the door on the right-hand side of the room. As she pushed the door gently, she gasped loudly. The bathroom was almost as big as the bedroom, but the whole left-hand wall was glass, with sliding glass panels leading onto the side of the decking area. Two ceramic basins sat neatly side by side, underneath a vast mirror, that covered the side wall and expanded to fill half the wall, floor to ceiling. There was a gargantuan walk-in shower, with a cerulean tiled bench in it. The blue tiles reflected the sun's rays and the ocean that sparkled beneath it. Enormous shells decorated the room and a ladder rail made from dark wood, held an array of fluffy blue towels, each the same colour as the surrounding tiles. There was a toilet, *(my goodness what a view you would have from there)* and an immense bath that looked big enough for at least two people. She blushed and quickly chastised herself for being shocked by the size of it all. She realised this must be for couples, honeymooners enjoying romantic, quality time with each other and suddenly she felt a deep sadness and an overwhelming feeling of being alone. She shivered and felt the unmistakable hole in her broken heart. She had not felt like this for a long time and she was certainly not going to let her sadness spoil this memorable occasion.

She shook her head, "Unpacking," she said out loud to herself and taking a sip of her pop, she busied herself with unpacking her belongings, charging her beloved iMac laptop and neatly hanging her clothes in the immense wardrobe.

She did have a moment of panic when she noticed the life vests neatly stowed at the bottom of the wardrobe. A small sign simply read 'For Tsunami use'. She closed her eyes and tried not to think about it. Her body was now tired and aching from the long journey, however, as enticing as the bath looked, she chose to shower quickly.

Figuring out the state-of-the-art display took a few minutes, but once she finally got it working, she let out a long sigh. Relishing the power of the incredibly powerful jets, that blasted her entire body, she was glad she had chosen to shower. The toiletries that were already in the shower also smelt divine, leaving her whole body smelling of coconut, her favourite scent. Revived in both spirit and mind, she dressed in a red halter neck dress and was just tying up her damp blonde hair, when Jez hammered on the door shouting, "Cocktails for two?"

It was early evening and the group had unwound with a large number of fabulous cocktails and a mouth-wateringly delicious, gourmet meal. They sat on huge cushioned chairs, sipping their drinks and watching the incredible sunset over the calm ocean. It was still clammy and hot, although the intense heat from the sun had gone for the day. The group hadn't seen any other wedding guests since they arrived, however, they had been told a small number had arrived late afternoon. The happy, weary travellers discussed their amazing accommodation, asking each other if they had seen this or found that. They all laughed heartily when they discussed the chocolate supply as Jez informed them all he had devoured three chunky KitKat like bars called Dido's, and four beers whilst getting ready. Where on earth he put it all, in his toned fit body, amazed the whole group.

They moved onto their plans for the next day and Lou was raving to them all, that she was going to get an all over tan. She apparently planned on sunbathing completely naked on her private sundeck.

Bella, who was completely mortified that her friend may expose herself to any would be passing swimmer, and indeed fish, was strongly advising her against such an action. She had declined the amazing cocktails and stuck to her usual diet Pepsi. She didn't like not being in control, plus she had work to do tomorrow. Delicate adjustments needed to be made to her beautiful works of art and, the dresses needed to be perfect. For that to happen she needed to have a good night's sleep and no hangover in the morning.

"You do realise that that's illegal?" She warned Lou.

"Illegal?" questioned Dan.

"Yes," she replied tartly, "we are not at home now you know" she countered.

"We're certainly not at home," smiled Rachel.

Feeling mellow and relaxed with the abundance of food and drink, she was now watching the surf as it gently ebbed and flowed against the deserted beach. The sun had set quickly and watching the glowing orange orb lower itself into the distant line of the ocean, had been the highlight of a truly wonderful day. Rachel loved her family, however, this wonderful group of people sat beside her, were the family she had chosen. Dear friends that she could not live without. She knew they all felt the same way about each other. A group of oddballs that somehow got on and stuck together through thick and thin.

"You look so happy Rach." Jez interrupted her reverie.

"I am." She let out a long-relaxed sigh. "How could I not be, somewhere like this. This has to be the poshest, most beautiful place I have ever been to."

She looked around at her travel companions and felt an overwhelming sense of love for them. How lucky was she to have an amazing family life, that included these gorgeous friends who knew her inside and out and back to front. She beamed as she took in each of their familiar features, in the dimly lit evening light.

Small solar lights had flickered to life on the glass covered, wooden drink's tables, dotted between the chairs. Lanterns lit the edge of the beach area, sending off a comforting glow. The moonlight gave off a bright light that provided the gently swaying palms with long dark silhouettes. It was still balmy; however, the gentle waves brought a slight breeze to the shore, for which everyone was grateful.

A shriek pierced the tranquillity as Lou suddenly stood up, spilling her drink all over Dan who, who was sitting the closest to her.

"Lou?" Ava who had been sitting quietly taking in the conversation whilst admiring the spectacular view, immediately raced over to her friends' side, "What is it, what's wrong?"

Lou pointed to a palm tree just to the right of them, all heads turned and as their eyes adjusted to the shadows, they could make out the silhouette of a large palm tree. There was a loud rustling in the leaves near the top, a sort of scratching noise, as the group gawped at it in silence.

"It's probably a lizard or something." Dan whispered, more to himself then anyone in particular.

"It's a bat!" Lou shrieked again.

"Yes, they have fruit bats here," Bella said nervously, still not taking her eyes off the palm tree. "They also have spiders, snakes, lizards, geckos, turtles, dolphins and sharks."

She reeled off the names confidently, as she had done her research, as always, and read several books on the Maldives.

Being an avid reader, Ava had also done the same. However, when she had said the last word, there was a sharp intake of breath from the whole group. The offending bat had been forgotten as all eyes turned to Ava. She was glad it was dim in the bar area, as she was hoping the blush, she felt creeping over her cheeks, was hidden by the poor light.

"I will protect you professor, don't worry," Jez reassured her.

He loved using her nickname and smiled lovingly at her as he stood, reaching over to her and gently stroking her cheek.

"I'm ok." Ava replied mortified, "I'm just getting tired now. I know it's early but it's been a long day."

The small group nodded in agreement; they were all knackered. Ava hated being the centre of attention and hated even more that her friends should feel sorry for her.

On finishing their drinks, the group donned their head torches, a real must-have for the Maldives and with fits of drunken giggles they made their way through the paved path, surrounded on both sides by tropical bushes and palms. There were a few screams when bugs and lizards ran out into the path in front of them. Maybe they were not as brave as they thought they were.

When they reached the end of the path, they were back on the beach where the jetty joined the water villas, they all stopped abruptly. The moonlight was assisted by large staked lanterns that were dotted around the beach front, highlighting where the sand ended and the plants and palms began. The start of the decking was lit by two huge lanterns, either side of the rustic pier entrance. However, the sight that had stopped them all, was a light emitting from the ocean floor. It went from the shore, right out to where the sea ended, under the moonlit sky. It was a neon-blue, glowing light, looking like a fluorescent sparkling stream going out to sea.

Ava had read about this and announced to the group, "It's called Noctilucent Scintillans, or also known as sea sparkle," she said brightly, taking in the marvellous spectacle.

"Thank you, Professor," smiled Jez as he admired his friend's stunning features in the moonlight.

She really was the most incredibly beautiful being he had ever met, both inside and out.

Bella sighed longingly and the group's attention turned to her.

"What?" she said defensively, "I didn't say anything" she countered.

Bella was the least romantic of the group besides Lou, and although she designed and created stunning wedding gowns for blushing brides, at no point would she be considered a hopeless romantic. Bella felt as though she was in a dream, looking out on this breath-taking scene, standing here on this gorgeous island, with her best friends. It was all too much, completely overwhelming. She decided that being travel-weary and jet-lagged, would all be contributing to the fact that her legs felt like jelly and her heart was turning to mush. Or maybe she could be romantic here. All she needed was to meet a man and fall in love. She snorted out loud at the preposterous thought. All eyes were still on her and she tried to change tack as she started walking towards the jetty.

Lou had decided to sing, albeit very badly and was dancing the can-can across the soft, cool, sand of the beach. Having veered off the wooden pathway Rachel and Dan were following her laughing, arms linked together to stop them falling over.

Jez curled his arm around Ava's toned slim waist and pulled her to his side, walking quietly across the boardwalk. Apart from Bella, they had all had more than enough to drink and realised that they had to now navigate the narrow wooden jetty. The left-hand side of the wooden path before them, was edged by a thick rope that hung low between the posts. At each water villa was a large lantern, adding light to the path way.

Lou was now tap dancing along the start of the jetty singing "Me old bamboo."

Dan and Rachel were trying copy her and Bella was doing her best to control them all. As Jez went to step on to the jetty, he felt Ava freeze. This must be a nightmare for her, walking over an ocean full of sharks. He knew she was scared and as they had all been upgraded to water villas, he also knew Ava would be too polite as to turn down such generosity and kindness. Although when he got the chance, he would discuss it with Kit, she must have known her sister would be petrified of this walk, let alone sleeping over the water, hiding all sorts of sea creatures. It wasn't like Kitty to be this thoughtless and he wondered briefly if she had been affected by the Pennington clan. They were ridiculously well off and he assumed that they were never told the word no. If they wanted something, they would have it. He hoped that this new found wealth and celebrity would not change his darling little Kit.

"I'm right here with you Ave, nothing is going to hurt you," he whispered softly.

She was staring at the dark waters lapping underneath the first villa, in the shadows where you couldn't see what actually lay beneath. She took a deep breath and bravely walked forward on to the jetty, with Jez glued to her side. They didn't speak and Ava tried to concentrate on the old bamboo lyrics being yelled out from ahead, although due to the curve, the rest of the group was out of site.

Suddenly there was a scream and a large splash. Ava felt psychically sick and held on tightly to Jez's hand they rushed forward. The screams had turned to raucous laughter and there on the path they found Dan, Rachel and Bella, kneeling on the edge of the boards, reaching their hands down to Lou, who was bobbing in the water below.

"Oh my god!" Ava said shocked.

"The water is lovely!" hiccupped Lou, "Come on in, me old bamboo."

She tried to wave her arms in time to the lyrics. In tears of laughter, she reached up and grabbed Dan's hand and tried to pull him in. Rachel and Bella grabbed Dan to support him and he managed to pull his sister up onto the decking, using the low rope as support.

Luckily, the water was deep enough that Lou hadn't hurt herself, although now standing, dripping with salty water on the path, she realised her Vivienne Westwood dress might not be ocean proof.

"It better not shrink!" She said suddenly all humour gone and frantically trying to wring the water out of her frock.

Ava smiled weakly as the rest of the group started laughing. Bella did try and point out the dangers of alcohol and the sea, but no one was listening so she gave up and joined in with the laughter. Ava kept scanning the waters below, wary of any movement or splash. Eventually, all had made it safely to their villas and there was just Jez and Ava left. He had walked past his villa to stay by her side and she let out a deep breath when they finally arrived at her door.

A smaller walkway led off the jetty to the right and he had gripped her tightly as they had made their way over it.

"Thank you," she said looking up into Jez's dark brown eyes. "I really appreciate you walking me back, I will get used to it don't worry." She smiled as Jez's concern showed on his face.

He held her face in his huge hands and scanned it, as if looking for the smallest mark.

"You can talk to me you know," he said softly, still holding her face, staring into her eyes.

Many a woman would have fainted from this proximity; however, Ava was used to him and his presence.

"I'm really tired, I need to sleep," she said quietly, smiling up at him, "…and so do you," she finished.

His beautiful face creased for a moment while he thought about what she had said and then the frown disappeared and his sexy lop-sided smile replaced it.

"Goodnight my darling girl," he said as he kissed her gently on the forehead.

"Goodnight my darling boy," she smiled.

As she walked through the door to the villa her entire body started shaking. The realization hit her that she was literally standing over the ocean and that she was all alone. The air con was amazing and refreshingly cool, but she felt hot and feverish. She ran to the bathroom and put her head over the immaculately clean, marble toilet. Her head was spinning and once she had been sick, she lay on the cool tiles, eventually falling asleep with large sea monsters and sharks filling her nightmares.

Chapter 4

Ava awoke around three am and as her eyes adjusted to the dim light in the room, it took her a few seconds to realise she was lying on the cool tiles of a bathroom floor. The light from the bedroom door gently lit the toilet she was lying by and she remembered that she was in a water villa and at this very moment, there could be a shark swimming beneath where she lay.

She sat up quickly and put her head over the bowl of the toilet. Although retching, she had nothing left to bring up. She rested her pounding head on her hands that were balancing on the toilet seat. Every part of her body ached and she felt exhausted. The night terrors had not aided a peaceful sleep. *Oh god did she scream out?*

She wasn't sure if she had dreamed it or not, thank goodness there was no one in the closest villas to hers. To be fair the villas were so spaced apart, Ava doubted anyone would hear her, even if she had any neighbours. An ugly thought crossed her mind about honeymooning couples making love and screaming out, surely the villas were soundproof. She felt nauseous again. *Come on, pull yourself together.*

She sat upright and decided on a plan of action. She stood and grabbed the large glass water bottle that was sitting neatly by the nearest sink. She poured some water into the glass provided and reached for her medicine bag. She had to put the bathroom light on, in order to find the ibuprofen, and the bright light hurt her eyes, making her wince.

Whilst routing around in the medicine bag, she realised the shutters were still open and the glass sliding wall was looking out into an abyss of darkness. A little of the decking had lit up from the bathroom lighting and she quickly pulled to and closed the dark wooden shutters. She didn't want to think about the ocean and anything living in it.

She stepped out of her dress and knickers, from the night before and gingerly tiptoed in to the huge walk-in shower. She hit the display pad and the jets sprang into action, with hot water streaming on to her aching body, God this felt good. She washed her hair and used the villa's own shampoo and body wash again. The coconut and honey concoction smelt divine and immediately lifted her spirits. When she felt like she had washed her aches away, Ava turned the powerful shower off and wrapped herself in the huge, fluffy bath sheet. She dried herself, applied a moisturiser to her face, brushed her teeth and put on deodorant.

Walking into the bedroom area she removed her towel and slipped under the cool covers of the enormous four poster bed. She reached out and pulled on the mosquito netting ribbon attached to the bedpost, loosening the wave of netting and enclosing her safely inside.

The others were already down in position. The ceiling fan spun above the bed and along with the air con it helped her feel so much better. She took a sip of the flat can of Pepsi Max she had opened earlier and switched on her iMac, might as well get some work done.

By five-thirty she had completed a whole chapter and tweaked another. She was happy with her work and suddenly felt hungry. She slipped out of the huge bed, pulling back an opening in the netting and padded gently across the wooden floor, over to the fridge. She retrieved a can of orange pop and what she thought looked like a chocolate bar, labelled 'Dido'. Much to Ava's delight she discovered a 'Dido' was very similar to a KitKat chunky, the one Jez had raved about. Along with a swig of fizzy pop, she savoured every heavenly bite.

She noticed the room was getting lighter and that she hadn't shut the bedroom shutters. Christ, she had been walking round naked, anyone swimming past might have seen her, although who would go swimming at this time of day? She picked up the soft throw from the back of the arm chair and wrapped it around her naked body. It was so soft and comforting it made her smile. She walked over to the gigantic glass doors and with one hand slid the panel open. It was surprisingly easy and once again Ava was impressed with what real money could buy you.

The heat was overwhelming, even in the darkness of the early morning. She gently closed the door behind her and took a seat on the large cushioned chair. Tucking her feet up under her, she gently pulled the throw snuggly around her clammy body. She was comfy and relaxed as she watched the most beautiful sunrise she had ever seen. As soon as the sun had risen the waters beneath became crystal clear again and were teaming with life. Both small and large. brightly coloured fish darted around as Ava peered nervously over the decking.

To the left of her view, she noticed a slower movement of a large object. As she strained her eyes all fears disappeared as she realised it was a massive turtle. A real-life turtle, swimming past her room. She jumped to her feet, the blanket falling off her shoulders but held up by her hands at her chest. The turtle was in no hurry and swam leisurely past her, through the teams off kelp and then the open sand bank pockets, where she could see it more clearly.

Ava smiled in wonder, what a magnificent sight. Just before the turtle was out of view, she heard a noise on the decking below. She cautiously moved to the wooden railing and saw a beautiful Bluey grey bird, perched on one of the sunbeds. He was huge and reminded Ava of the herons back home on the canals. She was just admiring him when she noticed another movement in the waters to her right. There was a lot of dark underwater greenery, but there streaming through it, was a black fin weaving a smooth line through the gentle slush of waves. The smile slipped from her face and she found herself holding her breath, as a large black tipped shark skulked past her in the waters below. It must have been five-foot-long and Ava glared, eyes wide with fright as the smaller fish darted out of this monster's way. The shark passed out of site and she let out a huge breath, just as there was hammering on the glass behind her. She jumped a mile and only just managed to keep the blanket around her tense body.

The glass slid open and Jez's handsome face peered out.

"Breakfast?" he said smiling broadly.

As he took in Ava's expression his smile dropped, the concern etched on his handsome face, as he quickly stepped out onto the decking and wrapped Ava up in to his strong, muscular arms.

"Sweetheart, what's happened?" he stepped back and held her arms while he assessed her.

"Shark," she said simply and her eyes darted to the left, where she had last seen it.

"Fuck," he groaned as he pulled her close again, squeezing her a little too tightly. "I knew I should have stayed with you last night," he whispered as he kissed the top of her head.

"I'll be fine," she smiled weakly. "We are here for three weeks Jez; I have to get used to it."

She hugged him back, grateful for the support. "Now did you mention breakfast?" her stomach grumbled as she spoke and Jez laughed.

"Sounds like you're in need of sustenance," he said smiling broadly. "Get dressed and we will go up to the pool to eat," he said masterfully.

"Yes sir." She laughed as she ducked out of his arms and made her way into the bathroom, thank goodness she had put the throw around her, note to self, do not walk around naked.

"How did you get in here by the way?" She called over her bare shoulder.

"I have my ways," Jez replied with a huge grin.

Laughing she made her way into the bathroom, her mood lifted.

Once dressed in a loose yellow shirt dress and the jetty navigated, it was a lot less scary in the daylight, they decided to walk around the shoreline. They could have used the network of paths or summoned a buggy, that could take you into the centre of the island, but they wanted to be alone.

No one else was awake yet, as it was only just after seven, so Jez and Ava chatted easily about how fantastic the island was and how excited they both were to see Kit, who would be arriving in a few days' time. She had had a lot of pre-wedding functions to attend with her future in-laws and Jez tried to explain to Ava again, just how rich and famous the Pennington's actually were.

Ava wasn't the least bit interested in celebrity gossip and as she had met Alfie several times before when Kit had brought him home to visit, she could see the love and happiness between them and any materialistic or money matters, were simply nothing to do with her. In fact, their joy was so infectious that Kitty's small and caring family, were soon as bowled over by Alfie as Kitty was and they had all accepted him with open arms into their lives.

Whilst making their way along the stunning, deserted beach, Ava would stop and retrieve shells that had been washed in on last night's tide. Each one more intriguing and beautiful then the last. Ava was beguiled by them and Jez nodded and inspected each one politely, as she showed him. His heart glowing that his beautiful Ava was happy. On their little adventure, they came across a beach bar, or shack might have been a better description. Considering the rest of the island was so exclusive and luxurious, this bar didn't seem to fit in with the smooth, polished, high-end look achieved elsewhere. The bar itself was clean and had a small thatched roof, from which hundreds of fairy lights were hung.

"I bet this place is lovely after dark," Ava commented, Jez nodding in agreement, as they walked up to the counter to peer over at the bottle selection.

"Good morning sir," a small gentleman popped up from behind the bar, and Jez jumped back clutching his chest.

"Bloody hell!" He gasped, "I nearly had a heart attack!"

He was smiling and finished with a wink.

"So sorry sir, so sorry ma'am, I did not mean to frighten you," he said apologetically, holding up his hands, one of which was clutching a tea towel.

"My name is Anju and I have the pleasure of running this bar," he nodded and glanced round the bar area, his pride obvious. "Please be seated and I will make you a breakfast cocktail" he announced with a flourish, waving his cloth theatrically.

"I'm in," said Jez with a huge grin and reached out his gigantic hand to shake Anju's much smaller one.

Anju was delighted and slightly taken back at Jez's friendliness and Ava could not help but smile, enjoying the very warm welcome.

"I'm in too, thank you," she smiled.

Anju looked at her a little longer than necessary and bowed slightly.

"My name is…" she was interrupted by Jez.

"My name is Jez and this is the Professor," he said turning proudly and raising his hand to show Ava off in style.

"Ahh a very warm welcome Professor and Mr Jez, please be seated and I will make you extra special delight" he smiled warmly and Ava and Jez were both immediately taken with him.

There were several cushioned, cosy-looking chairs with large canopy umbrellas, in front of the bar and the outlook was a stunning vista of beach and ocean. Anju busied himself behind the bar as his guests relaxed in the comfortable seats.

Ava rested her head back on the soft cushion and closed her eyes, although early in the day, the sun was already beating down and sitting under the canopy was a relief from the heat.

Jez studied Ava's face quietly and noticed how the skin under her eyes was slightly darker than her usual pale complexion. He gritted his teeth and shook his head to think of her having nightmares and him not being there to comfort her, made him feel sick. Without thinking he reached over and stroked her arm gently with the tips of his fingers, she jumped slightly and opened her eyes wide.

She turned and looked at him and as he opened his mouth to speak, Anju appeared with a small, black tray, containing two huge coconuts. Sticking out of the top of the coconut was a silver straw and an extravagant array of feathers, which on closer inspection, appeared to be a peacock.

They said a grateful thankyou to their attentive host and with great delight and a low bow he disappeared from view. Jez observed Ava didn't have any of her drink, but was admiring the peacock novelty bird and then the extendable solid silver straw that accompanied it.

"We are not in the West Mids anymore Toto," he said trying to encourage his peacock to fly, it hit the drinks table and crash landed, making Ava giggle.

Jez closed his eyes and smiled, her laugh was as beautiful as her soul and he loved to hear it.

"This cocktail is incredible," he took a big slug through the expensive straw.

Ava lifted the coconut and adjusted the straw to her mouth, gingerly taking a sip. She squeezed her eyes shut and tried to shake the memories of the past away. Jez watched her intently and again realised how pale and tired she looked. If she had had nightmares, she was probably as sick as a dog last night. He should have never have left her alone.

"Mm… it's delicious," she beamed at him breaking his thoughts, he beamed back. "Although drinking this early in the morning doesn't seem very sensible." She questioned.

He raised his coconut and shouted,

"A toast to not being sensible!" He finished with a cheer and Ava raised her coconut to his and shouted,

"To not being sensible."

They both burst out laughing. After several of Mr Anju's amazing breakfast cocktails, the slightly squiffy pair, giggled their way along the shaded pathways, getting lost a few times, even though the island was well sign posted. They had no idea what time it was, but they also did not care, as they had laughed and talked and had the best time.

Finally, along the fourth path they had followed, they made it to one of the outdoor restaurants, alongside an extremely inviting affinity pool, which was currently empty, apart from the huge heron-like bird, who was perched like a statue at the edge.

On seeing the couple, a member of staff rushed forward and greeted them, offering them a seat in the glorious sunshine, or in the shade of the restaurants canopy. Ava looked pleadingly at Jez, who was a sun god and adored the sun, however, she was a lot paler and easily burnt.

"Alright you win, shade it is… for now!" He winked and wiggled his eyebrows up and down.

They had just finished their brunch when they heard voices getting nearer. From the far side of the pool two women approached. Their loud American drawl commanded everyone's attention and as the area was so quiet, you couldn't help but hear what the approaching women were saying.

"It's so goddamn hot here, you'd think they would cool it down. I still want a tan and it has to be first class, or what's the point of coming?"

The disdain practically dripped off her, as the other one answered,

"It is fucking hot, I get it. We are here for a reason and we have to get started, don't forget what he said!"

A member of staff had approached the new guests and greeted them politely, however, the peroxide blonde haired one shooed him away like an unwanted fly.

Ava and Jez exchanged disgusted looks, just as the Americans spotted Jez and that was it.

"Oh my god, look Zara, its Jeremy Light... oh my god... he models for Gucci!"

The dark haired American immediately tottered over to where Ava and Jez were sat. Zara was not so impressed, she raised her hand to hush her companion, although she also made her way over to the canopy, in equally ridiculous high heels.

As they reached the canopy, Ava took them both in. They were horrendously thin apart from their boobs, bums, and lips, which looked completely out of proportion with the rest of their bodies. They both wore tiny neon-string bikinis, with matching neon, crocheted, ankle length beach dresses, although they didn't cover much. The skin around their chests looked painfully tight and Ava tried to keep eye contact and look at their faces rather than their rock-hard melon breasts. Their outfits were incredibly fitted and what little flesh they had, pushed through the gaps in the fabric, the look was not flattering. Unfortunately, their faces were not much better. Although they both looked like they were in their late thirties, they had obviously had a tremendous amount of plastic surgery. Not a line or wrinkle appeared on the over stretched skin on their skinny faces. Their lips and cheeks had been filled with God-knows-what, giving them a weird trout pout outline. Both of their faces were completely covered in heavy make-up, which looked like it had been applied with a trowel. The female who had raised her hand was now right in front of Jez's chair. She had so much mascara on, Ava wondered how on earth she kept her eyes open. Even though she was in heels, how practical around the pool, her gigantic bosom was literally eye level to Jez, who turned on the playboy charm immediately.

"Good morning ladies," he stood as he spoke smoothly, never breaking eye contact with the female before him.

"My name is Jeremy and I am delighted to meet you."

He took her skeletal hand to his lips and kissed it. He then turned to the more demonstrative female, who was practically bobbing up and down with excitement. He stepped forward and took her bony hand, kissing it, again never breaking eye contact.

"Delighted," he repeated, grinning like a Cheshire cat.

Ava grinned as well, as she knew that fake women would mean nothing to him and this was a game he played with adoring socialites. Most women wanted to sleep with him and sell their stories, or even better get pregnant and be kept in the lap of luxury with astronomical child maintenance payments. Nothing surprised her when it came to Jez's charms.

The blonde-haired skeleton spoke first, "I am Zara Blackwell, although you already know who I am." This was not a question "…and this is Jennifer La True," she gestured vaguely to her companion.

"Enchanted," Jez smiled a panty-wetting smile and then turned to Ava and introduced her as his 'very special friend'.

Both women looked down their pointed noses at Ava, instantly showing their dislike and disdain. They didn't acknowledge her, but simply redirected their attention to leer at Jez, who was in his element.

"Ladies I was thinking of taking a dip in the amazing looking pool over there, I am hoping that you will join me?" His voice husky and dripping with innuendo.

Zara, who was obviously the dominant female out of the two, glared at Ava. Her icy stare showing her that Ava was not welcome in this invitation.

"I have work to do," Ava said politely, glad of an excuse to get away from this plastic pair.

"Have a lovely afternoon," she smiled as she stood.

Jez grabbed her arm, with a serious expression on his face,

"Stay," he said genuinely wanting her to join in.

Ava could have sworn she heard the two women in front of her, suck their teeth in disgust. However, she ignored them and smiled kindly, as she kissed Jez's cheek and whispered,

"Have fun."

She winked and nodded in the direction of the plastics, turning and making her way to the 'jungle path' as Jez had nicknamed it.

As she disappeared down the path, she heard Jez shout after her,

"Don't get stuck at that shack, or I will have to come and find you!" he then sang, "I've got a lovely bunch of coconuts," very loudly in a terrible Cockney accent.

Ava was still laughing when she got to the beach, sobering quickly when she realised, she would have to walk along the jetty alone. Although nervous, she did eventually make it to the delightful coolness and safety of her villa. With a huge sigh of relief, she was safe.

Chapter 5

Ava had spent the afternoon and evening working on her latest novel. She was so motivated with her luxurious surroundings and stunning scenery, that she was actually noting ideas for her next book. She had enjoyed the solitude of her villa and had texted her friends and asked them to leave her to her work for the rest of the day, something which they had all promised to do if the mood took her. She was disturbed only once when she heard a commotion outside on her lower decking.

Nervously she had risen from the bed, where she had been engrossed in typing, to see a naked man standing on her lower deck. She recognised Jez's toned and bronzed bottom instantly, he was not shy, and she had laughed at the dance he was now doing for her. He didn't turn around, he didn't speak, he just danced. Then in a grand finale he wiggled his bum cheeks, threw his hands in the air and dived into the waters below. Hilarious. She hadn't once seen his face and she knew he was doing it to make her laugh. She took the opportunity to have a wee and restock her snacks and top up her wine, grinning broadly at Jez's antics. The wine was delicious and going down far too quickly.

She could get used to this, she thought as she fidgeted to get comfortable again, in the ginormous bed. Although invited for an evening soirée with her group, she had messaged her thanks and continued her writing, completing two whole chapters, editing others and making a glorious number of notes for the next best seller.

It was gone eleven when her vision was blurring and her tired eyes finally had had enough. She showered, brushed her teeth and for the first time in days, had a sound night's sleep, dreaming of characters and storylines. She was awake for the sunrise, which she had the advantage of watching from the sunbed of her top deck, sipping a can of iced coffee. She had again enjoyed the marine life that was vibrant and clearly visible in the waters below. The huge turtle made his way past again and she made a note of the time, in the hope of watching him tomorrow, she also decided to name him Tommy, which made her smile. There were two huge ugly looking fish lurking around today. They seemed to be very aggressive, chasing other fish of all sorts of shapes and colours away. She must look them up when she got chance.

She loved nature and learning about new places. She had already won the nickname of professor, before her local university had invited her to become an honorary Professor of literature. Having finished school at sixteen, Ava proudly accepted the title, with much teasing and banter from her family. Jez and Kitty had been by her side for the ceremony and although she had felt a twinge of sadness that her parents were not there to see it, she knew they would have been immensely proud of her hard work and achievements.

Suddenly the huge heron-like bird swooped down, landing on the rail right in front of her, making her jump. He was even more handsome close up and didn't seem bothered that a human was so near to him. She admired him for a while then decided he needed a name too.

"Good morning Henry," she smiled, gazing at him in awe.

This place was truly incredible.

A quick glance at her watch informed her it was just after eight. Realising that she should make an effort and breakfast with her neglected friends she jumped off the day bed. The sudden movement caused Henry to panic and he lunged forward, spreading his enormous wings, gliding effortlessly to perch on a raised sand bank out in the distance.

Happy and relaxed, Ava showered, covering herself in coconut sun cream and dressed simply in a red bikini and loose-fitting sundress. She donned flip-flops, sunglasses, a large sunhat and retrieved her iPhone. As she stepped out into the heat of the morning, she smiled and held her head up to the sky, closing her eyes.

The sun's rays felt so good on her body and when she opened her eyes, she took on the jetty walk with gusto. At the end of the jetty she paused, taking in the long-deserted beach before her. She thought of how lucky she was to be here, on this stunning island, with the people she loved. As her writing had gone well yesterday and she managed to get some much-needed sleep, she had a spring in her step and was looking forward to a pool day with her buddies.

Ignoring the tropical paths that led to numerous eating areas, she decided to walk up the deserted beach. Once on the cool sand that had been softened by the gentle lapping waves, she removed her flip-flops and enjoyed the glorious feeling of the sand between her toes.

Ava had always loved the beach and in particular beach combing. She was already on the lookout for new shells that may have washed on to the beach during the night. As she meandered around the shoreline, she collected as many shells as she could carry and admired the panoramic scenery.

"Come on missus we are starving," shouted Rachel from the cover of a large canopy up ahead.

Ava smiled and made her way over to the large table, surrounded by her little family.

"Hello stranger." Lou said sarcastically, as she sipped her breakfast champagne.

"Good morning everyone." Ava said smiling.

Jez had stood and pulled out the chair nearest to him and as she was sitting down, he kissed the top of her head.

"You look much more rested today," he said beaming.

"I managed to get a lot of writing done yesterday, plus I had a better night's sleep." She answered honestly. "Although it may have had something to do with all the wine I consumed whilst working, I bet the last hours' writing will make no sense at all when I read it back!" She laughed and the others joined in.

"I did the same as you Ava." Bella spoke quietly, "I was up until midnight working on Kitty's dress, I really hope she is happy with it" she said nervously.

"Oh Bella, Kit loves it. You could not have done us prouder," Ava said genuinely delighted at the stunning gown her clever friend had created.

"I still don't know why us fellas can't see it," grumbled Dan.

He was chomping on a fresh croissant which looked delicious and made Ava's belly rumble with hunger. She grabbed a croissant and started to eat it.

"The men will have to wait until the big day," said Lou. "Bella has only shown me and Rachel the design, we haven't seen the actual dress on yet" said Lou, she threw a look at Ava, who was smiling whilst eating her delightful pastry.

"Kitty wants you all to see it on the day, with the shoes, makeup hair etc." Bella cut in.

She had worked really hard on the design and even more so on bringing her creation to life. She had also designed bridesmaid's dress for each bridesmaid, including herself. Kitty had wanted Ava as head bridesmaid, matron of honour sounded so old fashioned. The other bridesmaids were Lou, Rachel, Bella and Sophia, Alfie's sister. Sofia had told Ava that she was relieved that they were the only ones asked, as Alfie came from a large family and social circle and she was happy that Kitty had kept it small. Although five bridesmaids could hardly be considered a small party. The groomsmen included Dan and then Alfie's two brothers, Gio and Ethan. Jez had been given the huge honour of walking Kitty down the aisle. Something that had shocked him into silence, He was so touched by the gesture, when Kitty and Alfie had approached him about it. He had decided that even though he wasn't keen on weddings, understatement of the year, he would do his absolute best to ensure his little KitKat and his beloved family, enjoyed and made the most of every minute of the festivities.

"That reminds me that over the next two days, I need the ladies to try on the bridesmaid's dresses, just so I have chance to make any last-minute alterations before Kit arrives and then I can concentrate on her dress," Bella announced seriously to the group.

The women all nodded in agreement.

"Ladies," snorted Rachel, as she knocked back her large cut crystal glass of fizz, the whole table laughed again.

"What are the plans for today then?" Lou piped up. "I was thinking of going diving," she said earnestly, the whole table became silent as they looked at Lou.

"What?" She said slightly annoyed.

Dan bravely spoke first "You, in a wetsuit…with an oxygen tank on your back…in the ocean?" he asked incredulously.

"Yes." She said sharply.

"Umm Lou?" Rachel said, not hiding a smirk, "I don't suppose this involves a male diving instructor?"

Lou shot her a tedious look.

"Well obviously there will be an instructor, I have never dived before," she said waving her arms about.

"…and would this diving instructor possibly be extremely good looking?" asked Bella secretly enjoying the teasing as it was usually her that it was aimed at.

"So, what if he is?" Lou stated, slightly exasperated by all the questioning.

With knowing nods, the group fell silent and just sat smiling watching Lou. Even Dan was smiling, his sister would never change. After a few minutes sat in comfortable silence, Lou could stand it no longer.

"Alright!" She shouted, making Bella choke on a piece of mango.

Dan slapped her on her back.

"Saved your life," he said good naturedly.

"Alright…" Lou spoke a little softer, "…his name is Heath and he is a twenty-six-year-old, Australian diving instructor, with thighs that could crush a walnut." She ended dreamily.

The whole table laughed at this and then stories were swapped about diving, Australians and of course sexual exploits, these coming mainly from Lou. Dan excused himself and went to dive in the stunning infinity pool to cool down.

Rachel watched Dan's lithe body, dive expertly into the cool inviting swimming pool. His head popped up and he shouted over to them all, telling them how glorious it was. She stood and made her way over to the pool area, half of which was covered with a huge white sail canopy, sunbeds sat idly in the shallows underneath it. Rachel's ideal spot, as you could swim and lie down without getting burnt.

"Meant to say to you all, the psycho barbies from last night…reminded me of toxic waste." Jez said to the table. "You all need to steer clear of them," he said sternly, "or they will seriously spoil our time here." he finished.

"What Barbies?" asked Bella innocently.

"Oh my god Ave, they were vile," joined in Lou, "I went to sit by Jez last night at the bar and they were so rude, they didn't want me to sit by him." Lou continued rolling her huge olive eyes.

"They're apparently friends of Alfie's, so I was really good and stayed as polite as I could, but Kitty had better watch out, they were not very pleasant about the wedding."

Ava had stopped smiling and Jez held her hand tightly.

"Nothing to worry about, just a pair of jealous wannabes who have the hots for Alfie," he countered.

"That's awful," said Bella. "Why come to a wedding if you are going to be nasty about it," she was most upset even at the thought of it.

"Anyway." interrupted Lou, "Blara, Blara needs mascara and her little side kick La Fou, were smitten with our super model here, so I have given him the job of keeping them busy whilst we are here." She finished with a broad knowing smile.

Bella looked horrified and all Ava could say was, "Blara, Blara what?"

Lou laughed, "Blara, Blara needs mascara, Zara whatser name, she looked like she had her make up applied with a trowel…" Lou pulled a face. "…and her little side kick La Fou, you know Gaston's servant out of Beauty and the Beast!"

The ugly face fell and Lou grinned broadly, Ava could not help but return a smile. Ava was a kind hearted person, however, the thought of anyone not liking her sister was uncomfortable, the thought there may be others objecting to her sister's happiness, was even more so.

"Its fine, I've got this," Jez smiled and squeezed Ava's hand.

"I bet you have, you dirty dog…anyone for a threesome," shouted Lou, much to Bella's embarrassment.

Both Ava and Jez were used to Lou's outlandish behaviour, but Bella always seemed to be shocked by it.

"Ave, if you have no plans, would you like to come to the spa with me?" Bella was now trying to change the subject with distraction.

"I would love that Bell." Ava smiled back. "I'm sure these two are going to pin themselves out in the sun for the next few hours and I can't wait to see the treatments they have here, although I bet, they cost a bomb" Ava said thoughtfully.

"That's the thing Ave they are all free, I rang yesterday to see about booking and all the treatments for all the guests are free. Can you imagine that?" Bella said excitedly and with great reverie.

"Wow, that's amazing," said Ava in shock.

"It is a different world my lovely girl, we are not in the West Mids anymore Toto!" said Jez standing, his favourite phrase dropping into the conversation again.

He was still holding Ava's hand tightly.

"Jeremy… Darling!" Came a shriek from the poolside.

Ava instantly sat up straight and was on alert. By Ava's movement, Bella knew instantly that the shriek must belong to one of the toxic Barbie dolls. The click clack of perilously high heels, and a god-awful fishnet stocking dress in neon green was coming towards the table. Jez held Ava's hand firmly as she tried to move away and the look on Blara's face was a picture when she observed it.

"Good morning Zara," he said coolly, "I hope you and your friend are enjoying this beautiful morning," he practically oozed sex appeal and it always fascinated Ava that woman actually responded the way they did to him.

"Actually, Jenifer is at the spa, she had a little too much sun yesterday and is getting a rub down and then a treatment that is said to take inches off those who need it," came Zara's high-pitched American twang, with a sneer she turned to glare at Lou.

It was as if Lou was something disgusting stuck to the bottom of her tiny heel. Lou stood up, took off her brightly coloured sarong, showing her curvaceous, fabulous body in a teeny, tiny green bikini that literally only covered the essentials.

"Well, I'm off to get some of these rays on my smooth, Botox free skin…enjoy the spa you two." She said with a huge smile that basically said fuck you to Blara.

Lou sauntered past the hideous Barbie doll, with a super sexy stride as she sashayed her way to the pool. Unperturbed that Lou had just completely ignored her, Blara glared at Jez who was still holding Ava's hand.

"You two are going to the spa?" She spat out, as if she couldn't stop the bile leaving her throat.

"Actually, Ava and I are going, we are going to have our eyebrows shaped and…"

"Oh well that makes sense," Blara rudely interrupted. "Although you have to realise that they cannot work miracles," she said tilting her head and offering what looked like a pitying glance in Ava's direction. Jez's hand was now uncomfortably squeezing Ava's a little too tightly, so she stood before he lost his temper.

"Well Bell we had better get going, I'm so looking forward to this." She said brightly and with huge enthusiasm.

Jez kissed her hand, a flicker of a frown crossing his gorgeous face before he turned and smiled his extraordinary, panty-wetting smile at the four ladies left. Ava grabbed her iPhone, completely unaffected, Bella blushed the colour of a beetroot and then clumsily spilled a glass of water as she stood, catching her foot on the bottom of her sarong almost falling over. She reached for her obligatory designer sunglasses and huge sun hat. Jez chuckled at Bella's uncomfortableness around men, he really should stop teasing her. Rachel had wolf whistled, encouraging him to be naughty as usual and Zara stood stock still, icily regarding this Adonis before her and relishing the wetness she suddenly felt between her legs.

44

It was after they were long clear of the pool area that Ava and Bella let out a sigh of relief and laughed at the nicknames Lou had given the American plastic dolls. Although Ava had an uncomfortable feeling that they could be trouble for her sister, she stowed it to the back of her mind as she entered the incredible, luxuriousness of the spa.

Chapter 6

As they walked into the entrance of the welcoming spa, both Ava and Bella were completely in awe. The cool air, from the more than efficient air conditioning, chilled their hot skin and the smells of relaxing lavenders and exotic blossom oils filled the air. Soothing monastic music played quietly, with the mesmerising chimes of a tongue bell. The expansive floor was tiled in intricate mosaic patterns, surrounded by walls, in muted natural tones. Hung on the expansive walls were large detailed paintings of exquisite tropical flowers.

On the left-hand side of the vast room, was a luxurious seating area. Stunning flower arrangements adorned the immaculate magazine tables and the soft, comfortable looking chairs looked like a great place to curl up with a good book. Dominating the middle of the room, stood an impressive water fountain, which Ava recognised from the thick folder she had skimmed through on arrival to her room. It was a huge stone masterpiece depicting a naked man resting along the bottom with his hand raised to a naked woman, who was lithely leaning over the middle section, barely touching hands. The bottom well was full of water and held a number of small, brightly coloured fish, which seemed to be enjoying the slow pace of life, swimming idly round the softly splashing waters. This constant sound of the water added to the amazingly tranquil ambiance.

The two friends looked at each other, grinning widely, already loving this place. They made their way around the magnificent fountain towards the elegant reception desk that had been partially hidden behind it. A petite lady, dressed in a neat cream tunic dress, dark red sash around her tiny waist and a matching dark cherry blossom clipped in her hair, greeted them politely and asked for their names and room numbers. A younger woman, dressed identically to the receptionist appeared from nowhere with a tray. It contained four long elegant cocktail glasses, with expandable silver straws, Ava loved this extravagant touch, with delicate flowers attached to the side of each rim. She greeted Ava and Bella with a small nod of the head and polite smile. She indicated to the glasses with her tiny well-manicured hand.

"Alcohol…no alcohol," she said proudly, as she showed off her wares.

Ava took the alcoholic option, with a thank you and a polite smile. Much to Ava's surprise Bella also took the alcoholic beverage, although slightly more apprehensively than her friend. They clinked their glasses together, with a hearty cheer. They both sipped the pink looking concoction apprehensively, it was so delicious. It had a hint of mint, orange and melon and Ava also knew it had a good drop of rum in it and with a huge sigh whispered,

"It really cannot get any better than this."

Bella grinned and agreed with a bob of her head, reluctant for her mouth to be parted from her straw.

"Do you know which treatments you wish for?" the older lady behind the desk asked her friendly face beaming.

Bella reeled off a list of waxing treatments as Ava stood and ogled the receptionist's beautiful skin. She must be in her fifties and yet her complexion was incredible, her skin was actually glowing. Maybe staff were allowed to have treatments too, she contemplated this for a moment.

"Ava?" Bella interrupted her thoughts.

"Sorry, I was just admiring your beautiful skin," she looked at the receptionist and touched her own cheek to help her understand. "If you have a treatment that would help my skin look as good as yours, I would like that please" she said earnestly.

The lady smiled broadly and bowed her head slightly as a thank you.

"You do have an amazing complexion." Bella added, "Do you mind if I ask you your age?"

"My age is sixty-two," the lady answered, smiling politely and both Ava and Bella gawped in shock.

"No way," said Bella.

"Yes way," the lovely lady responded, making them all giggle. "I can offer you relaxing facial, scalp massage and full body massage, if you wish," she informed them, directing her gaze at Ava.

"Yes please," whispered Ava.

She was finding it difficult to believe this was all supposedly included in the holiday. She had made up her mind she was going to make the most of this spa and have whatever treatments she wanted and just pay the bill at the end, surly there had to be some cost.

"Don't you want anything waxed?" Bella asked with concern.

"I had everything waxed before we came out," Ava replied with a grimace.

Bella understood the meaning of the grimace but went on, "Are you sure?" her perfect eyebrows raised.

Ava realised her friend was a little apprehensive.

"Bell, you have had something waxed before?" Ava asked discreetly.

Bella bit her bottom lip and shook her head.

"Lou has been going on about waxing forever and even Rach has had everything waxed for this trip. I want to look my best for the big day," she said sincerely.

Bella was a beautiful, intelligent woman and Ava was slightly taken aback that she should feel she needed anything waxed, just because her friends had it done.

"Bella, this is your holiday, if you want to have every single hair waxed off your body then it's your choice......if you don't want to let hot wax anywhere near you, then, once again… it's your choice." Ava spoke slowly and quietly as if conversing with a child.

Bella responded with a cautious smile and turned to the receptionist who had been taking all of this in with a knowing smile.

"What will it be?" she asked politely.

The next few hours went past in a blur of unadulterated luxury. Ava had felt slightly uncomfortable about being naked and lying on a bed with nothing but a warm towel over her at first, however, she soon relaxed and enjoyed every second of this exquisite treatment.

The facial consisted of warmed oils being massaged gently into her face, with small agile fingers. Warm damp cloths followed, wiping the oils away, with each movement, encouraging circulation and rejuvenating her skin. Then ice-cold cloths invigorating and sealing the pores on her face. She had been asked what her favourite oils were before starting the massage and of course she opted for coconut. She had also chosen honey, vanilla and cherry blossom, which in the hands of her talented masseur were incredibly sensuous and relaxing. In fact, this wonderful lady called Tee, had the most incredible, skilled hands and Ava was delighted that her masseur was so adept at her job. She had been rubbed and massaged to within an inch of sleep, although there were two minor interruptions. Just as her treatment was starting, Ava had thought she heard a mobile phone ring, a loud trilling noise, much to the annoyance of Tee, who had tutted softly at the distraction. Then when having her back rubbed, she thought she heard a dubbed scream, however, as she was so blissfully relaxed, it was soon put out of her mind. Tee had chimed a small cymbal, notifying the end of the massage and had exited the room quietly. This left Ava blissfully relaxed, her body feeling warm and heavy as she lay on the comfortable bed.

As she lay there, she decided to try and concentrate on her latest storyline, imagining characters and how she could describe them. She ran through conversations her main characters could have. Her latest novel was a romance, although she was finding the leading man's character difficult to write. She just couldn't quite get him right. Picturing a romantic scene in her head, the relaxing treatment soon overwhelmed Ava's brain, which switched off completely and she finally nodded off to the sound of soft, meditative chiming bells.

The peace was suddenly shattered with a loud scream from outside the room. Ava sat bolt upright and gripped the soft towel to her chest, as the door burst open and Bella ran in. She was wearing a white fluffy robe and was sobbing with her hand over her face.

"Oh my god Bella, what's happened?" Ava felt sick as the sudden noise had wrenched her from her light sleep.

"Look!" Bella practically shouted, as she moved her hand from her face. "Look what she's done!" she sobbed.

Ava studied Bella's beautiful face; her own face scrunched up in scrutiny. Suddenly Ava realised that one of Bella's eyebrows was completely missing. Ava's mouth dropped open and she had no idea what to say. Bella swung round to face the large ornate mirror on the wall beside them.

"The whole thing is gone…my whole eyebrow!" she said hysterically.

"How did they manage to take the whole thing off?" Ava questioned and Bella spun back around, a manic look on her face, which wasn't helped by the missing brow.

She didn't speak.

"It doesn't look that bad" Ava wondered if she should cross her fingers as she spoke, but as her hands were gripping the towel to her chest, it just wasn't possible.

"The wedding!" Bella cried, "I'm a bridesmaid for god's sake!" her tone was getting higher as she spoke.

Ava tried to calm her down.

"You know Lou is amazing at makeup, she will be able to create an eyebrow for you and I bet the others would never know," she said soothingly and Bella let out a deep breath.

"She is good at that sort of thing," Bella conceded.

She let out another long breath through pursed lips.

"This was supposed to be a relaxing treat," Bella whispered, tears threatening to fall from her huge olive eyes.

"Oh Bell," Ava jumped off the bed and whist clinging to her towel with one hand, she hugged her with her free one.

"It will all be fine," Ava said reassuringly, "I promise we will sort it out."

Bella whimpered slightly and then turned away from Ava to ogle herself again in the mirror.

"Let's face it Bell, you still look like a Super model" Ava looked at her friend's reflection as she spoke.

Bella's mouth twisted a little into an almost smile.

"A bloody short supermodel," Bella countered.

Ava laughed, "Yes, a short one."

At this Bella smiled wearily.

"Why me?" She said, shaking her head gently, "Why is it always me."

Then to finish off her words of woe, her favourite mantra,

"Well, worse things happen at sea," she said with a sigh.

With that they decided to change and make a swift exit of the spa, although the Spa manager had hurriedly chased after them in the reception area sincerely apologising. She said that the member of staff concerned had been reprimanded and removed from her post. She wanted to know how she could possibly make it up to their valued client. She gave Bella a Reethi Lobe logoed baseball cap, which she immediately pulled on her head to try and cover the accident. Ava was holding Bella's large sunhat and encouraged Bella that she could not see her brow, due to the low peak of the cap.

Bella wasn't a spiteful person and very kindly informed the spa lady that everything was okay and that she wanted the young girl concerned to keep her job, after all we all make mistakes.

With that Ava took Bella to her favourite bar, the Tikki shack, still not knowing its proper name. It was completely deserted apart from the ever-delightful Anju. He greeted them warmly and with much admiration from his new customers, did not mention the missing brow, which was glaringly obvious.

They sat and drank the most beautiful cocktails, ignored the many texts from the rest of their group, especially Jez who wanted to know where Ava was. Snacking on a meze of amazing food, they talked and laughed their day away. As the sun started to set, Bell proclaimed she was ready for bed and Ava thanked her wonderful host and with an arm holding up her drunken friend, they somehow made it to the water villas without incident.

Although Ava had sobered instantly as they had stepped foot on the jetty. For the first evening since her arrival, she tried to concentrate on Bella getting to her room safely, instead of what lay lurking in the waters beneath them. Ava had secured her friend in her bed, placing a large glass of water and two ibuprofens on her bed side table. She also moved the waste paper bin to the side of the bed, just in case Bella was sick. She was not a big drinker and although Ava had enjoyed the time with her friend, she knew Bell would regret the cocktails in the morning.

Ava made her way to her room, cursing the fact it was one of the farthest villas on this long jetty. Darkness had descended quickly and with no Bella to take her mind off the sharks below, she was relieved when she reached her door. The cool of her room was delightful and after a shower, she put on her PJs and fired up her iMac. She poured a huge glass of red wine and as she plonked herself on the gigantic bed, she was ready for a few hours of writing.

As she took a bite of her Dido bar, she flicked through her last few texts. All of which were from Jez. The last one made her choke on her chocolate. It read

Well, I hope your happy, I am pissed and having to sit with some of the extended Pennington family that arrived today. I'm off clubbing, enjoy your Dildo!

Chapter 7

After another unsettled sleep, Ava had risen early to continue to work on her latest manuscript. The leading man was still giving her some difficulties, as she wanted him to be warm and alluring, but with a tough exterior. Although an accomplished writer, for some reason she had lost the fluidity of thought with this particular fictional man. The only reason she could think of as to why, was that she was surrounded by kind and loving men and therefore they were not helpful muses.

After completing another chapter and closing her laptop, she enjoyed the magnificent sunrise, showered and liberally applied the island's own coconut-scented sun cream. She dressed quickly in a bright yellow bikini and a loose shirt, keen to start her day. Quickly piling her damp blonde locks on top of her head in a messy bun, she grabbed her phone and sunglasses and opened the door.

She was greeted by Jez's dripping wet, tanned, muscular body, in a pair of extremely fitted royal blue swimming trunks.

"Wow, you're up," she said adjusting her sunglasses down her nose, to take him all in.

"Of course," he said smiling his gorgeous (would unsettle the fairest of maidens) smile beaming on his gorgeous face.

"I'm just going for breakfast, are you joining me?" She asked ignoring the smouldering look Jez was giving her.

Seriously any other woman would spontaneously combust! With his six-foot five frame dominating the doorway and nothing left to the imagination in the trunk department, Ava just laughed at him.

"Damn you woman," he said pulling a face, "Here I am in my teeny weenies, giving you my best 'Come to bed' eyes and you just laugh at me!" he said pouting and with that he stepped forward and grabbed Ava around the waist, lifting her easily, swinging her around.

She squealed as his wet body stuck to hers, making the pair of them burst into laughter.

He hadn't bothered with a shower, but had quickly donned a Boss soft, pale blue t-shirt and snug fitting shorts, over his damp swim trunks. They walked arm in arm along the jetty, Ava's confidence was growing with each crossing in the daylight, however, at night her demons returned and she was petrified of the sharks that may be skulking beneath.

They made their way to the nearest pool area and settled at a table under a magnificent white sail canopy. Very quickly a tea pot and coffee pot were produced by the ever-efficient staff as they buzzed about the beautiful couple, offering freshly squeezed juices and fresh pastries along with the leather-bound breakfast menu.

One by one their friends joined them, Lou and Dan were slightly worse for wear, after last night's session in the nightclub. Rachel was her ever-happy, outgoing self and greeted everyone with a huge hug and a kiss. Bella appeared last, making a silent approach, wearing her huge Jackie Onassis sunglasses. These were Belles's trademark along with a designer sun hat. Today however, she had teamed it up with an American university baseball cap, which was very unusual. A cap was something which no one around the table had ever seen her in before.

Bella loved her designer head gear and had brought a range of hats in her case. The puzzled group stared at her.

"Umm … Anyone going to mention the elephant in the room?" Dan queried, as Bella solemnly took a seat.

"What elephant?" asked Rachel innocently.

"The all-American play girl at the table," Lou said through slatted eyes.

The sun was very bright, she was ridiculously hungover, but she knew Bella would never be seen dead in a baseball cap and that something was up. Bella sank low into her seat and grabbed the menu that had been sitting innocently on the table in front of her. She put it up in front of her face endeavouring to become invisible.

"Bell?" Dan said as he leant over to put his arm around her.

Bella stayed hidden behind her menu, pretending to be engrossed in making the decision, of what to have for breakfast.

"Bella, are you ok?" Rachel asked concerned about her friend's odd behaviour.

The peak of the baseball cap and huge, dark sun glasses peaked over top of the menu.

"You haven't told them?" she whispered from behind her safety screen.

"No," answered Ava gently and all eyes were redirected to her.

She shifted uncomfortably in her seat, hating being the centre of attention. Jez's hand immediately grabbed hers as he looked at her with concern. As Bella remained tight-lipped and half-hidden behind her menu, Ava took a deep breath.

"There was a slight incident yesterday at the spa and Bella's a little upset about it."

"A little!" Bella snorted, slamming the menu down on the table, making everyone jump.

At this, the attention returned to Bella, with all sorts of scenarios going through their heads, they waited with baited breath. With great effort, Bella took off her baseball cap and slowly lowered her sunglasses to reveal her secret spa disaster. It took a moment for the others to realise that one of Bella's perfectly contoured eyebrows was completely missing.

There was a long pause where you could have heard a pin drop. Slowly her friend's mouths started twitching and they began biting their lips to try and stifle any outbursts. No one could make eye contact, although Ava could make out Rachel's shoulders shaking, which in turn started Lou off sniggering, then Dan was laughing, until in the end all of them, including Bella, were doubled over with laughter.

"What's so funny?" Came a high-pitched American drawl.

As if someone had suddenly pressed the mute button on a remote control, the group fell instantly silent. Bella quickly shoved her glasses back on and sharply pulled the cap back on her head, in order to hide her face. It was one thing to laugh at herself with her friends, but quite another to embarrass herself in front of this Yankee Doodle nut job.

"Well...someone let us in on the joke," Blara's voice trilled loudly, as she glared at each of the group in turn, landing on Jez, eyes widening slightly at the sight of him again, holding Ava's hand.

She had outdone herself in regards to today's outfit, as she was dressed in a shiny silver, sliver of a bikini, barely containing her rock hard, watermelon breasts and a matching, loose fitting kimono.

La Fou was doing her sidekick duty and wore exactly the same, although at least one size smaller than her friend's. Her outfit was bronze and both reminded the English contingent of foil wrapped turkeys, before and after the oven, and scrawny ones at that.

The overly efficient staff produced extra chairs around the table, without request. There was no thank you from either of the new guests, as they perched their bony arses on the edge of the chairs, uninvited and definitely unwelcome.

Ava caught Lou's expression showing the complete dislike she had for this prissy pair of wannabes. Jez squeezed Ava's hand and she turned to see his quizzical expression and realised she must have been frowning. In a fresh attempt to keep up the festive atmosphere, she decided to try and be friendly.

"Good morning, how are you both today?" Ava asked politely.

"Well, there was the biggest bug in my room this morning," La Fou answered immediately with an overly dramatic pout.

Ava wondered idly, that if this woman had all of the Botox drained from her skeletal face, would she still have that alarmed expression? *Be kind Ava,* she scolded herself inwardly and really tried to think more positive thoughts.

Blara turned to her sidekick with a sneer and took over the conversation, something that must happen often, as La Fou promptly closed her mouth tightly and said no more.

"I am so disappointed with 'my' room," she emphasized the word 'my'. "It's so small, I am used to having a private suite," she droned on.

The whole table stared at her, not knowing what to say, so Ava tried again.

"I am sure they have given you the best room available and that they are all incredibly luxurious," she said trying to sound enthusiastic.

Blara actually sucked air through her teeth, visually affecting all around the table, as their eyes widened in shock.

"You English are so gullible" she raised her hand; palm face up and gestured around the table as if to prove her point. "None of you would ever complain, you just smile and put up with this crap!"

Her face looked like a bull dog's arse chewing a wasp. She had had a large number of surgeries to 'improve' her features, however, the result was unnatural and severe. There was no beauty in the overly made up, artificial facade.

"Maybe it's because there is nothing to complain about," piped up Lou, smiling sweetly and directing a withering look at Blara.

Blara regarded Lou carefully, sizing up her opponent and it was a few minutes before anyone spoke. La Fou just looked nervous and uncomfortable at the silence and kept opening her mouth as if to start a conversation, before closing it again.

"Well, I'm going to go and have a dip in the pool and cool down," Rachel interrupted the awkwardness, "You coming?" she turned to face Lou as she stood, obviously wanting to get Lou away from the American snipers.

"No thanks, I'm good here." said Lou smiling sweetly.

Oh god, Ava thought, *this is going to be a battle of the wills.*

"I'll come," said Dan standing quickly and moving away from the tension, both Blara and La Fou quite obviously eyeing him up.

He was wearing a pair of red swim shorts, showing his toned six pack and his caramel skin had darkened in the sun, he looked amazing.

"Me too," said Bella as she stood awkwardly, almost tripping over the chair leg.

Then there were five.

"So, we hear the 'bride' is arriving tomorrow."

The word 'bride' was said with such disdain that Ava actually flinched and felt her politeness start to slip.

"Yes, her plane gets in around three pm and Alfie's sister and husband should be arriving too," Ava tried to keep an even tone.

She couldn't wait to see Kitty and she had met Sofia, Alfie's sister, before. She was quiet compared to Alfie, but Ava had really liked her. She hadn't met the husband, however, from chatting to Sofia she had gotten the impression that her marriage was not a happy one. Most wives would be gushing about their husbands, especially as she was a newlywed. On trying to find out more about Alfie's sister, Ava found her nervous and uncomfortable when discussing herself and her new husband, so had given up and focused their conversations on Alfie, Kitty and their upcoming wedding, something Sofia seemed happier to discuss and was genuinely warm and enthusiastic about.

"Our friends are on that plane too," Blara's drawl interrupted Ava's thoughts.

For some reason the evil pixies were now both staring intently at Ava.

"Let's hope they are happier with their accommodation then you are..." smiled Lou, turning to look at La Fou, "...and that there are no bugs in their rooms," she said sickly sweet.

This went straight over La Fou's head and she nodded furiously, as if Lou had just made a very good point. Blara glared at Lou, trying to think of a nastier comment, she squeezed her mouth into a tight pout, as if sucking a lemon covered in salt.

"Tell me…do people like you ever have to put sun cream on?" she said this with a sneer.

"Excuse me," said Lou briskly, the surprise at the question showing on her face.

"Do-people-like-you-ever-have-to-put-sun-cream-on?" Blara repeated slowly, her trout pout mouth enunciating every syllable.

Lou tilted her head slightly and somehow managed to smile.

"Yes, of course I do," she said surprisingly calmly.

Ava knew Lou was staying polite for her sake and was secretly thankful to her friend, but would have not judged if Lou had punched Blara in her plastic face.

"Do you?" It popped out of Ava's mouth before she could stop it.

Blara directed her attention back to Ava, once again noting that Jez was still holding her hand, something that seemed to offend her greatly.

Her glare was icy as she responded, "I have 'white' skin" as if that answered the question.

Oh my god, Ava thought of slapping this bitch herself, but again felt a squeeze of her hand. She turned to Jez who, as usual, was studying her face.

Instead of getting angry, Ava smiled sweetly back at Blara and said "Actually you're orange," to which both Jez and Lou let rip with raucous laughter, closely followed by the rest of their group who were listening intently by the pool.

La Fou just looked confused. The end of Blara's nose flared fractionally and Ava realised that this may be the only movement her surgically altered face allowed her and again smiled sweetly at the thought.

Blara changed tact, "It seems the bride-to-be is out clubbing before travelling," she said sarcastically. "As if the Pennington's want a drunken party girl in their family." Her mouth was now set in a line of contempt, "Poor Alfie." she finished falsely.

La Fou looked as if she was going to faint and Lou's mouth hung open in shock.

"On the contrary, Alfie is a very lucky man," Jez spoke up, breaking his silence.

His attention was now solely focused on Blara and his now thunderous look alone was enough to silence this evil woman. Although his expression was serious, it made him look even more devastatingly handsome than usual.

"Ava, Lou…" they both turned to look at him "…care to join me at the shack?"

Still holding Ava's hand, he bent his head and kissed it adoringly as he stood. Ava also stood, following his lead and Lou nodded her head as she got to her feet.

"I have a theory," she said to nobody in particular, "I think too much Botox affects the brain cells."

She looked directly at Blara and then La Fou who were both gaping with silent outrage.

Lou followed Ava and Jez with a huge grin on her face, showing off her sexy, curvaceous body as she swaggered out of sight. At the safety of the shack, the threesome downed a few of Anju's special breakfast cocktails, before they could even contemplate eating. Lou was extremely wound up and threatened to do all sorts to the American plastic dolls, as Jez laughed heartily at every suggestion, trying to relieve the tension that had built. Ava was quiet and reflective, whilst smiling and joining in where appropriate. She couldn't help but feel protective of the bride-to-be, because if those were Alfie's so-called friends, then God help her when she met his enemies.

After what had turned into a fantastic brunch and lots of cocktails with her dear friends, Ava needed some alone time. She waved them farewell as they disappeared in search of the nearest pool and Ava decided to go back to the spa. The coolness in the reception area was a welcome relief to the heat of afternoon sun. She was greeted like an old friend by the kind receptionist, who again was so warm and endearing. Ava asked politely if they could fit her in for a massage. She had thoroughly enjoyed her massage yesterday, until Bella and her missing brow incident.

She was ushered into a treatment room and once again relaxed, as another skilled masseur worked on her tight muscles. She felt the stress and tension leave her body and decided to block out all thoughts of the American trolls, for now. Maybe the wedding was taking its toll even though she thought she had it all under control. Blara and her sidekick seemed to have it in for Kitty and this really bothered her. Once again, she lay in the peace of the room, breathing in the coconut and honey oils that had been rubbed so expertly into her body. The masseur chimed the small cymbal and discreetly left the room after completing the massage and the next half hour was all hers, to unwind and relax even more.

She must have dozed off, as she was disoriented when she opened her heavy eyes. She felt so tired. Suddenly, she realised there was someone else in the room with her, breathing heavily. She sat up abruptly, again clutching her towel to her chest. As she spun round on the table, she saw a young girl, dressed in the white tunic and dark red sash.

She had red, puffy eyes and on seeing Ava's shocked face, she began to weep quietly.

"Can I help you?" Ava asked her politely, not knowing what to else to say.

The weeping turned to sobbing and the girl shook her head.

"I so sorry ma'am," she sniffed out.

Ava carefully got down off the warm bed, ensuring the towel was covering everything it should. She tiptoed over to the girl, who looked no more than nineteen years old and put her hand on her shoulder.

"Can I get someone to help?" she asked quietly and again the girl shook her head, the little red blossoms trembling in her hair.

"I need to give you this ma'am" and with that the girl produced a large wad of American dollars.

There was a pause.

"I don't understand," Ava was so confused, although her heart was still beating ten to the dozen from the intrusion.

"I took it ma'am, took it to do bad thing, I so very sorry ma'am," she whimpered.

Ava didn't have a clue what was going on about, but walked over to the table and poured a glass of ice-cold water, with as much dignity as she could wrapped only in a towel, and took it back to the distressed girl.

"I'm sorry, but I'm not quite sure why this involves me?" Ava questioned gently.

It took a few moments for the girl to stop crying, Ava stood patiently.

"You are Miss Hart?" She asked sniffing in a most un-lady like fashion.

"Yes," replied Ava gently, handing the young girl a tissue from the box in front of her.

"You were supposed to have me yesterday," she gulped and took a huge steadying breath. "I was supposed to wax you," she said, now blushing and overheated.

"No, I wanted a massage, but my friend Bella had the wax," she answered.

Then suddenly Ava realised the girl was upset due to the missing brow drama.

"Please don't worry, Bella will be fine and her eyebrow will grow back… we all make mistakes, please it is nothing to worry about it," she said kindly.

The girl looked up at Ava and her bottom lip trembled as she began to speak again, "I did on purpose ma'am, for this." she stretched her arm out again with her hand full of money. "She pays me to do ma'am, I feel so bad as Miss Ricci so kind," she started crying again.

"I'm sorry, but are you telling me that someone paid you to remove Bella's eyebrow?" Ava asked incredulously.

Once again, she had to wait for the reply until the tears had subsided. The girls arm fell limply to her side again and she looked up into Ava's beautiful face.

"No ma'am… someone paid to remove your eyebrow ma'am." She whispered in between huge gulps of air.

Ava was dumbstruck, who on earth would… Blara! Ava stood a little taller and straightened her shoulders.

"May I ask who paid you to do this?" she was slightly sterner than she meant to be and the young girl's eyes opened wide in horror.

"I'm sorry, but I need to know," Ava said a little gentler.

The girl looked frightened now.

"It's okay, this will be between you and me," she said trying to control her dismay.

"It was Miss Le True. Ma'am," the girl looked down at the wad of cash, there must have been hundreds of dollars there, "this is more than I make in a year ma'am," she said in a mournful tone, "I thought it would be worth it, but your friend was so upset, then so kind telling my boss to not fire me," she gulped again, trying to hold off the onslaught of more tears, "but its dirty money ma'am, I did not sleep last night, I have been bad ma'am," and with that she held out the money again.

Ava took a deep breath and pushed the girl's hand back down to her side and said gently, "Keep it."

The girl now stood with both eyes wide and mouth open in stupefaction "but."

"No buts," Ava replied firmly, "Thank you for being honest with me, you are not in any trouble, but I hope you have learnt a lesson from this and if asked again, you know to turn such a request down."

The girl lunged forward and squeezed Ava tightly.

"Oh ma'am," she cried, the tears flowing again.

"Please calm down, it's okay," Ava reassured her. "Go and put your money safe and don't upset yourself..." she paused, "I'm sorry I don't know your name?" Ava asked.

"My name is Detin," she said shyly.

"Right, thank you Detin, you may go now."

The girl smiled weakly and looked at the money in awe.

"Go and put it safe," Ava instructed firmly.

"Yes ma'am, thank you ma'am," and with a final sniff and gulp of air she left the room, leaving Ava alone to her thoughts.

Once again, the relaxing effects of the spa had dissipated quickly. Ava dressed and after leaving a good tip for her masseur, even though you weren't supposed to, she made her way out of the coolness of the reception to walk up the empty shoreline in the late afternoon sun.

She knew more guests had arrived, however, as they were all on the groom's side of the family, she was happy to stick to the quieter side of the island, especially at this moment in time, where she wanted to be alone to contemplate the events of today.

She decided to concentrate on looking at shells and spent the next few hours filling her shell bag, which had been a little gift from Jez, whilst trying to think why Zara Blackwell and Jennifer Le True hated her and her family so much.

Chapter 8

"What the fuck do you mean she hasn't signed it?" He growled down his cell.

There was a pause, then Sidney replied calmly, "Like I said, she has yet to sign the documents. I have tried to discuss the situation with him and he is adamant that it is his decision and no one else's."

"No one else's?" he interrupted," It's the family business and it will be his inheritance he is pissing up the wall, when this marriage goes south."

He was barely containing his anger. How could Alfie be so stupid? He himself was used to gold diggers. In his youth he had fallen for it a few times, females flirting outrageously with him and draping their arms all over him, coming on to him, in some high rolling casino or hot night club. The photographs would be in the papers the next day, with some exclusive about a hot night of passion that had never actually happened. He didn't stand for it any more. Now he had money and power and although that occasionally dragged the lowlifes out of the gutter, he had learnt to protect himself from these psychotic money grabbers.

How could Alfie be fooled by her? Fair play, this girl was pretty enough and she was English, something Alfie found attractive, he had always loved an accent. He could not just stand by and watch Alfie throw his life away. He had only been seeing this woman for a short time, surely that wasn't long enough to know if you should marry someone. Sofia had called it a whirlwind romance and she had been swept up into the whole nonsense. He had tried to make her see sense, as Alfie refused to discuss the pre-nup with him, but he might listen to reason if Sofia had talked to him about it.

He made a mental note to speak to her first thing in the morning.

"Son?" Sidney was waiting patiently on the line, waiting for Ethan to speak.

"I'm still here Sid… I have over a week to get her to sign or I swear there will be no wedding."

He was so wound up, missing important work back home due to this sham of a wedding. The whole Pennington clan had agreed to spend the run up to the wedding on the island and enjoy some much-needed family time. Everyone was so busy with their own lives. It was damn near impossible to get everyone in one place at the same time.

Sidney sighed down the phone. He had been the family lawyer for more years than he cared to remember, working for Pennington Senior before he had retired and passed the reigns over to his children. Sidney was more like family and was trusted implicitly and although frustrated that this latest gold digger had not yet signed the pre-nuptial agreement, he knew it wasn't Sidney's fault.

"I will try and talk to Alfie again in the morning and ensure that he is aware of the importance of his future wife signing the documents." Sidney was still calm and steady.

The handsome American had been walking back from the main reception of the hotel, avoiding the lavish evening buffet that had been laid on for the arrival of some of the Pennington family, who had just arrived on the island. He had walked along a pathway that ran adjacent to the shore line and had managed to happen across, what can only be described as a shack. The outside was lit with strings of fairy lights, giving a soft, enigmatic light to the area, however, there were no guests about and as he approached, he could see a small man preparing drinks behind the bar.

"Thank you, Sidney, I appreciate that," he finished, all anger gone and genuine appreciation of what his old friend was doing for him, trying to protect Alfie and the family.

"Get some rest son, you've had a long day, goodnight," he could hear the smile in Sidney's voice and did not answer him, he simply ended the call and stood at the bar, ready for a strong drink.

Anju had heard his customer approach and turned to greet him.

"Good evening sir, the wedding party is celebrating at our main bar," and with a gentle wave of his work worn hands, he gestured behind him and to the left.

Anju gave his best smile to welcome this new gentleman and hoped it would make his new guest and friend happy.

"Yes, I am aware the main event is over there..." he looked over the barman's shoulder and nodded his head "...and that is why I am over here. I wanted to avoid the party, it's been a long day and all I want is a large JD over ice."

He grimaced and tried to use his non-existent telepathic powers, to tell the barman he wasn't here to chat, he just wanted a quiet drink. Anju understood the facial expression and that the new guests may have been travelling days to get to his beautiful island. The man before him looked tired and agitated. He had overheard some of the telephone conversation, he was obviously a big boss. He could see this man needed to unwind. Anju instantly produced a drink and placed it on the bar in front of him.

"Uh no, I wanted a JD over ice,"

A frustrated reply as he really wasn't in the mood for trying a local liquor or whatever had already been sitting in the glass for God knows how long.

"Yes sir, large JD over ice, just for you sir."

He smiled again, showing his perfectly straight white teeth. Boss man frowned and took the glass. As he sipped the spirit, it warmed his throat and instantly lightened his mood.

"How did you do that?" he questioned, "I didn't even see you pour it."

Anju laughed, a hearty genuine laugh that made his new guest's mouth twitch up into nearly a smile.

"That was for the Professor, sir, I was just about to take but then you came here and wanted same drink, it is like magic sir," he said laughing again. "My name is Anju and I am the manager of this bar sir. If you wish assistance with anything during your stay, anything at all, please you only have to ask Boss man." Anju finished with a flourish of his hand and gave a small bow.

The moody stranger briefly thought about getting Anju to speak to Alfie about the pre-nup, but it was a fleeting idea, that went just as quickly as it had come into his head.

"I will make the Professor a new drink sir and all is well with the world," and with that Anju turned and busied himself with pouring another Jack Daniels. The ice cubes were impressive, transparent orbs that took up half of the low ball, crystal glass. The suave stranger was admiring Anju's bartending skills, as he moved around the bar. It was as if he was doing a dance.

"Professor is watching the ocean lights, very bright this evening Boss man, you would like." Anju stated as he walked around the front of the bar and stood in front of his new guest. "You come sir, you see," Anju implored.

Exhausted from the travelling he was about to turn down the offer, when Anju added, "Very quiet place, no wedding talk Boss man."

At this they both stood and listened to the sounds drifting across the island towards the little bar. The loud music, hubbub of people talking and laughing.

"That sounds good to me," he agreed and with a triumphant smile Anju led the handsome new guest, to a winding path aligned with dim lanterns and dense palms and vegetation.

Whilst walking, Anju suddenly stopped. "Oh, dear sir I have forgotten walkie phone, I must get it sir, very important."

He pointed in front of him and gestured to follow the path, "I will follow quickly sir, this path brings Boss man to the beach, the ocean lights and the Professor," he pressed the full glass of Jack Daniels into the Boss man's free hand and with that disappeared quickly up the path back towards his precious bar.

Intrigued, the Boss man continued down the path, sipping his delicious drink as he walked. The noise from the party was dissipating with every step and he found the solitude relaxing. He had had a busy day at work, full of meetings and agendas. Then the tedious and very long journey to get to this island, in the middle of nowhere and on top of all of this, the worries and concerns that were racing through his mind, regarding Alfie's up and coming wedding. He was shaking his head trying not to start his mind racing about Alfie again, when he stopped abruptly. The pathway had ended and he was now on a beach front, where the palms had thinned to expose the most spectacular site. There in the moonlight the ocean was indeed lit up. It looked as if thousands of tiny blue twinkling lights were making a pathway in the ocean, from the shore, out in to the deep waters. It was simply stunning.

As he took in the scene starting from the left, where he could see the shadows of water villas out in the distant waters, then a wooden jetty, arching its way past the villas and snaking its way on to the beach. The jetty was illuminated by small dimly lit lanterns. This was followed by the stunning ocean lights just to the right. He strained his eyes as they adjusted to the moonlit shoreline, where he could make out a large cushioned seat with a small figure sat on it. As his eyes grew more accustomed to the darkened area, he could see the figure more clearly.

It was a woman. She was sitting with her feet up on the seat, her arms wrapped around her legs, her chin resting on her knees. With the faint glow of the lanterns that were setting the scene behind the seating area, the blue lights emanating from the sea and the bright moonlight, she looked iridescent and ethereal. Her hair was piled on top of her head and she sat like a marble statue, staring out to sea. She was the most beautiful creature he had ever seen and the word angel sprang to his mind. He walked silently towards her and when only a short distance from her, he just stood and watched her, ignoring the surrounding tropical paradise.

Chapter 9

A small movement to her left made Ava turn her head, as she realised someone was approaching. The stranger walked slowly towards her out of the shadows. She took in his handsome features, in the bright moonlight. He stopped besides her looking down at her and she noticed his face was serious and slightly drawn.

"Good evening, I was looking for the Professor."

His American accent didn't surprise her, as most of Alfie's family and friends had arrived during the day. To be honest that was why she was hiding, trying to be invisible, it obviously wasn't working.

"You've found her," Ava replied smoothly, reaching for the glass at her side and taking a last sip of the amber liquid.

The stranger tilted his head slightly.

"You're the professor?" he sounded unconvinced.

"Don't tell me, you were expecting an old man with a beard and pipe?"

Ava couldn't help the hint of sarcasm as she answered. The stranger took another few steps forward, to stand in front of her looking down. His full lips had curled into a smile that had also reached his eyes.

"My apologies, I should not have assumed," he said quietly, shaking his head.

"I am returned Boss man, Professor," came Anju's voice from the darkness.

He walked up to Ava and with his well-practiced bow. He took the full glass from the Boss man and held it out to her.

"Professor, we have brought you a drink," he was beaming.

"Thank you, Anju, that is very kind of you, but I was just going to go to bed," Ava smiled politely.

"Oh no Professor you must stay with Boss man and admire the ocean lights," Anju insisted, pushing the glass towards her.

She handed him her empty glass and took the full glass, smiling and shaking her head.

"You can both hide from big wedding together," he finished with a wink.

Ava looked up at the stranger, who let out a genuine laugh. Anju's walkie talkie beeped into action and a garbled message came through to which he responded quickly.

"My apologies Boss man… Professor… I have been called," he nodded at each of them in turn and then with a flourish and bow he was gone.

Ava shifted uncomfortably as this American stranger sat down next to her, uninvited, on the cushioned beach chair. It was larger than a settee and there was still enough room for another person, however, Ava felt he was a little too close for comfort. She had been enjoying her personal space in peace.

Ava turned to face him, God he was gorgeous. Lou is going to wet her herself if this is how hot all the male wedding guests are.

"I will leave you to it," she smiled a shy smile and went to stand.

He grabbed her arm and immediately felt a jolt of electricity shoot from where he touched her skin, he felt it right to his core.

"No please stay. I have disturbed your solitude and it seems as though I am not the only one on this island who is trying to escape this wedding," his smile was dazzling and it was a moment before Ava could gather her thoughts and reply.

She sat back in the comfy seat and turned away from him to look out at the stunning ocean.

"I'm not avoiding the wedding, just all the hoo-hah it involves," she smiled and thought of all the air kisses and fake boobs that had no doubt arrived today.

"You're avoiding the Pennington's?" he questioned looking serious again.

"No," it was Ava's turn to laugh. "I have met most of them and they're lovely, it's the hangers on I'm not keen on," she looked at him directly and once again his beautiful mouth was turning up at the corners.

"Hangers on?" he questioned.

"You know the ones, like Blara and La Fou," she smiled as she said their names, he frowned trying to recall who they could be.

"They are like evil Barbie dolls on speed, you must know them if you're Alfie's friend? They are nasty, plastic dingle berries" Ava could not contain her laughter and as this handsome stranger tried to understand the meaning of the word dingle berries, she suddenly stopped and looked at him horrified.

"I am so sorry," she whispered. "The plan was to find some shells, walk back to my room and hide before the party started. I got carried away with the shells as I walked along the beach. Then I realised the sun was setting, so I sat here to watch it," at this she turned to face the ocean again, still sparkling and twinkling with the hypnotic blue lights. "Anju saw me and brought me a drink…he is very kind," she turned back to face the American. "Once the sun set, the ocean lit up and after several top ups…" she lifted her glass in her hand to show him, "I'm afraid I lost count of how many refills I've had, so I'm sitting here, smelling of sea salt and coconut sun cream, insulting your friends……once again… I do apologise," she looked sad as if her words may have offended him and he just laughed.

"You don't have to apologise, I'm sure Alfie wouldn't be offended either, he does share some rather odd company."

Ava returned his genuine smile.

"Thank you… and due to your kindness, may I present you with a refill," she held her glass out to him, "I really can't drink anymore and I don't want to waste it."

He took it from her and poured the liquid in to his own glass, managing to stop the large ball of ice going in too.

"I don't like all the falseness, but I am looking forward to the actual wedding itself," she looked serious now and he could tell that she was being honest with him.

He didn't often sit and talk to strange women, this was a new experience and one he found himself enjoying.

"So, what is so false about Blara and what was her name…foo foo?" he was rewarded with another heart stopping smile.

"La Fou," she returned.

"Ah yes La Fou."

"Well shall I just say everything? False personalities, false bodies, false everything," she bit her bottom lip as she tried to stifle a giggle and he found himself shifting in his seat.

His look had darkened, she noticed the movement and misinterpreted his uncomfortableness to the fact that she had just insulted his friends again. She clasped her hand over her mouth and shook her head.

"I really shouldn't drink, once again, my apologies," and with a deep sigh she leant forward and retrieved a net bag bulging with shells.

She fiddled within the bag and produced a beautiful shell, which she blew gently to get rid of the dried sand. She wiped the shell on the bottom of her shirt and placed it on the seat between them.

"In the way of yet another apology and before I say anything else offensive, I'm going."

After retrieving her flip-flops, but making no attempt at putting them on, she stood up.

"I am going to now attempt to walk the very slim, wobbly boards, whilst slightly pickled… and try and avoid falling into the shark infested waters, where they will probably have a field day thinking there's a very large seal for the eating," she stopped and turned to look down at him. "Enjoy your evening Boss man," she said with a beautiful smile.

He was completely stuck for words. He watched her turn and walk away, with a bag full of shells in one hand and her flip-flops in the other.

As she reached the start of the decking that led out into the ocean, she paused for a moment. He found himself praying that she would turn around and look at him, not realising he was holding his breath. After pausing, it seemed as though she were summoning the courage to step up onto the jetty. Her shoulders straightened, she held her head a little higher and stepped up onto the wooden jetty.

Chapter 10

Ava tried her best to look sober, as she walked away from the handsome stranger. She felt his eyes burning into the back of her body, as she tried to not hyperventilate and walk in a straight line, both at the same time. As she reached the start of the jetty, she took a deep breath. The bourbon had relaxed her, but she still had some wits about her and was well aware that at this time of the night, the sharks would be feeding. She would be crossing the shallow waters over a few planks of wood, with the occasional lamp on a pole, offering a dim light to show the way. Ava was petrified of sharks. As a child, she loved swimming and snorkelling, enjoying all the delights the ocean could bring.

This had all changed, on the eve of her eighteenth birthday, a moment in her life that she tried desperately not to remember, but which haunted her dreams. Some would consider it an irrational fear as she lived in the Midlands, and couldn't quite understand why the terror was so great. Her fear of sharks, however, was not as paralysing as the fear of befriending a man. A fear garnered later in life, when she had suffered another heart-breaking event. Yet a handsome American stranger, had just sat by her and made conversation. Instead of being shy and withdrawn she had actually chatted to him, thanks to the emboldening effects of the liquid courage.

She had stood tall, straightened up and took her first tentative steps onto the jetty, her mind racing with 'Boss man's face', his smile, his body...... *oh my god Ava, concentrate or fall in the water and become shark bait!*

She carried on walking past the first few water villas, which were all in darkness. The only light was from the moon and the pirate ship effect lanterns dotted along the jetty. The moon was bright enough to show the fish darting through the waters below, Ava tried not to think about the bigger fish that might be lurking underneath the villas, hiding in the shadows.

Suddenly there was a noise behind her, a creak of one of the jetty's wooden boards. She spun around to see the American stood stock still a few meters away.

"Professor," he nodded his head to acknowledge Ava.

Her newly found bravery slipped instantly away. There was literally no one else around, it was just the two of them. The villas were all unoccupied as their guests were either up at the party or had not yet arrived on the island.

"I don't need you to escort me home you know, I am quite capable of walking over a few planks," even Ava was shocked at how harsh she sounded and as the handsome stranger raised an eyebrow, she once again apologised.

"Sorry, I'm a bit jumpy about the…"

"Sharks," he interjected with a heart melting smile.

She smiled nervously back at him, but it did not reach her eyes. She was scared.

"Yes, sharks."

"Well, I didn't want you to end up as fish fodder," he said smoothly.

"Really I'm okay, thankyou though," she replied, ever polite.

Ava nodded her farewell and turned a little more carefully to face the direction she was going in. She carried on until she had rounded another bend and her villa was the next in sight. Relief flooded through her as she congratulated herself on making it home safely, even after a few drinks and more importantly avoiding a seriously close encounter with a tall, dark, handsome American man.

As she approached the smaller walk way on the right of her which led to her villa door, she noticed a movement in the water, a huge shiny fin breached the surface out of nowhere and she panicked. Turning quickly, dropping the shell bag and flip-flops as she did so, she went to run full pelt.

Something blocked her escape, as she ran into what felt like a brick wall.

"What is it?" a serious American voice came close to her right ear.

She realised she had her eyes squeezed tightly together, her whole body shaking. She slowly opened her eyes and turned her head to look up at this handsome stranger peering down at her with concern.

"What's wrong?" he demanded again.

He had a tight grip on her upper arms and kept her steady.

"Shark," she whispered and she watched him drag his eyes to the right of her searching for the beast she had just seen.

"There's nothing there," he said quietly, relaxing his hands slightly, but not letting her go.

She heard water splashing and watched his soft expression change to shock.

"Holy fuck!" he breathed, as he abruptly pulled Ava to the left of him, whilst his arms tightened around her, enclosing her body to his.

She closed her eyes and leaned into him, her muscles immobilised with fright.

"I thought you were joking," he said incredulously. "Surely that's not right, a shark that size being so close to shore?"

At this Ava heard another splash and felt his embrace tighten even more.

"It's okay, you're safe. It can't reach us up here," he spoke gently.

Ava suddenly felt stupid. Of course, the shark wasn't going to jump up on the jetty and eat her. His grip relaxed a little and she pulled back from him, creating a slight gap between their bodies, his hands now firmly on her waist. She bravely looked up at his gorgeous concerned face and opened her mouth to make yet another apology, but the door of her villa swung open with a loud bang, causing both of their tense bodies to jolt. They turned in unison to see Bella strolling out of the villa.

"Bell!" was all Ava could manage as she gawped, staring between Bella and the now calm waters beneath the bridge.

The sea monster had gone, the bang of the door probably frightened it off. Ava took in a deep breath to settle her nerves and looked back from the water to her friend. Bella had stopped in her tracks, an odd expression on her face, it was a cross between shock and euphoria.

Ava looked puzzled for a second and then the Boss man spoke.

"Good evening, we were just shark watching," he said with a polite smile and a nod.

Ava was mortified. She was standing outside her villa, in the arms of a man, she had only just met.

What must Bella be thinking?

She made to push away from him, but he held her firmly to his chest. Ava looked at her friend and for once in her life she didn't know what to say.

"I was just checking up on you Ave," her friend announced as she breezed effortlessly across the small walkway on to the main jetty.

She was now standing in front of them and Ava was glad it was night time as her face felt like it was on fire, she must be as red as a beetroot.

"Thought I'd find you working or cuddled up with your kindle and a glass of wine… how wrong was I." She retorted and actually winked, with her perfectly drawn on eyebrow.

Ava was so embarrassed. She once again tried to make some space between herself and this smoulderingly, sexy man. She splayed her palms and tried to lever herself out of his vice-like embrace, but once again he maintained his firm, hold and did not let her go. If anything, he tightened his grip.

Ava turned her head to face him. How dare he hold onto her in front of her friend, how dare he not let her go, how dare he have a body like an Adonis and have it so close to her like this. She could feel the firmness of his chest muscles and the smell of his aftershave, which was intoxicating.

She briefly wondered what he would look like with his shirt off… and his trousers. Ava shook her head to try and clear her erratic thoughts. His piercing blue eyes held her gaze, as if he were trying to read her mind. A small line ran across his forehead, his face held a serious expression, as if any movement would not be tolerated. As if he wanted her to stay in his arms forever.

"Well, I can see you're both busy, have a great evening and Ave, can you check on us all in the morning? They are planning on getting smashed and spending the night on the four posters," Bella smiled broadly and edged passed them.

Not looking back, or waiting for a goodbye, she disappeared around the bend of the jetty.

Now they were alone. He was still holding her incredibly close, her hands still splayed on his chest. Their breathing had slowed and was now in unison, all thoughts of sea monsters forgotten. Ava could feel her stomach turning over with nerves, she hadn't been held like this for years.

"You can let me go now," she said quietly, not meaning a word of it.

His strong, lean body pushing against hers was heavenly.

"No," he murmured.

They gazed into each other's eyes and just as he was bringing his face close to hers, she realised he was about to kiss her. Panic struck her and she pushed him hard on the chest, this time surprising him and their bodies parted.

"Why did you follow me?" her harsh tone was like a slap on the face to him.

He took a deep calming breath.

"I was not following you, I was simply walking back to my room," he said patiently as if talking to a child, his mouth twitching with humour.

"There's only one water villa after mine and it's the honey moon villa," Ava responded curtly.

"Yes… that's mine," he paused and pointed in the direction behind where Ava was standing, as if for clarity.

"Hey neighbour," he smiled trying to break the tension that had suddenly manifested.

Ava looked thoughtful for a moment and then spoke slowly and quietly.

"You're in the honeymoon villa?" she questioned.

"Correct Professor," he replied mockingly, but she did not smile and averted her eyes from her feet, which for some reason she had found easier to look at, back to his face.

"Of course, you are…" she shook her head gently as she spoke "…of course you're in the honeymoon villa."

She grimaced, as the realisation hit her like a punch to the stomach.

"You had better get back to your wife then," she failed miserably to keep the bitterness out of her voice.

He smirked and she felt like smacking him across the face, a feeling that surprised her as she was not an aggressive person.

"I am not married," he replied, still smirking.

"Girlfriend then… or boyfriend," she frowned as if she had made a grammatical error that annoyed her.

She should know by now not to judge people, although the thought of Boss man being gay was depressing. His response was a heart-melting laugh and for a moment she zoned out of the conversation they were having and concentrated on his beautiful face. Chiselled cheek bones, long dark lashes and the bluest of eyes.

"Professor," he was enamoured now, "I am single and the villa is mine and mine alone. I have no one waiting in my bed," he purred.

This snapped her out of her reverie and she looked appalled. He is single, he has a whole honeymoon water villa to himself and he thinks I'm going to sleep with him, shit!

"Professor," he interjected, now a little concerned.

He was expecting a swoon or at least a smile, but she looked horrified. Not the usual response women had to him. He took a step towards her and she instinctively took a step backwards making him scowl. He took two large strides towards her and put his hands on her shoulders. She looked like a rabbit caught in the head lights, again not the usual reaction women have to him. They stared at each other, not moving. Their bodies close, but not quite touching. She could feel his breath on her face as her insides squirmed. Feelings that had been locked away for years began to surface. He brought his face closer to hers and just as their lips were about to touch, they were startled by a shrill voice coming from the honeymoon villa behind them.

"Darling…is that you?" Ava's eyes opened wide and her blood ran cold.

Oh my god, she would recognise that voice anywhere, she'd heard enough of it all week. Blara!

"It's not what you think," he said sternly feeling her body tense in his hands.

She broke their gaze first and turned to look in the direction of the last villa, where she saw the surrounding area suddenly light up. Blara had found the porch light, the jetty suddenly illuminated.

"Where have you been darling?" the voice came again, but this time it was clearer and Ava knew Blara bitch face was now behind them, watching them.

"Listen-to-me…" he began slowly, not hiding the anger in his voice.

Ava misinterpreted this as anger at her, as he had been caught out. She had nearly kissed him for god's sake, she is the one who should be angry. She took another step away from him and he made no attempt to move.

Not so keen now your girlfriend is watching us, she thought bitterly.

"Goodnight," she said curtly, as she turned and almost ran to her door, opening it and shutting it quickly behind her.

How could she have been so stupid? After all these years she had finally felt the need to kiss someone and he turns out to be Blara bitch face's boyfriend. She flumped down on the bed, suddenly feeling tired and incredibly lonely. The whole episode had exhausted her and it had all taken part within the last hour. She felt ridiculously embarrassed, she had deterred a lot of interested men over the last few years. Her heart really couldn't cope with 'love' again, so she had built her barriers well. Yet this evening, this evening she had felt attracted to someone. She had felt that odd sensation in the pit of her stomach, that you get when your body craves to be touched. She had ignored her head screaming at her to run and for once listened to her heart, which wanted her to stay in his arms and kiss him.

She felt like screaming out in frustration, of all the men she could kiss, she'd wanted to kiss Blara's boyfriend. She felt sick at the thought of it, they were probably having a good laugh at her expense. She pulled the duvet over her head. Eventually she fell asleep, although that was more thanks to the Jack Daniels she had consumed. She was in for a restless night, where a shark was not the only dangerous creature to dominate her dark dreams.

Chapter 11

After a night of tossing, turning and heart wrenching nightmares, Ava had showered extra early and had sat on her huge bed, staring at the blank screen of her iMac. Upon her arrival on the island, she had written prolifically when in her room. She had also brought her kindle with her, however, the surroundings had been so inspiring, she had wanted to get her thoughts down and had had no time for reading. This morning she had a lot going on her head, but nothing relating to her novel. Writing usually freed her mind of any worries and concerns and she would lose herself in her characters and their world she created so brilliantly.

Last night's encounter had shaken her to the core. She hadn't even asked the Boss man what his real name was and he had managed to turn her world upside down. The way he held her tightly when she'd seen that shark, her body shuddered at the memory. Although the way his arms embraced her, his firm toned chest pushed against her soft curves. Christ what was wrong with her, *get a grip Ava*, she silently scolded herself. Then her memory flicked back to his handsome face gazing intently at her, concerned about her. It had felt incredible. So incredible in fact, that she had almost kissed him. She, the perpetual singleton, sworn never to fall in love again, had almost kissed a strange man. Then her mind reeled as Blara's voice shattered her hot memory. She had been waiting for him, in that huge honeymoon villa. Ava felt slightly nauseous. How pathetic was she being? She needed to pull herself together.

She closed the laptop, slightly harder than she had intended. She didn't really know this man, he was free to have whoever he wanted in his villa, it was none of her business and she needed to get a grip. She turned to look at the clock on her bedside table, it was just after 6 am. She liked to watch the sunrise, so this gave her the boost to get up out of the comfort of her cosy bed and back to the real world. She would put the gorgeous stranger out of her mind and get on with her day.

She showered and dressed quickly, gathering what she needed, placing it in a canvas beach bag. One last, quick look in the dressing table mirror, where she observed that she looked presentable, although maybe a little tired, at this time in the morning the place would be deserted, so who cares. Her hair was up high in a messy bun, damp tendrils clinging to her neck. She wore a loose white, buttoned up shirt, over her favourite red bikini. She looked acceptable and as she turned to walk out of the villa, she straightened her shoulders and stood a little taller, in readiness to see what today would bring.

The sun was slowly rising over the stunning ocean shedding the light of a new morning, onto this island paradise. She felt a little more confident on the jetty during day light hours, although remaining vigilant, scanning the ebbing tide, for any large fish that may be swimming below.

As she had left her water villa, Ava hadn't been particularly quiet, as her only neighbours were ensconced in the honeymoon villa. The handsome stranger she had encountered last night and Blara, were no doubt tucked up in bed, which was a depressing thought. She really didn't care if she woke them by closing her door a little too keenly.

The noise of the door closing had stirred the Boss from his half slumber. He opened his eyes and took a few seconds to register where he was, which was lying on a sun lounger on the decking of his luxury honeymoon water villa. He liked the suite as it had plenty of room and it was away from the hum drum of the rest of his family and wedding furore. Up until last night.

Last night he had been introduced to the Professor. Her beautiful features and curvaceous body had plagued his dreams. His broken sleep had been interrupted by a door closing loudly, it must be her. With this thought he jumped up quickly and strode determinedly into his villa. He quickly swilled some water over his face, roughly dried it on the soft cotton towels and left his villa via the main door. He couldn't see anyone, but could have sworn he had heard a villa door close. He walked quickly using huge strides rounding the curve of the jetty where the villas also curved, echoing the contour of the beach.

Then he saw her. She was walking to the left of the jetty along the white powdery sand of the beach. The sun's early rays shone against her incredible body and he paused, admiring her long-toned legs and briefly closed his eyes as he remembered her pressed against his body last night. He groaned as he became hard at the thought.

It had been a long night. If only he had kissed those full lips, that long neck and basically the rest of her amazing body. Thanks to Zara, the Professor had moved out of his grasp and into her villa, before he had had time to even blink.

He opened his eyes wide and watched this English beauty walk along the beach. Something caught his eye on the right-hand side of the jetty. It was Rogers. He nodded a greeting and turned his attention back to the Professor.

Moving swiftly along the jetty, he never once took his eyes off her beautiful figure, making her way around the shoreline. He followed and curiosity consumed his thoughts. What if she was having an early morning rendezvous with someone? His forehead creased and he became annoyed at that thought. *For fucks sake you don't even know her name*, he chastised himself.

Just as his thoughts were running wildly away from him, she veered away from the edge of the newly dampened sand, she had been carefully walking on and made her way to a huge cabana bed. He could make out at least three bodies lying on the huge mattress and then remembered the little brunette last night.

These bodies were the Professor's friends, sleeping off the party spirit from the night before. She was now at the first of two beds and had placed the bag she had been carrying, onto the cushioned mattress. She had put her hands on both hips and looked like she was gently shaking her head. He sucked in his breath as her hands reached her sides. The loose shirt she was wearing was raised to show where her long legs ended and her curve of her sexy behind began. She didn't seem to be speaking, but he had stayed well back.

The sounds of the waves could have covered any quiet talking. She reached into the bag and pulled several bottles of water and placed them on the bed. She then moved to the bottom corner of the bed, fumbling with the tied-up material. Freeing the soft, white muslin, she pulled it to where she had been standing by the bag. She walked to the top of the bed and did the same with both corners.

Just as she pulled the material down to meet the other, a tanned, muscular arm rose off the bed and grabbed her around the waist. She let out a squeal of delight and then laughed. The sound felt like balm being poured over his soul. He then checked himself as he took an instant dislike to the man this arm belonged too.

The Professor bent over the male, exposing the base of her red bikini briefs and sublime butt. From this distance, he couldn't figure out if she had kissed the man on the bed, but there was no more interaction, she stood up, drawing the curtain across and tying the sun shade together. She made her way around the

80

back of the bed and presumably did the same. He now registered that he could hear soft voices, but they were female and then after a few minutes he saw the Professor edge around the decking and close and tie the front muslin curtains.

With her friends safely protected from the sun, she turned to face the ocean. She stepped down off the wooden base of the bed and walked towards the damp sand. Just as her feet touched the water's edge, she stopped. She tipped her head upwards and closed her eyes, as though enjoying the warmth of the early morning rays. Suddenly she dropped her head facing forward, her eyes wide and alert. He wondered briefly if she had seen a shark. Abruptly she turned her head in his direction and he realised she had discovered her stalker. They glared at each other for a moment. She turned her head to face the other way. It was as if she was debating whether to go towards him or run in the opposite direction. He didn't want her run, she had done that last night and he had had a sleepless night because of it. He wasn't used to not getting what he wanted. She turned back to look at him again. Her decision made, she straightened her shoulders, held her head high and walked towards him with purpose.

Chapter 12

"Good morning," she said looking him squarely in the eyes.

He had watched her walk towards him and now she was literally within touching distance, he was for once in his life lost for words. A hugely successful business man, he commanded respect and could handle himself in any situation and yet this beautiful English woman had completely messed up his head. She was still staring at him, as he admired the sparkling topaz blue of her stunning eyes. They were the most incredible luminous pools, in which he felt he could easily loose himself forever.

Her head inclined slightly to the left, her eyes narrowed, as she studied his handsome face. This small movement brought him out of his reverie. She opened her mouth to speak, but closed it quickly as if changing her mind. Unexpectedly, she went to walk past him. His hand shot out like a barrier, his arm stretching across her flat stomach, his fingers grabbing her left hip and preventing her from moving forward. She spun round to face him again, her mouth open in shock, an incredulous expression on her face. She did not speak.

"Why were you going to run?" he questioned under his breath.

Her mouth closed and her shoulders relaxed slightly. Christ she was the most beautiful creature he had ever seen. He had slept with famous actresses, super models, some of the most incredible looking women on the planet and they were all at his beck and call. Yet this stunning woman before him, wore no makeup and yet her skin was iridescent in the gentle early rays of the morning sun. Her full lips were begging to be kissed and the natural movement of her expression, showed no chemical injections or implants had touched her beautiful face. Most of the women he knew, including his family, had all indulged in medical procedures in order to so call 'improve' themselves, however, he could see now, the true meaning to the words 'natural beauty'.

"Do I need to repeat myself?" He growled, lines deepening on his forehead as he spoke.

"No… but maybe I do," she answered seriously. "I did say good morning?" She questioned and he realised he had been staring at her and hadn't answered

"You did. Good morning Professor," his eyes had darkened. "Why were you going to run?" he repeated.

She turned towards the gently lapping waves and let out a slow calming breath.

"I was debating whether to avoid you," she answered honestly. "However, the island is full of guests and we haven't had the wedding yet, so avoiding you is impossible."

When he didn't respond she continued.

"Last night I," she shut her eyes tightly as though searching for the right words, "last night I had had a little too much to drink and I apologise for talking about your girlfriend the way I did, I had no idea," she trailed off.

There was a pause she opened her eyes again and looked at him. It was as if she was peering into his very soul and he was again lost for words.

"And then on the jetty, I thought… I thought you were going to… that we were going to," another soft sigh that melted his heart and stirred his groin.

He suddenly realised that his arm was still around her and he wanted nothing more than to pull her closer to him and kiss her fiercely.

"I'm sorry," she said quietly, looking down at her feet.

He raised his left hand to her cheek and guided her face to look at him.

"Zara is not and never will be my girlfriend. I do not have 'girlfriends'," his voice was seductive and intense. "Be assured she was not in my room by my request. In fact, she had evaded security, lied to the villa staff and I had no idea she was in there. I have spoken to her and made it clear that she will not interfere in my life again. She is a mere family acquaintance who I tolerate out of respect for them. She left shortly after your swift exit and will not be pulling a stunt like that again," he said seriously.

He was peering into her eyes, as if needing assurance that she understood last night was not what it looked like. That Zara really meant nothing to him. In fact, he couldn't see why his family put up with her. Last night's actions had made him angry and he had told Zara to stay away from him, in no uncertain terms. She had broken into his villa in an attempt to seduce him, but she was not who he had wanted in his bed. Thanks to Zara, the woman he wanted had run into her own villa and away from his embrace. Both Zara and her foul friend were obviously gold diggers and he could never understand why his family tolerated them both. What did the Professor call them last night? Blara and La Fou. He smiled at the thought of the nicknames lifting his eyes again to hers, he was telling the truth and for some reason he really wanted her to believe him. For some unidentifiable reason, this mattered, she mattered.

Ava was good at reading people and against her better judgement she trusted what he was saying and for some unknown reason, she was extremely relieved that this wonderful specimen of a man was not sleeping with the enemy. Although enemy seemed too strong a word to use and she mentally chastised herself for even thinking like that.

Ava smiled a shy, warm smile and then looked over his shoulder to see a tall well-built man, dressed in a short-sleeved shirt, tailored shorts and a baseball cap. His eyes were covered by expensive looking sunglasses. His focus seemed to be fixed in their direction.

Boss man turned and called over, "It's okay Rogers, she's a friend." He turned back to her.

A flush of pale pink had touched her cheeks and he realised that she was blushing. Fuck she was beautiful. He wanted to throw her on to the sand and have his wicked way with her here and now.

"I'm going for breakfast… you would like to join me?" She asked quietly, watching his face very carefully as if trying to weigh him up.

Although his thoughts were otherwise engaged, he responded quickly, in case she changed her mind.

"I would like that, thank you Professor," he smiled a huge genuine smile and she felt her insides turn to jelly, as she gazed into his striking features.

Neither moved a muscle. She felt his grip tighten slightly on her waist and once again she found herself in a compromising position with this stranger. Oddly the thought made her smile and this had the same effect on him, as his groin twitched in reaction.

"Come on then, I'm hungry," she said, her words making his groin strain even more.

Christ, he wanted to rip off her clothes and kiss her beautiful body from top to toe. He let out a long breath he hadn't realised he had been holding, and reluctantly let go of her waist. He briefly debated telling her that he was hungry if she was breakfast, but then thought the better of it.

He stood to the side with his right arm raised, guiding the way.

"Shall we?" he smiled,

"Thank you, Boss man," she replied politely and walked slowly past him in response.

As they walked along the stunning shoreline, she pointed out different shells that had washed up overnight. As she bent to pick up each treasure, he felt the pull in his shorts as he grew harder with want. He watched intently as her face lit up with each new shell. They were both more relaxed now and the conversation started to flow easily.

He told her he was a CEO of a business that had been passed down from generation to generation and briefly explained what the company did. Quite simply they brought businesses and either invested in them or asset stripped, which ever was to make the most money for them.

She listened and commented where appropriate, asking questions that he thought were interesting and intelligent. Not the type of conversation he was used to having with a woman, except his sister, mother or grandmother. He spoke passionately about saving the environment and how important it was to give back.

He mentioned a project taking part in the Maldives, interlinking marine life and keeping the oceans clean and plastic free. She was impressed with this and they discussed the project intently. He was enjoying himself and for the first time on this trip, he started to unwind. They spoke of how little time off he usually had and that this vacation was a rare break in his hectic business schedule.

After veering off the subject of business, he began to talk on a more personal subject of the upcoming wedding. He commented on how he was not happy with being a wedding guest and how this was an unwanted interruption on his valuable time. They had been sitting in the sand, watching the waves gently lap the uninhabited beach, not having made it to the restaurant for food, as they had both been enjoying each other's company.

He commented on how this event was costing a fortune and that the bride and groom hardly even knew each other.

"They have been together for over a year," she countered, her voice not betraying the emotions that were going through her head.

The shell she had been trying to focus on, seeming completely unimportant anymore, falling from her hand. He raised a quizzical brow and firmly shook his head.

"Bible," she said her eyes wide and honest.

God she was beautiful, but she obviously doesn't know the bride well.

"Bible?" he questioned, she briefly looked down at her feet, something he realised she did when she was embarrassed, a move that was endearing and also alluring.

When she looked back up at him with her huge cerulean eyes, gazing through her long black lashes, it made him want her even more.

"Bible means honest, it means I'm telling you the truth," she said willing him to believe her.

"It's barely been three months and they hardly know each other; they are from completely different worlds… she is of no consequence." He said sternly, ignoring the look of horror on her face he continued. "She has no family to speak of and little money behind her."

The look of disdain on his face made Ava angry. She was not a volatile person and usually the grounded, calming influence come any confrontation, but this was not on.

"For your information they have been a couple since March last year…" she said trying to keep her tone calm. "…and she 'has' got a family who love and care for her and she is also a hardworking, independent woman," she finished, glaring at him.

They were sat incredibly close to each other and the tension was unbearable. He leant in even closer to her, making the distance between them a hairs breadth and with a furrowed brow he spoke.

"If I said bible, would you believe me?" he replied defiantly. "I assure you I know exactly what is going on and I am trying to stop it."

Ava literally stopped breathing. It took a few seconds for her to realise and force herself to take a huge breath. She pushed her hands into the sand and stood quickly, feeling a little dizzy for the speed of her ascent. He immediately jumped up and gazed at her. Her face had paled and he realised that it was due to him and his words. She looked as if he had literally punched her in the stomach, knocking all of the breath out of her striking body.

He moved his hand to her face to comfort her, but she flinched away and quickly took a step back.

"I'm sorry, I didn't say that to upset you, it's the truth… bible," he added with a tight smile, trying to lighten the mood, which suddenly felt positively polar.

She did not smile.

"You wouldn't know the truth if it bit you on your arse," she replied quickly blanking images of his firm, sexy bottom out of her mind. "Who do you think you are to say you are trying to stop the wedding?" She was really angry now and stood her ground. "How dare you interfere with a relationship that has nothing to do with you!" Her fists were clenched and she was shaking with fury.

He took a step back and raised both hands as if to calm a wild animal.

"Just calm down," he said soothingly.

"Calm down?" she almost screamed, "…are you joking?"

His brow furrowed as he stepped forward and looked down into this beautiful woman's face.

"I am the groom's brother," he said firmly, as if that was all that was needed to justify his opinions.

He watched her carefully as her mouth closed quickly and her eyes widened. He noticed Rogers appear in his eye line, obviously concerned about the raised voices. It seemed like an infinity before either of them spoke or even blinked.

She straightened her shoulders, stood a little taller and stepped so close to him he could feel her breath on his face. He was so turned on, he actually smirked. In an almighty effort not to smash this arsehole in the face, again she was not a violent woman however, this man!

She took a deep breath and, in a calm, and even tone responded with,

"I am the bride's sister."

With that she turned on her heels and strode determinedly back down the beach, leaving the shells she had been admiring in a pile, on the sand where they had been sitting.

'Boss man' stood and watched her as she made her escape, Rogers running over to him to ensure he was alright.

Chapter 13

Ava stormed across the jetty at super speed, only briefly acknowledging that sharks may be lurking in the crystal-clear waters below. She was absolutely livid. *How dare he speak like that about her beloved sister!* She slammed the door as she entered the coolness and solitude of her villa. The nerve of the man. Saying he was trying to stop the wedding, that Kit was some way inadequate for his brother.

Who did he think he was?

Ava stormed over to the fridge and retrieved a bottle of red wine. She knew it was too early in the morning, but she needed something to help her calm down. Shakily pouring a huge glass of the delicious looking liquid, she took a big slug. She usually had her red wine at room temperature, but when in Rome, or in this case the Maldives.

She continued pacing holding her glass tightly. She caught a glance of herself in the dressing table mirror and stopped stock still. She was flushed and sweaty, with a face like thunder. *Fuck.* She thought to herself, *what a bloody mess and it's all his fault.*

She didn't even know his name. Bloody Boss man. Well, he wasn't the boss of her and she was certainly not going to let him try and stop this wedding. Maybe she should have paid more attention to Jez, when he was telling her how prominent the Pennington dynasty were. Lou had said they all appeared in her posh magazines. Bella had mentioned Alfie's sister, Sofia, had married a few months ago, in a huge society wedding that apparently was covered by the media. Ava had taken it all with a pinch of salt, as Kitty and Alfie had seemed so down to earth and at no point did Kit mention any aggravation with Alfie's family.

A knock at the door broke her train of thought and a wave of nausea swept over her as she realised that Alfie's brother might be standing on the other side of the door. She slowly walked towards the door. Someone hammered on it again, this time with a worried voice.

"Ave?"

She let out a sigh of relief as she recognised Jez's concerned tone. Ava opened the door to find him leaning on the frame, squinting at her in the sunshine. His short-sleeved shirt was completely open and his tailored shorts hung on his toned and muscled hips, he looked like he was on a fashion shoot for Vogue. She knew he was a bloody supermodel, but it was so annoying that he always looked so glamourous and sexy.

"Wow that bad?" he said nodding at the loaded glass in her hand, immediately seeing the tension in her face.

"Come in," she said sharply and he winced, placing his hands on his heart.

"I'm wounded by your tone," he pulled a sad, schoolboy's face.

As angry as she was, Ava's temper faded for a moment and she sighed.

"Come in you idiot." She sat down on the end of her huge, four poster bed.

Jez sauntered in and made his way to the fridge, helping himself to a can of orange pop.

"You have no idea how much my head is hurting," he smirked and drank thirstily from the can, whilst flumping down on the bed beside her.

"Good night then?" Ava asked politely.

"Would have been better if you were there," he said with a pout, "I missed you."

He paused and sat bolt upright, turning to Ava with a serious look on his handsome face.

"Come on then, tell me who he is?" he questioned.

Ava looked confused, how could he possibly know she had just had a row with a man?

"The gorgeous stranger you were snogging outside your room last night?" he said, his quizzical brows raised.

"Snogging!" she shouted, making him wince.

"Alright, alright, blimey Ave, calm down." That did it, the words had been used just minutes ago by someone else, the American Boss Man, Alfie's brother.

She stood up a little too quickly and tried to blink the spots out of her vision, suddenly feeling far too hot, in what was an icily cool room. She felt rather then saw arms wrap around her and focused on steadying the glass in her hand, then realised the glass was no longer there. Feeling extremely dizzy and nauseous, she felt herself being lifted and placed flat on the cool bed.

Ava could hear the whirring of the ceiling fan and water running in the bathroom. She closed her eyes tightly trying to sort her feelings out in her head. She was so angry at Alfie's brother, yet so attracted to him, how was that possible? She flinched as she felt a cool, damp cloth on her forehead, opening her eyes carefully to find Jez, face to face, with concern etched on his gorgeous profile.

"What just happened?" he spoke quietly and waited patiently for a reply.

"I didn't kiss him." Ava said slowly, realising how stupid she was to have knocked back red wine on an empty stomach.

"Okay…" Jez said slowly, he paused and she saw the concern in his eyes.

He was really worried about her, no wonder when she was acting like a complete nutter.

"I'm fine really," she said unconvincingly, even she didn't believe herself.

"Mmm." Jez said, plonking himself on the other side of Ava and sprawling across the humongous bed.

"Start at the beginning my angel," he said, softly grasping her hand for support.

For a moment she couldn't speak, her emotions were running riot. So, she began her story with watching the ocean lights last night and the handsome American aka 'Boss Man', who had sort of escorted/followed her back to her villa. She mentioned the shark and he tightened his grip protectively. She was completely honest, as she always had been with Jez and as he was with her. She told him how he was holding her when Bella appeared. He snorted with laugher at this bit, but stopped abruptly when she turned to glare at him.

"Sorry!" he said quietly regaining his composure.

Ava continued and described how Bella had disappeared on the jetty and they were about to kiss, when Blara appeared from the Boss Man's room. Jez sat up at the mention of Blara.

"Blara, Blara needs mascara?" he said incredulously.

Now it was Ava's turn to smile grimly. She placed her hand on the cooling flannel that was still lying on her forehead and turned it over, giving some relief to her now pounding head.

"I said goodnight and practically ran into my room and locked the door."

Jez was now leaning on one arm, gazing down at her, the concern still etched on his handsome face. He asked her to go on. She explained that after dropping the water off at the cabana beds, she had bumped into the mysterious stranger again and went on to explain how the events had unfolded.

Jez *eww'd* and *ahh'd* in all the right places, but when she told him the stranger was Alfie's brother, he slapped his hands over his mouth, his eyes wide with shock.

"No fucking way... Boss Man is Alfie's brother?"

Ava closed her eyes, now that she had said it all out loud to Jez, there was no escaping it. This had actually happened.

Jez took in Ava's pale complexion and realised how hard all of this must be for her.

"My darling girl," he said quietly, "I knew it was only a matter of time before some handsome stranger swept you off your feet." He began seriously.

"Stop... please... I don't want to talk about that. I want to discuss what we are going to do about Alfie's brother, trying to stop my sister's wedding." She said gravely.

Jez pondered for a moment and then said carefully, "Do you know which brother it was?"

He produced his iPhone from his back pocket.

"I haven't got much charge left in it after last night, but there should be enough to google him?"

At this Ava sat up, again a little too quickly and regretted it immediately. Jez tapped furiously onto his phone and there in the world of cyberspace, appeared a picture of what must be the Pennington clan.

Ava studied the picture carefully. The high-class group were all dressed up to the nines in tuxedos and ball gowns. There were two sets of elderly couples and a younger, beautiful couple that could possibly be Alfie's parents. They were all seated and behind them the most gorgeous set of people Ava had ever seen, besides Jez.

There was a handsome gent on the left-hand side, with his hand connected to the elderly lady sat in front of him. He looked a lot like Boss Man, the same serious, daunting eyes, however, he had silvery, white streaks either side of his head, breaking into the otherwise dark brown hair. It gave him a distinctive, devastatingly, handsome look. He was smiling and although strong-featured, he looked like he had a kind face. Next to him was Alfie. Younger in years, he had the same features, only his dark-brown hair was short and spikey. A strong jawline, softened with the most dazzling smile. She could see why Kitty had fallen head over heels for him. Next to him, a man, who seemed to have missed the Pennington genes completely as there was no strong jaw or handsome features. He was tall, with cropped, jet-black hair and looked completely inferior to all of the other men in the photograph. He had an expression that Ava didn't like the look of and next to him stood the beautiful Sofia Junior. A stunning siren, who had obviously inherited all the best genes of the women along the front row. Although smiling, it didn't quite reach her eyes, giving her a sad appearance. The moody interloper on her right, had his hand around her waist, pulling her close to him, must be her new husband.

Before scrutinizing anyone else, Ava saw him, 'Boss Man'. Even on a photograph, on a mobile phone screen, he seemed to dominate the rest of them with his handsome and serious features. Ava pointed at him with a shaky finger.

"Shit Ava," Jez whistled through his perfect teeth. "You have only fallen for one of the most eligible bachelors on the planet, besides me." he added with wink.

Then stoical and with great regale he said, "Professor… let me introduce you to Ethan Pennington!"

They both sat there for a few minutes, staring at the image.

"You seriously think he's going to try and stop the wedding?" Jez questioned.

"That's exactly what he said," Ava said sadly.

Jez could see that Ava was torn, she obviously liked this Ethan, which in itself was to be discussed, but she also loved her sister and she would never put anything before Kit's happiness, not even her own.

"Maybe Blara fancies him and that's why she has been so malicious and underhanded?" Ava was talking to herself, but Jez picked up on the underhanded bit.

"I know she's an evil bitch, but she has been quite open about it," he said honestly.

Ava then filled Jez in on the spa treatment and Detin's admission that she had taken money from Blara to deliberately remove Bella's eyebrow, only Blara had meant for Ava to have that treatment. Jez was literally gobsmacked. He had met some psycho women in his time, mixed up and nasty. They would say or do anything to try and keep him, something it seemed, he had in common with the Pennington men.

Ava watched very little television and never read the showbiz magazines. Her life was writing, helping Bella in the bridal shop and spending time with her little family. There was no real downtime to catch up on what was happening in the real world, as Jez called it. He tried to fill her in about the latest showbiz drama or celebrity showdown, but he knew she had no interest in it. As long as it didn't affect her or her loved ones, why should she care about it.

A few years ago, a skanky woman had sold a story to a tabloid paper, saying Jez was the mother to her unborn child. He had never even met the female stalker, who had gone to great lengths to trick her idol. Of course, Ava was livid and vowed to help in any way she could. Jez had camped out in her home for weeks, in the end he had gone stir crazy.

As soon as the police had arrested and charged the maniac, he went on a romp around Europe to celebrate with his showbiz pals. Ava and Jez had always been there for one another and loved each other unconditionally. The worst thing in the world was if one of them was sad or upset, the other would turn their whole world upside down to help. In fact, Ava had met up with Jez in Paris, just to make sure he was really okay, after all of the upset and drama of the court case.

He was seriously one of the world's most eligible bachelors and although women would drop at his feet, Ava was the one woman he truly loved and her happiness was paramount. The fact Blara had tried to hurt Ava had made him not only uncomfortable, but really angry. She had already tried it on with him the first time she had set eyes on him, by the pool. Even La Fou had made it obvious that if he wanted to have sex with her, she was more than willing and available.

They lay in an easy silence on the massive bed, the wooden fan whirring contentedly above. Slowly and silently, they both tried to process the events of the last twenty-four hours.

Ava woke to a gentle snore coming from the side of her pillow. She opened her eyes and blinked several times, realising Jez had moved closer to her and fallen asleep on her pillow. She smiled and was glad that he was next to her, it made her feel stronger, not so lonely.

Her thoughts immediately strayed to a time when she really wasn't alone and she felt a warm tear fall over cheek. She was not one for being an emotional wreck and very rarely cried, but as she lay there, she felt overwhelmingly sad. She closed her eyes tightly to try and block out the pain the memories were bringing.

"Hey," Jez's gentle voice broke her contemplation and she felt his soft fingers wipe away the tear.

"You're thinking of him?" he questioned gently, she nodded not wanting to speak.

His strong arms were around her instantly, pulling her to him and holding her tightly to his body. She snuggled up and felt the warmth flow from his torso to hers, keeping her eyes closed and letting sleep envelop her once more. They were both bleary-eyed when Ava's phone pinged into life.

Jez reached over to check it as Ava lay still, not wanting to break this contact.

"Shit!" he sat up abruptly, "It's nearly time for KitKat to land," he said, smiling with excitement.

Ava also sprung up on the bed with a huge grin. His excitement was infectious and all sadness was forgotten. She took her phone and replied to Lou, who advised that she was waiting at a small bar, by the water plane jetty. As this was the other side of the island and Ava and Jez did not want to greet Kitty, as hot, sweaty messes, they quickly called room service and ordered a buggy.

By the time they had walked the length of the jetty, the buggy was on the nearest path, waiting. They laughed as they whizzed round the paths, the upset from earlier put aside, for now.

When they arrived at the start of the sea plane jetty, the others were waiting for them, cocktails in hand. Bella was holding a rolled-up banner she had made to welcome the bride-to-be. She was still wearing that baseball cap and sunglasses, along with a long, black, maxi dress. As a petite, Italian woman, she had perfect bone structure, which was enhanced by her short pixie cut. She would have usually donned a fashionable floppy straw hat, so the baseball hat still looked odd. Ava thought it looked familiar, but was distracted by the sounds of propellers getting nearer and everyone cheered as the sea plane landed.

As it bobbed along on the crystal-clear waters, the group made their way along the jetty to greet their missing family member. The door of the plane opened and a young lad in a white t-shirt and shorts, jumped out bare-footed. He efficiently and expertly tied off ropes to the jetty keeping the plane as stable as was possible.

The Australian pilot appeared. He was the one Lou had tried it on with when they had been flown to this beautiful paradise. Lou whooped with excitement getting his and everyone else's attention. The bronzed, bare-foot pilot smiled wolfishly at Lou and then offered his hand into the cabin. Like their own disembarkation, it was not easy climbing down the small steps of a bobbing sea plane, on to a moving jetty.

The first to appear from the hatch was Sofia. Ava, like the others, had a huge smile plastered on her face as she leant down onto the moving floating platform, to help Alfie's sister. Instead of reaching for Ava's hand, Sofia smiled politely and shook her head. She waited on the unsteady platform as she helped the next person disembark.

"Sofia!" An American gruff voice shouted from inside the cabin.

An angry face appeared, it was the interloper from the picture Jez had shown Ava.

"You gonna leave me on this shit heap?" he growled and Sofia put her arm out to try and help him.

As he made his way down the steps, he smacked her hand away and she stood back. Her dark brown eyes wide with alarm and embarrassment.

"What a fuckin journey, this place better be worth it," he growled as he traversed the moving platform and made his way to the steps on to the main jetty.

Ava looked back at Sofia, completely appalled. Dan jumped down to help this beautiful woman, who had just been spoken to like a piece of dirt.

"So, who are you?" The gruff voice was now right next to Ava and as she turned and looked up at him, she smelt the stale stench of cigars and whiskey and tried not to vomit.

Ignoring what he said, she turned back to Sofia, who was now being helped by Dan across the rocking boards below. She held her hand out and helped Sofia on to the solid area of the jetty, underneath the huge white sail canopy, where they had all gathered.

As she did so the rude American growled nastily in her ear, "I don't like to be ignored."

She didn't turn and reply, but a chill ran down her spine. Sofia was now in front of her and they hugged each other warmly.

"I'm afraid your sister is unwell," Sofia spoke gently and an alarmed Ava turned to stare at the hatch.

Two women had now emerged, arguing about who should have had a window seat and the best view. *Blara and La Fou's friends,* thought Ava, trying not to dismiss them as useless, plastic trolls, but finding it hard to be polite.

"This is my husband Brody," Sofia tried to make introductions, but Brody had already turned and skulked off down the jetty in search of the nearest bar.

Sofia turned back to Ava, shrugging gently.

"Oh my god!" shouted Rachel, dropping the welcome banner she had been holding with Bella.

The whole group turned their attention to the sea plane's hatch, as a dishevelled looking Kitty appeared. Her pale skin was positively grey and she looked terrible. Clutching what looked like a sick bag to her chest, she gratefully reached out for the Australian pilot's hand.

"Kitty!" shouted Ava alarmed.

"She will be fine when she has rested," said Sofia kindly.

"She was out drinking with us last night," chimed in one of the American plastics, who was on all fours, crawling across the moving platform below.

Dan grabbed Kitty's arm, holding her tightly. Along with the pilot's assistance, they guided her down the steps of the plane and on to the floating platform. Both then practically lifted her up to the main jetty, where Jez took over and lifted her off her shaking legs into his strong, capable arms.

Ignoring everyone around him except Ava, he nodded at her to follow and started striding down the jetty, heading for terra firm. Ava was still holding Sofia's hand as they followed Jez and Kitty down long boardwalk and on to the soft sands.

There Jez stood Kitty up and supported her on either side of her waist, as Ava hugged her tightly.

"I feel so ill," Kitty whimpered, clinging on to her older sister.

"I'm so sorry Ave," she whispered.

"We have all been there Kit," said Lou stroking Kitty's head "Boozing and travelling never mix." Lou confirmed with a knowing nod of the head and a warm smile.

Kitty let out a beleaguered laugh and Jez realised her legs were giving way and scooped her up again.

"Come on you lot…" Lou took charge, "…we can all say hello properly later, when Kit's had a rest and hair of the dog."

She smiled lovingly at Kitty who was like a little sister to her and then marched the group in the direction of the main bar.

"Why don't you join us, Sofia?" Dan implored her. "We can say thank you to you for looking after our little KitKat," he smiled broadly and Sofia returned the smile and agreed with a small nod.

Jez carried Kitty to the waiting buggy and instructed the driver to take things steady, as she was unwell from travelling. No one spoke on the short journey as they trundled down a deserted path, with tropical foliage spilling out on either side. The path led them out into a beautifully tendered garden, in front of a huge villa.

The staff were waiting in line to greet the bride-to-be and Ava thanked them all kindly, but explained her sister was not well. She too blamed the exhaustion of travelling, opting not to mention the alcohol consumed beforehand. With no fuss, they had all smiled politely and the two male staff holding the flower leis, disappeared quietly around to the side of the villa out of sight. The female who was left there, guided the threesome in through the main door.

Jez carried Kitty and Ava carried her sick bag.

"The bedroom is this way ma'am," the housekeeper kindly led the way and without taking in any of the surroundings, Ava followed Jez, grateful for his strength, that her sister didn't have to walk when feeling so ill.

Once laid on the bed, Jez disappeared and reappeared with a cool, wet flannel which he laid gently on Kitty's forehead, just as he had done with Ava earlier that day.

"My darling KitKat," he said kissing her gently on her cheek.

Kitty opened one eye and peaked from under those long lashes, something she had in common with Ava.

"I'm so sorry Ave, Jez. I was so looking forward to seeing you all so much and I've ruined it," she said miserably closing her eye again.

"Don't be silly Kit, we are just so happy that you are here." Ava said, desperately happy that she was with her sister, albeit Kitty was feeling the ill effects of going out on a session, the day before travelling on such a long journey.

"Alfie gets here tomorrow morning," she groaned. "We are supposed to be going on that boat trip."

"Boat trip?" questioned Jez.

"Yes, we all have to go…" Kitty said through gritted teeth. "So, both families can meet each other properly," she said yawning.

"Well, there's not a lot for them to meet on our side." smiled Jez, teasing.

"Although Ava has met Alfie's brother already," he smirked, as Ava hit him with a pillow.

Kitty didn't hear any of this, she had closed her eyes and fallen fast asleep.

"Ahh the delights of alcohol." Jez teased.

Ava covered her sister with a blanket, the air con obviously working well in this colossal villa. Jez closed the electric shutters with a flick of a switch and Ava clicked on the intricately carved lamp that sat on the ornate bedside table, leaving Kitty asleep, in a soft glow. She poured her sister a glass of water, which she left beside the lamp. They both kissed Kitty's cheek and quietly left the room.

They introduced themselves properly to Akilah, who was the head of staff at the honeymoon garden villa. Akilah was in her sixties and was very softly spoken, with excellent English. Ava and Jez said they would stay with Kitty, but Akilah insisted they carry on their evening and that she would look after the bride-to-be, as if she was her own. Ava felt drained after the day she had had and decided it might be best. After all Kitty could sleep for England, especially when she was hungover, as Ava remembered well from her little sister's clubbing days. She advised Akilah that she would be in her water villa if Kitty awoke and needed anything, no matter what the time was. With a gentle bow of the head, the kind lady escorted them out of the stunning villa and onto the waiting buggy.

The pair walked in an affable silence, arm in arm along the jetty. They were both absorbed in their own thoughts when they came to Ava's door.

"I hear your sister is unwell," the sarcasm in the words meant it was a statement and not a question.

Ava and Jez both turned at the same time, to see Ethan Pennington leaning on the doorway of his villa, at the very end of the jetty. Ava wanted to speak, but found she didn't know what to say. This man, Ethan Pennington, had made her feel something. Vulnerable maybe? Something she had sworn she would never be again. Turned on? Something she thought she would ever feel again. She looked down at her feet, not wanting to look at him.

Jez glared, not saying a word. Ethan unfolded his crossed arms and stepped forward, a whole speech prepared, Ava had opened her door quickly and slipped through it, into the safety of her villa. Jez nodded politely and followed her in. Ethan was left on his porch, alone and angry. His whole world had been turned upside down.

Chapter 14

Ava and Jez enjoyed a quiet meal on the decking, whilst attempting to put the world to rights. They started with Kitty and made the promise that they would both do anything they could to ensure the wedding went ahead with no stress or worries for the bride and groom. If Blara and La Fou, or any of their cronies put an expensively, pedicured, plastic toe out of line, Ava and Jez would deal with them.

Jez asked her how she felt about Ethan Pennington and why she didn't listen to what he had to say, when entering her villa earlier. Ava was still trying to figure that out in her own head. She told him simply that the wedding came first and that any feelings she had for Ethan would have to be dealt with after the nuptials had taken place.

Jez knew there was more to Ava just liking this Ethan then she was letting on, but didn't push her on the subject. She had only ever loved one man and after having her heart completely shattered, she had vowed she would never allow anyone in again. She was not strong enough to go through that sort of heartbreak a second time.

As Ava, had never met another soul mate, Jez was taken aback that this Ethan character had affected her so strongly. She was obviously struggling with her feelings for him, even more so, as he was making threats that would affect Kitty's happiness. He didn't push her to talk about him, only discussing that she may possibly have to speak to Ethan's parents to gauge their opinions. She hoped they did not feel the same way about Kit, as Ethan and the plastics did.

They also discussed the boat trip tomorrow and that they all needed to be on their best behaviour, as they wanted to impress the Pennington's and not let Kitty down. They had enjoyed a few bottles of red wine, whilst watching the fish darting around in the spotlights below.

Late into the night, Jez ordered Ava inside to bed, as they had an important day tomorrow. In truth he had spotted a huge black fin and the shadow of a massive shark swimming beneath and as Ava had enough nightmares to deal with already, he wanted her inside before she saw it. They brushed their teeth and Ava washed her face quickly, before they snuggled up in the cool bed.

It wasn't long before Jez was gently snoring, something Ava found comforting and as she lay there, contemplating the events of the day and going over every word Ethan Pennington had ever said to her.

Another restless night, left Ava feeling exhausted. She had showered and dressed in a loose white V-necked, t-shirt and knickers. Quietly retrieving her iMac, iced coffee and a 'Dildo' (as it had now been lovingly renamed by their group) chocolate bar, all without disturbing Jez.

She was studiously tapping away at her keyboard when the huge glass wall slid open and Jez appeared. He closed the doors behind him and sauntered over to kiss Ava on top of her head. She shook her head in envy, how could he look so good when he had literally just woken up.

His hair was tousled stubble had covered his strong jawline and his hazel eyes were shining brightly. He wore nothing but his CK hipsters that left nothing to the imagination. He was toned, muscled and tanned all over. His skin a luscious dark, honey colour, he looked incredible.

"You didn't sleep well."

It was a fact not a question. She smiled up at him as he stretched his arms above his head.

"You did," she replied, noting the time on her laptop, it was just after seven.

"This is ridiculously early, actually," he said yawning. "Oh, and this was under the door," he said, producing an envelope from the back of his pants.

Ava opened the silver envelope and inside was an invitation to the boat trip Kit had mentioned yesterday. The silver, oval card, had small, white flower blossoms, which looked as though they had been painted around the edge.

In silver and white italics was written,

Sofia & Blake Pennington cordially invite Ava Hart, to a pre wedding brunch on their yacht, La Sofia. Please be at the sea plane jetty at nine forty-five this morning, to set sail promptly at ten o'clock. We look forward to meeting you and ensuring both of our families can be introduced.

Ava took a deep breath.

"I don't suppose there is any way to get out of this?" she asked hopefully.

"We will show them all how amazing we are Ave, stop worrying. I'm going to go and have a shower and sort out what to wear." He paused and looked her up and down, the white low-cut t-shirt looked amazing on her sun kissed skin.

"Shame you can't wear that, they would all fall in love with you," he winked and then ducked as she threw the invitation at him.

"I will sort out a dress for you before I go, but put a bikini on underneath it..." he instructed, "...they will probably stop somewhere and give guests a chance to swim and snorkel."

He couldn't keep the excitement from his voice.

"I can assure you I will not be swimming," she said solemnly.

"Well, you can sit on the side of the 'yacht' and look sexy then," he offered as she shook her head and laughed.

"Later tater," he said as he disappeared out in to the heat of the morning.

It was still early, but already very hot. She would have to plaster herself in sun cream before getting on this boat, as she did not want to get burnt. She mentally chastised herself for calling the Pennington yacht a boat. She must not do that today if she didn't want to offend them. Smiling to herself at the thought of a family owning their own boat... fuck... yacht. That really was an extravagant purchase.

After another hour of writing, Ava packed up her belongings and went into the villa. Laid out on the bed was one of her favourite sun dresses. It was soft and flowing, covered in rainbow-coloured stripes. A full-length, halter-neck maxi dress, which was backless and accentuated every curve of Ava's toned body. The delicate silk meant it was a joy to wear and although she had only worn it a handful of times, she had actually brought a blue swimsuit to fit underneath it, which meant that not a single strap would show from under the dress. Jez loved this dress too and she wasn't surprised he had chosen it.

She showered again, however, this time she dried and straightened her hair. Luckily, Bella arrived just as she had finished getting dressed and plaited Ava's hair on both sides, twisting the end of the plaits into a neat bun at the base of Ava's neck.

Bella whistled.

"You look fantastic," she said genuinely impressed with her friend's whole ensemble.

"So do you Bell, although you always do." Ava said honestly.

Today, Bella was wearing a dark-green, chiffon sun dress, which wrapped around her tiny body perfectly. It was knee-length and had tiny spaghetti straps. She was wearing a strapless bikini, in the same colour and had paired her outfit with a huge black floppy straw-hat, perilously high wedges and her Jackie O sunglasses. She had already nipped to Lou's room to have a fake eyebrow drawn on. The makeup job looked so good that she was sure no one would notice.

"What shoes are you wearing?" Bella asked thoughtfully, whilst looking at the bottom of Ava's wardrobe at the array of flip-flops and sandals.

"These." Ava sat on the bed and held up a pair of flat sandals, with tiny diamantes glistening in a V-shape to her toes.

"Oh," replied Bella in dismay. "Are you sure you don't want heels?" She prompted.

Bella loved shoes as much as hats and sunglasses. She always encouraged her friends to wear high heels.

"Firstly Bell, we are going on a boat, shit, I mean yacht. I don't want to fall over and break my neck. I know…I know, you look amazing in your heels and you can actually walk in them too, but I can't." Ava continued as she walked around the room throwing things in her white straw bag, which had a huge sequin pineapple on the front. "Also, I really don't need the height," she laughed at her own joke and Bella gave up.

"All right, enough with the height jokes, you still look incredible in flats." She hugged Ava and Ava hugged her back.

"Let's go impress the in-laws." Bella chuckled.

As Ava closed the villa door, she grimaced at the day that lay ahead of her. She did not want to see Ethan and she did not want to see Blara or La Fou. Having to be on your best behaviour for people you were not sure you even liked, just seemed a waste of time. Although, she would get to spend time with Kitty and Alfie, that was a positive. Ava would also get to see the Pennington yacht, she liked the idea of nosing around it.

They knocked on their friend's doors as they made their way down the jetty. Jez looked smoulderingly hot, in Givenchy tailored khaki shorts. He had paired it with a crisp pale pink, short-sleeved polo shirt. The neck buttons left open and a pair of mirrored Ray Bans finished his scorching hot, sexy look.

Lou and Rachel didn't answer their doors, and the others assumed they would be at the jetty. Dan looked devastatingly handsome in navy tailored shorts, navy and white stripped t-shirt and white canvas deck shoes. He was in a bubbly mood and was very excited at the thought of spending time on the Pennington yacht.

They laughed and joked on the buggy ride to the jetty and Ava began to relax. She had truly amazing friends and if the Pennington's didn't like them or her, then tough. The buggy took the happy gang right the way down the sea plane jetty, to where the impressive boat was waiting. Ava could see a lot of crew, all dressed in smart, white t-shirts and shorts and matching baseball caps.

"Wow," whistled Bella, "Looks amazing."

Dan stayed quiet, smiling broadly.

"I bet you can't wait to have a nose around Dan" she said looking at Dan's beaming face, as they stepped off the buggy and thanked their driver.

As they went to actually get on to the vessel, Ava recognised the man on the beach, the morning she had seen Ethan. Rogers, wasn't it? Oh my god, what was he doing here, surely nothing scary can get to the Pennington's on a yacht when out at sea? Why have security at sea, it didn't make sense unless the Maldives had a band of drunken pirates, marauding about.

Both Jez and Dan made their way along the small gangplank and on to the deck of the yacht, with little effort. Bella however, was wearing those high-heeled wedges and the body guard helped her, grabbing her waist and lifting her like a china doll, from the plank and onto the deck beside him.

Ava watched them intently and caught a glimpse, a strange look between Bella and this handsome, muscle man, before Jez shouted,

"Come on Ave or we will leave without you."

She held the offered hands, firstly from Jez and then from Rogers, the body guard. She said a polite thank you and turned to look up at his clean-shaven face, still wearing his mirrored sunglasses and baseball cap.

"Is he here?" she asked anxiously.

She could see him frown from behind his sunglasses.

"Ethan," she whispered, "is he on this boat?" she questioned.

"No ma'am," he said. The frown remained as if he was going to add something else, but he said nothing more.

"Thank you," Ava said with a nervous smile, as her phone pinged several times and distracted her.

Thank God for that, he wasn't on the boat, shit, she had said boat and it was a yacht.

She retrieved her phone from her bag and read several texts, the first from Rachel. Apologies that she wasn't coming on the boat, but she was feeling a bit delicate after a good night out last night and didn't want to vomit on the future in-laws. Ava smiled. The next was of Lou, it just read *'Busy'* and a winking emoji. Ava shook her head gently and carried on through the texts. One was from Kitty. Ava let out a disappointed sigh and advised the others that although Alfie had arrived safely on an early flight, Kitty and Alfie were going to be staying in the villa as Kit was not feeling up to a boat ride…yacht ride. She corrected herself quickly.

Bella glided over with glasses of champagne that she had procured from somewhere. Ava felt the boat moving and suddenly realised they were the only ones on the lower deck. There was a large, canopied area that was also empty and steps up to a second deck, which also looked deserted apart from the crew milling around.

Jez was at her side in an instant, his arm gently around her waist, supporting her as the yacht picked up speed.

"You don't think this is a hoax trip?" she asked worriedly.

Bella looked round.

"I was just thinking the same thing, I can't see any Pennington's although why would anyone fake a trip?" She laughed as if the idea was preposterous.

Dan appeared raising his glass of champagne in a toast.

"Here's to meeting our new family," he said with a beaming smile, the others just looked at him.

"What's up?" he said, still smiling.

"We think that Blara has sent us out to sea, to keep us away from the Pennington clan," Jez said waving his glass dramatically about in the direction of the ocean.

"Umm guys," Dan had lowered his voice, "you do know this is not the Pennington yacht?"

They looked at each other, confusion written all over their faces. Dan laughed heartily and shook his head in wonder.

"Oh my life, you lot should do your homework," he paused shaking his head and then huddled closer to his family, before he whispered, "We are on a sea taxi…" his eyes were wide and excited. "…the yacht is over there." He nodded his head in the direction the boat was going in. "I say yacht, it's more of a super yacht," he said conspiratorially, not hiding his excitement.

"So, this is a water taxi and not a yacht?" Bella questioned seriously, with her mouth gawping open whilst looking around the opulent, well equipped, luxury craft they were stood in.

"We are not in the midlands anymore Toto," Jez whispered teasingly in Ava's ear and squeezed her waist.

She looked up at him and his lips were pursed and he was letting out a long whistle. She followed the direction of his gaze and her mouth dropped open, like Bella's, this was definitely not the Midlands! The so called 'water taxi', (they were all still in shock, except Dan) started to slow, as it made its way towards a gigantic yacht.

In this exact moment, Ava began to realise just how rich the Pennington's actually were. Hiring a whole island for a wedding was extravagant, but the Pennington's actually owned this gargantuan yacht. Having been on very few boats in her lifetime, even Ava could see on approach that this was the bee's knees.

Ava took in the massive yacht, which had at least five levels that she could see. The gentle sound of classical music and the chatter of people grew as they made their way slowly to the back end of the yacht. It was as if their little boat was paying homage to this incredible supersized model, as it gave all aboard a chance to gaze in wonder at the sleek lines and curves.

On the huge back deck were some of the yacht's crew, all men. They wore the same tailored white shorts, white, short sleeve shirts and white hats with gold braids.

"They think they're in the Navy," Bella scoffed and then fell silent as she caught Roger's eye, she quickly sipped her champagne.

"I think they look very smart," said Jez, not the least bit intimidated, although having spent time on many yachts in his playboy life, this one kicked all the others arses.

As they docked smoothly, a small gangway was placed between them as their boat was secured. Rogers made his way across it first and then stood on the other side waiting patiently for their small group to cross. Dan went first, like a bull at a gate. Striding over boldly, he was smiling with eager anticipation of checking out what he knew was the most expensive super yacht in the world. He hadn't shared his knowledge with the others, as he knew they would feel even more intimidated, but he for one was delighted to have the opportunity to look around and take in every detail. He was also secretly hoping to accidently bump into a certain Pennington whilst on board too.

Bella was a lot slower in crossing the bridge, making sure each footstep was placed properly as she did not want to slip and fall into the ocean. Rogers held his hand out and Ava could have sworn she saw a hint of a smile cross his lips when Bella's hand finally reached his. Jez held Ava's hand whilst crossing together, making it slightly awkward to manoeuvre. When they reached the deck of the yacht, Rogers again held his hand out to assist her.

"Thank you, Rogers," she said sincerely, remembering his name from the beach.

She was sure he had more pressing things to do, instead of helping her off a gangplank.

At that Ava turned to focus on him.

"You guys carry on and I will meet you shortly," she said firmly, not even turning to her friends, keeping her focus on this burley brute in front of her.

Dan took Bella's arm and immediately whisked her up the steps on the left-hand side of the large back deck. Jez didn't move and was still holding Ava's hand.

"Ave?" he spoke quietly.

"It's okay, I just need a minute," she didn't turn to look at him and kept her tone even, trying not to freak out.

Jez lifted her hand to his lips and kissed it gently, before stalking off up the same stairs as his friends. The crew had dispersed quickly and she was now alone with Rogers.

"Is he on this boat?" she shook her head, "I mean yacht?" She spoke quietly.

"Yes ma'am" Rogers said simply.

"Oh," was all Ava could manage.

She turned and gripped the shiny silver bar that ran around the edge of the deck, for support. She observed the water taxi pulling away.

"Is it coming back?" she asked with alarm, staring at the boat that had brought them to the yacht.

"It will return in a few hours, ma'am," he said seriously, watching her response.

Her head turned to face him and she was now gripping the support pole like a vice.

"A few hours?" she whispered horrified.

She turned to look at the island they had just travelled from, it seemed like minutes on the ride over, but it looked so far away now.

"I'm guessing it's too far to swim back?" She was still whispering.

"It is a fair way away ma'am… you are not thinking of trying to swim back?" he asked seriously, his head inclined slightly, with an expression she couldn't make out, as he had his sun glasses on.

Ava let out a slow steadying breath and was about to inform him of her fear of sharks when he suddenly put his hand to his earpiece and spoke clearly.

"Yes, I can confirm that sir," and then his attention was back on Ava. "May I escort you to your friends, ma'am?" he said courteously, not wanting to leave her on the back deck, alone.

She looked like she was going to jump over the side to escape. He felt an overwhelming urge to protect her, even though this was part of his remit, this felt personal. He was actually concerned for her. Ava didn't reply, she was staring back at the island, as the yacht vibrated softly and the engines kicked in, the La Sofia began to move.

Ava's knuckles were white, gripping on to the bar for all it was worth.

"I remember the first time your sister came aboard," Rogers spoke softly and Ava turned to face him bravely letting one of her hands release the bar.

She looked up and could see her own reflection in his sun glasses, huge topaz eyes imploring him to go on.

"She was totally in awe, like you," his face softened.

"Miss Hart had Alfie here and they ended up having a great time," he said kindly, trying to put her at ease.

"It's not just the boat…I mean yacht," Ava began, but was interrupted by a vision in red sweeping across the deck towards them.

"Ava," Sofia's voice made them both turn.

"Sofia." Ava was glad to see her and she let go of the bar completely, hugging her warmly.

Rogers took a discreet step back and was about to leave them when Ava called after him.

"Look after her."

He stopped and turned back to look at her, still embracing Sofia.

"Look after Bell," she said quietly.

He looked surprised, nodded his head and disappeared across the back decking, through a glass panelled door. She then realised that Sofia was not just hugging her but clinging to her tightly.

"Are you okay?" she whispered as her new friend began to sob. "Oh sweetheart, what's wrong? What's happened?"

Sofia continued to cry and Ava simply held her. After a few minutes, all tears exhausted, she finally loosened her grip on Ava and rested her hands on her waist. Ava held her shoulders waiting patiently for her to take a few deep, calming breaths.

"I am so sorry Ava; this is the last thing you need," she said sadly.

"You can talk to me about anything, we are going to be family soon," Ava said softly, "I hope," she said as an afterthought and Sofia's beautiful face creased slightly.

"Kitty and Alfie are very happy, why would they not be married?"

Suddenly her sadness evaporated and concern now filled her voice. Ava sighed.

"It's a long story… but at this moment in time, I'm more worried about you," she said honestly.

Sofia let out another deep breath and took Ava's hand, pulling her over to a plush, seating area, adjusting her floor length dress.

Fuck, Ava felt completely underdressed. Sofia elegantly took a seat and gestured Ava to do the same, next to her. Ava sat down beside her and took her hand.

"If you don't want to talk about it, we can just sit here and get drunk?" Ava said, with a small smile.

Sofia giggled and for the first time in her life, decided to trust someone she hardly knew. An hour later and with a slight headache, Ava made her way to the first floor of the yacht and through the first opulent room, to get herself a drink and God knows she needed one. Sofia had gone to freshen up and Ava realised she couldn't hide out on the back deck for the entire trip, as Kitty and Alfie were counting on her to impress his family and that was exactly what she was going to do.

With a spiced rum and coke in hand, she introduced herself to a lively group of Americans, who were talking enthusiastically about the Maldives. There was a mix of Pennington extended family and some of Alfie's friends, who Ava liked instantly. They went on to discuss the wedding, with such happiness that Ava found herself actually relaxing and enjoying the conversation. Bella appeared and linked arms with her. One of Alfie's friends wolf-whistled and got a kick in the shin from his pal next to him. Bella smiled her sexy Italian smile that melted the younger men's insides, as she turned to the group and said politely,

"I need to borrow Ava," with a polite goodbye to the group, she pulled Ava out of the room.

Bella led her to a balcony which had yet another luxurious seating area, running along its internal wall.

"How amazing is this yacht," Bella said excitedly Ava smiled and nodded, "I mean how amazing are the Pennington's," She almost squealed with delight.

"Actually, Bell those were the first new family members I've said hello to, but I'm going to work my way around the boat…I mean yacht," she shook her head, correcting herself again. "…and try and to introduce myself to everyone." Ava said earnestly.

"Have you seen the loos?" Bella's eyes were wide and full of bewilderment. "Oh my god, they are magnificent! Good job Lou's not here she would steal all the goodies!" Bella laughed at the thought.

"Goodies?" Ava questioned, wondering what possible goodies you would get in a toilet.

"Ave there's super posh perfumes, branded makeup everything!" Bella gushed.

"Do they have chocolate?" Ava asked smiling and raising an eyebrow.

"No," Bella's face fell.

"Then they don't have everything Bell, and they call this a super yacht," they both laughed.

A polite cough to their right, made them both turn to see Jez. He was standing alongside a tall, devastatingly handsome man. Ava held her breath for a split second, as she thought it was Ethan Pennington. He had the same blue sparkling eyes and thick, dark brown hair, however, silvery white streaks ran along both sides of his head.

"Here she is," Jez said smiling broadly and raising his hand towards Ava.

Ava recognised the man from the picture Jez had shown her, and this was confirmed as he stepped forward, with a wide, genuine smile. He spoke chivalrously.

"Ava Hart, I have been looking forward to meeting you."

His gaze was as intense as his brothers, and he took Ava's hand kissing it gently. Ava reminded herself to breath. His eyes were like Sofia's, blue with hazel flecks. He had the same intenseness in his manner as Ethan. A glimpse of Ethan's face whirled through her mind and she could see clearly his fierce dazzlingly blue eyes. Ava smiled politely, as Jez introduced this handsome man.

"Ava, this is Giovanni Pennington, Alfie's brother," Jez introduced him politely.

"Please, call me Gio," he smiled graciously, "and you must be Bella, wedding dress maker extraordinaire," he turned and took Bella's hand, kissing it too.

Bella blushed like a belisha beacon, nodding. He had rendered her completely speechless.

"I have to say, the family were particularly concerned not to have a well-known designer making the dress, however, when Alfie told us you were an Italian dress maker, all was forgiven," he smiled broadly.

Bella was also smiling, totally under his spell. Ava was taken aback by his comment.

"Actually, Bella is a couture designer and anyone who questions that will have me to answer to," she said firmly, a serious expression etched on her beautiful face.

Everyone turned to look at her and Giovanni spoke first to break the awkward silence.

"I am sure Bella has created a spectacular dress and that KitKat will look absolutely stunning in it" He spoke earnestly, sensing he had misspoken, but Ava was already affronted.

The words 'the family' had rubbed her up the wrong way and she knew she should just smile sweetly and nod, but she couldn't help herself.

"I suppose 'the family' have had a lot to say about 'Kitty' in general?" She asked with a polite veneer, ignoring the fact that this stranger had just called her sister, by her pet name, KitKat.

Jez stepped forward, "Ave, you need a drink." he chided.

"Spiced rum and coke," she said seriously, not breaking her gaze with Giovanni and ignoring Bella's horrified expression.

Jez paused for a moment, stepped close to Ava and kissed her forehead gently. Before turning and advancing through the nearest door, presumably to get her a strong drink. Ava closed her eyes slowly and then reopened them hoping everyone had disappeared, sadly they were still there. Giovanni was staring at her, a quizzical look on his brow, a mortified Bella had found her tongue and began talking about the complications of creating wedding dress for such a hot climate. Giovanni turned his attention politely to Bella and they carried on the conversation, leaving Ava to stand there like a spare part. Her mind drifted to what the Pennington's actually felt about Kitty.

Her reverie was interrupted by a warm finger running from the nape of her neck, trailing down her spine, the length of her naked back. She relaxed at Jez's touch, knowing with him there, all would be well and this difficult introduction may soon be forgotten. The stench of stale cigars and whiskey came just as the finger turned into a palm, rimming the low-cut waistline of her dress.

She turned sharply and came face to face with Brody 'wannabe' Pennington. His hand hadn't moved and as she turned to face him it was now on her stomach. She wanted to scream at him to get his filthy hands off her, but she was on a boat full of Penningtons' and had already offended Alfie's oldest brother.

Brody sipped his crystal-glass, full of whiskey, which he was gripping with his other hand. He smirked evilly as he took in Ava's angry face and continued leering down the rest of her body.

"Excuse me," Ava said as tactfully as she could, moving to her right and trying to get away from him.

He grabbed the top of her arm tightly and yanked her towards him, bringing her closer to his foul breath.

"Hurry back, or I will have to come find you," he muttered viciously.

Ava was frightened, but stood her ground. She looked down with disdain at where he was gripping her arm tightly, stopping her circulation.

"Excuse me," she said more firmly, making eye contact with him again as he let go.

She didn't look back at Bell or Giovanni, she just walked quickly in the direction of the nearest door. She was sure she heard someone follow behind her, but at this point wanted to get as far away as possible from everyone and so she kept moving.

Darting down a corridor, she found stairs leading to both higher and lower levels. She could hear music and chatter from the floor above. Behind her, she heard a door slam and her flight or fight mode kicked in. She decided to fly, and she ran down two sets of stairs and then along another long corridor. Her heart was racing and she felt like she was going to throw up. She heard hurried footsteps on the floor above her. Running full pelt down the corridor, she saw the first door on her right. She pushed the door open and ran into the room, slamming it shut behind her.

She spun around, resting her palms and head against the door. She tried to calm her breathing down, straining to hear any noise from the other side of the door, in case that disgusting animal was following her.

"Ava?"

A man's voice came from across the room and she spun around in shock.

"Ethan!" She whispered.

Chapter 15

Ava was still out of breath, her heart pounding with fear. She had spun round to see Ethan standing there, in the same room as her. He was frowning, an angry expression on his captivating face. He went to approach her, but she put both hands up in protest, stopping him abruptly.

"Are you okay?" his voice deadly serious.

"Fine," she blurted out, her hands still up in the air.

"You are not fine," he retorted angrily. "Now are you going to tell me what's going on, or am I going to have to find out for myself?" He looked like he was David Banner, trying his hardest not to turn into the hulk.

Ava wondered if she might not be safer on the other side of the door, with that slime-bag Brody. She dropped her hands to her sides, risking a brief glance back at the door handle behind her. It was still and she let out a slow breath to try and steady her over-beating heart. She looked at Ethan, he looked formidable and handsome, and she realised she was safe in this room whilst he was with her.

"Allo," a loud, musical voice came from the right-hand side of the room where a little old lady was walking towards Ethan, smiling at them both.

"Nonna," Ethan turned and the frown almost disappeared, as the elderly lady approached him.

She was at least half Ethan's height and had a rotund, soft appearance. Wearing a simple royal blue, shift dress, a sparkling antique broach, pinned to the left of her chest, she looked elegant and rich. Her dark grey shoulder length hair, full of bouncing curls as she walked. With a warm smile and a twinkle in her wizened eyes, she turned and took in Ava.

"Allo you," she spoke in a thick Italian accent.

She beamed at Ava and Ava couldn't help but smile back.

"Ava, this is my grandmother, Aurora," he nodded at the little lady, who now had her arm wrapped around his waist and had rested her head on his firm stomach.

Before Ava could speak, he continued, "Nonna this is Ava Hart......Kitty's sister," he turned to look at Ava and her insides turned to jelly.

His grandmother raised both arms straight into the air, her face full of joy, as she started talking loudly in Italian. Before she knew what was happening, Ava was being hugged tightly by Aurora, who was surprisingly strong for a little old lady.

She turned back to her grandson and shouted, "Drinky Drinky," and made a drinking action with her hand.

Ethan nodded and smiled in compliance making his way over to a well-stocked drinks bar.

"Leta me seea you face," Aurora said putting her hand on either side of Ava's clammy face.

She frowned and began shouting, flitting between broken English and fluent Italian. Ava tried to follow the conversation, whilst having her cheeks pinched.

"Is no good," Aurora was saying emphatically, then reverted to Italian.

Ava looked up at Ethan for a translation, he was actually laughing now.

"She doesn't like me?" Ava questioned, with a sinking feeling in the pit of her stomach.

"On the contrary," he said with humour, "she likes you very much. She is just saying you are beautiful, but that you need feeding up."

Ethan had walked forwards and placed three elegant looking drinks on a small table. He walked over to stand next to Aurora, who was gently holding Ava's face in her hands. Ava who had been bending forward, due to the height difference, took this charming lady's hands in hers and stood up properly.

"...is beautiful like er sister," Aurora was still gazing at Ava's face and continued on in fluent Italian, nodding at Ava, as if Ava could understand every word.

"Nonna, Ava non capisce," Ethan spoke gently and his grandmother frowned, folding her arms across her ample bosom in frustration, lips pouting like a child.

"I am so sorry Aurora, I do not speak Italian, however, Kitty has told me all about you and I am delighted to meet you at last." Ava said kindly.

She was nervous, she wanted all of Alfie's family to like her and her own little, odd family.

"Ahhh, Kitty isa good girl," Aurora spoke slowly as if wanting to say the correct words. "You were mamma and papa..."

This was not a question and Ava continued to hold her gaze, although she felt Ethan's eyes on her and had to resist the urge to look up at him. "...youa did a good job... Kitty isa beautiful, good girl... my Alfie isa lucky man."

Aurora once again beamed up at Ava and she returned the expression. Kitty had spoken fondly of Nonna Aurora and Ava liked her instantly.

"Join us for a drink?" Ethan broke Ava's reverie and she looked up to see his handsome face, although she could not read his expression.

Ava remembered that she was here to meet the Penningtons and that she really needed to make an effort and find the others, despite their family lunatic stalking her.

"That is very kind of you, but I've taken up enough of your time," she said politely, "Aurora, I am delighted to have met you and my apologies for interrupting your time with Ethan," she finished.

"Aww my Ethan isa my favourite in alla the world." She replied, turning and hugging Ethan tightly.

Ava was surprised that he made no move to stop her, instead he held her back, just as tightly. For some unknown and inexplicable reason, Ava felt like crying at the sight of unconditional love of a man and his grandmother. Ava had never known her grandparents, as they had all passed away before she was born. *Pull yourself together Ava,* she mentally chastised herself. This is the man who is trying to stop the wedding. My bloody hormones are running riot, she thought to herself.

"Well good bye," Ava forced a tight smile.

Aurora let go of Ethan and grabbed Ava around the waist, hugging her tightly too. Ava felt a warm glow spread through her whole body and couldn't help but smile. Why couldn't all the Penningtons be like this, warm, friendly, loving.

Ava suddenly pictured being held by Ethan and had a flash back, to the jetty where his firm toned body was pressed against hers. She closed her eyes briefly and then opened them, remembering where she was and who she was with, looking at Ethan in alarm.

"I have to go," she said apologetically, wanting nothing else but to create some distance between her and this annoying man.

He was staring at her, an odd expression on his face.

"Ohhhh nooo, bye," Aurora said despondently, obviously enjoying this new company.

Ava turned as the old dear made her way over to the table, where Ethan had placed the drinks he had made. She paused, her hand raised to turn the handle of the door, as she recalled the reason, she had entered the room in the first place. Ethan hadn't moved and she felt his eyes boring into her back, so she straightened her shoulders and stood a little taller. Opening the door again, she slipped silently into the corridor and without turning back, closed it gently behind her.

The corridor was empty and she could hear the chatter of people and music playing above. Ava decided to follow the corridor to the right, as she could see a staircase at the end. As she walked along the plush interior, she realised she was full of emotions and could really do with some alone time to think all of these events through. She resigned herself to the fact, that at this present time she had to do her best to impress Kitty's in-laws-to-be. Alone time would have to wait.

Suddenly, Ava's whole body was pushed violently to the left, her head smacking off the wall with a sickening crack. Pain exploded on the left-hand side of her skull and then she felt excruciating pain on the right-hand side of her waist. She went to scream, but a large hand was forcefully covering her mouth. Her eyes squeezed shut in pain, she had an overwhelming urge to vomit. She smelt the stale cigar and alcohol breath of her attacker. The sweaty hand moved from her mouth to clamp tightly around her throat and her eyes opened wide in terror. His face was so close to hers, she could feel his warm stinking breath on her cheek.

"I know he's fucking you!" he spat out. "Sending his fucking henchman for you… he's so fucking obvious," he hissed venomously.

Ava was trying to focus, the pain she felt in her head and side was immense and with his hand so tightly around her neck, she was struggling to breath.

"Well, he's not having you all to himself," he sneered and to Ava's horror, he licked the side of her face.

Terrified, she realised she couldn't run and so she would have to fight. Summoning an enormous amount of courage and using what little strength she had, she raised her knee sharply and with purpose, coming into contact with his groin, then dropping her foot hard onto the instep of his foot. His vice-like grip fell away immediately, as he howled and clutched his privates with both hands. Ava fell to her knees, gasping to take deep burning breathes, into her oxygen starved lungs. She had her arms wrapped around her waist, which was also burning with pain and her head was throbbing. She was completely unaware of the commotion happening to her right. She felt dizzy and put both hands on the floor in front of her, trying to concentrate on her breathing. She felt two strong hands grab her under her arms and then felt her body lift into the air. The pain in her right side was unbearable as her body straightened out.

She forced her eyes to open and there holding her up was a pale and angry looking Ethan.

"Ava," he growled, his voice demanding her to answer him.

Her head was spinning and the pain too much, as she opened her mouth to answer him, nothing came out. Ethan's gorgeous dark blue eyes, were the last thing she saw before her whole world went black.

Chapter 16

Ava was on the edge of her villas deck, looking out at the incredibly calm ocean. She could see brightly coloured fish darting about below and smiled at the sight of her favourite turtle approaching from the left, on its way to swim past her, as it did every morning. Henry the heron was perched on the edge of her sunbed on the lower decking, taking in all of the movement of the fish below.

Just as Tommy the turtle swam in front of Ava's lower deck, she leaned over a little too far and the wooden railing fell away, leaving Ava's body fall helplessly into the waters below. She was screaming as she fell, hitting the water with such force, it caused unimaginable pain, everywhere on her body. She went under and struggled to hold her breath, as she tried to emerge from the crystal-clear waters. Frightened fish scuttled away from her and she saw the turtle swimming slowly towards her.

Still submerged, she had forgotten about struggling to breathe and watched in awe as the turtle approached. He was so close she could see the vivid scales on his face, glimmering shades of translucent green. As she studied him, the waters around her grew darker and slowly the green of the turtle faded to a shiny, silvery, grey. The scales slowly faded to leave a smooth, sleek skin. Its body began to morph and change shape.

Ava, suspended under the water, watched in a trance, as the turtle's flippers disappeared, along with its colossal shell. It began to form a long, fish-like body, now only an arm's length away from her. It opened its huge mouth to reveal two rows of sharp, blood-stained teeth. Shark.

In terror she opened her mouth to scream, but nothing came out. She was flailing around, arms and legs flying everywhere, trying to get to the ocean's surface, before this hideous monster attacked.

"Ava," Ethan's voice penetrated through the water and above Ava's screams, everything went black.

He must have jumped in the water after her. Ava suddenly realized she had put him in danger, he doesn't know there's a shark, oh my god,

"Ethan!" she screamed into the blackness.

Nothing.

Ethan sat on the edge of the bed, gripping Ava's delicate hands in his. She was still now. Bailey had given her something to help her rest. He watched her face intently, straining to hear her slow rhythmic breathing, over the sounds of the ocean and the party makers on the floors above.

Rogers entered the room and stood at the end of the bed.

"Collins has been removed sir," he said, stoically trying to not let the sight of Miss Hart, lying there helpless, affect his ability to do his job.

"That bastard!" growled Ethan, not taking his eyes of Ava. "Get him off the island and ensure he has no contact with any of the family or wedding party." Ethan directed sternly.

"Does my sister know?" as an afterthought.

"No sir" replied Rogers.

Ethan's thoughts were all over the place, his mind racing. Collins had attacked Ava and physically hurt her. Had Collins ever done this to his sister? Surely not, Sofia had always been close to her brothers and she would have told one of them.

Surely?

Christ, how could he have let this low-life into his family? All security and background checks had been done as routine, when his sister had said she had met and fallen in love with Brody Collins. An up-and-coming politician, he had big plans for his future and had passed all background checks with flying colours. No red flags and not one word from Collins had given Ethan or the Pennington security team any cause for concern. He never particularly liked Collins, but as his sister had pleaded with them all to give him a chance, the whole family had tried to be polite and had welcomed him into their tight knit family, just to make Sofia happy.

Was she happy? Ethan thought about her looking a little paler and thinner than usual. She also seemed a little quieter than her normal outgoing self. However, she had not long had a huge society wedding and all the stress that brings. Ethan was trying to convince himself that his sister had not been hiding any unhappiness. He tried to think of the last time he had spoken to her without her husband being present, Collins always seemed to have been with her. Ethan had been so preoccupied with work and then Alfie announcing he had fallen in love and wanted a whirlwind wedding, he now realized that he had neglected his sister. He hadn't seen her since her wedding day, that was two months ago.

He squeezed Ava's hand tightly and felt sick to his stomach that his brother-in-law had done this.

"Sir, is there anything I can do?" Roger's voice interrupted Ethan's thoughts.

"Make the team aware of what has happened, I want them on high alert, extra patrols, you know the drill." Ethan said firmly.

"Already done sir," Rogers replied efficiently and with a nod of the head, left the room.

"So…" Ethan had forgotten Bailey was still in the room.

Bailey was a childhood friend and was the Pennington's family doctor. He was also a trusted and valued member of Ethan's inner circle, of which there were few.

"So?" Ethan's intense gaze never left Ava's face.

"So who is she?" Bailey asked gently probing.

"She… is Kitty's sister, Ava" he replied, his voice breaking slightly.

Bailey was now the other side of the bed and leaned over to pick up Ava's wrist. Ethan glared at him and Bailey explained he was just checking her blood pressure. Ethan nodded and waited for his friend to update him.

"That's good," Bailey said nodding with approval, "Good strong pulse, blood pressure returning to normal. The sedative will wear off in an hour or so."

He leant over and gently turned Ava's head to the side, there was blood on the crisp white pillow. Ethan stood up in shock, not letting go of Ava's hand. He stared open mouthed, not daring to speak, as Bailey felt the side of Ava's head with gloved hands.

"She's had a nasty knock to the head, I will feel happier when she's had a scan, but for now, she's doing well," he smiled reassuringly at Ethan to try and break some of the tension that had built up in the room.

"Her head is bleeding," he said sharply, "That is not good!"

He glared at his friend. Bailey had grown up with Ethan and as his best friend, it was obvious he was upset and the woman lying here meant something to him, for him to be acting like this.

In fact, Bailey had never seen his friend behaving in such a concerned way, about any woman before, except his family. Ethan Pennington was the coolest, most together man, Bailey had ever met.

"You need to calm down or I will have to sedate you." Bailey smirked.

Ethan looked at Bailey, still tightly holding Ava's hands.

"Sorry," he said earnestly. "It's just…"

He broke off, his eyes once again fixed on Ava's pale face.

"You know her well?" Bailey questioned, not able to contain his smile.

Ethan said nothing.

"How have I not heard about her before? Why hasn't Kitty told me she has a stunning older sister?" he said frowning.

He really liked Kitty and had met up with her and Alfie several times in the last few months. Alfie had grown up quickly since he had met his bubbly, gorgeous British girlfriend and Bailey had a lot of love and respect for them both. He was now a little hurt that Kitty had neglected to tell him about her equally beguiling older sister and the fact that Ethan seemed to be completely smitten.

"I met Ava the day I arrived here," Ethan spoke softly now, as if not wanting to wake his sleeping beauty.

Bailey tried and failed not to act surprised.

"And…" was all he could muster for a response.

"She came into the library when I was with Nonna and I knew there was something wrong, she looked…" he paused, "…she looked frightened," he finished.

Bailey stayed quiet, slightly overwhelmed at the fact that the great Ethan Pennington was actually showing some emotion.

"When she left the room, I made my excuses to Nonna and went after her, but when I looked down the corridor Rogers was pinning Collins down and he was fighting him. As I got closer…" again his voice broke.

Bailey moved to his side and having removed the vinyl gloves, placed a hand on his shoulder in support.

"Ava was kneeling forward on the floor, struggling to breathe, he really hurt her Bay," he said gruffly.

"Do we know why he attacked her?" Bailey asked gently.

"No idea." Ethan replied. "But I will find out and god help him if I ever set eyes on him again." Ethan muttered, gently rubbing his thumb across Ava's hand.

As she slowly opened her eyes, Ava took in the room she found herself in. The ceiling was painted in muted creams and golds, with the most delicate glass chandeliers hanging from delicate ceiling roses. They swayed gently, creating small, rainbow-like prisms of light that flickered around the large luxurious space. She was lying on sumptuous metallic gold covers, which were soft underneath her fingers. There were paintings of beach scenes on each wall and pale wooden furniture dotted around.

Ava wanted to move her right hand, but it was heavy and weighted down. As she lifted her head slightly off the soft pillows, pain shot across the left-hand side of her head and the right-hand side of her waist.

"Ahhh," she let out in a whisper.

Ethan lifted his head abruptly off the bed, where he had been dozing, eyes wide in alarm. He stood over her.

"Ava," he said quietly and let go of her right hand to cup her face.

"Sofia, Collins?" she whispered, suddenly recalling that Collins had attacked her and that Sofia could be in danger.

"It's okay," he consoled her, "he is off the island. You're safe now and Sofia is safe," he was so serious that Ava couldn't help a weak smile.

"Safe?" she asked slightly confused.

"We don't know why he attacked you, the security team are looking into previous checks we had done, to see if they can find anything," he said gently.

Ava raised her left hand off the bed and touched the side of her head softly. There was a large bump and what felt like dried blood.

"You have concussion," Ethan spoke solemnly. "Bailey, a friend of mine, checked you over."

Ava looked mortified.

"He's a doctor," Ethan added, as if reading her mind.

She sighed, "Thank goodness for that," she said jokingly.

"This is serious Ava," his eyes were black whirlpools, the blue had gone completely.

His face was taut with overwhelming anger.

"You've been hurt!" he said angrily. "I swear to god if I ever get my hands on him…"

Ava reached out and took his hand, squeezing it to reassure him.

"I'm fine," she said, trying not to wince as her head felt as if someone had hit with a hammer.

"Really…" she said trying to convince him "…I'm okay."

She sat up trying to ignore the pain in her side. Ethan rearranged her pillows behind her expecting her to lie back down. As she sat up straight, she took in more of the room.

"This is a beautiful room," she said quietly, in awe.

Ethan was staring at her, his handsome face creased in a frown. He sat on the edge of the bed and with his hand, guided her face to look directly at him.

"Hello" she said, smiling. *God he was so good looking it should be illegal.*

"Ava," he said shaking his head, "you need to rest, you have had a nasty bang to the head."

Ava closed her eyes briefly, as she flashed back to the moment where her head had been smashed off the wall.

"Like I said, I'm ok," she said unconvincingly. "I have Penningtons to impress," she said suddenly, eyes opening wide, as she had just remembered her duties for the day.

"You have to rest," he spoke gently, as if she did not understand what had just happened to her.

He still had his hand cupped around her beautiful face and she took it gently in her hand and held it on her lap, looking down at her hand entwined in his. She bit her bottom lip gently, whilst deliberating whether she should divulge exactly what Collins had said to her. She knew there were things she could not tell him, as it was not her business, but she felt he deserved to know why Collins had attacked her.

"For Christ's sake Ava, stop biting your lip," he pleaded, closing his eyes briefly to try and regain control.

"Sorry," she was appalled that biting her lip had offended him in some way, but when he opened his eyes, the anger had gone.

They were back to their exquisite Topaz blue, it was as if they pierced her very soul. Ava had to remind herself that this was not the time and place to jump on him. Although they were in a bedroom, maybe it was his bedroom and no-one else was there.

"Ava," he interrupted her carnal thoughts and when she looked at him, his brow was furrowed with concern.

"When you bite your bottom lip... it makes me want to bite it," he said simply.

Ava's mouth opened to respond, but she didn't know what to say. She had no idea how to flirt and as for love, she had only ever truly loved one person. She shook her head at her own thoughts, *love, why would she think of that word.*

As she shook her head, the pain resurfaced and she stopped with a sharp gasp, closing her eyes tightly, in an attempt to subdue the pain.

"For god's sake Ava, lie down and rest." Ethan demanded.

She opened her eyes again and spoke quietly, looking down again at their hands still entwined.

"There is something you should know…" She took a deep breath and he found he was holding his in anticipation.

"Collins said something…"

The memory was not pleasant, but she knew it could be important, not only for Sofia's, but also for Ethan's own safety.

"He said he knew we were together and that…" she paused trying to find the words, "he thinks we are together and that's why you sent Rogers on the sea taxi for me."

Ethan stayed stock still and didn't speak, he wanted her to say what she needed to tell him.

"He… he," she sighed a long, slow sigh and after staring at their hands, she closed her eyes.

"He said he was going to have me too and that you had to share."

She spoke so quietly that Ethan took a few seconds to take in what she had just recounted. With her eyes still closed she squeezed his hands tightly, suddenly she felt his warm lips crush against her mouth. She kept her eyes closed, not wanting this to be a dream. She started to kiss him back, all the feelings they had been harbouring for each other overflowing into a passionate embrace. She placed her hands on his face to hold him there, not wanting to break the kiss, their tongues probing, as they wanted more from each other.

He wanted her closer, to feel her body beneath him, so he moved both hands to either side of her waist.

"Ahh," she screamed in his mouth tipping her head back quickly, as he opened his eyes wide in horror.

Her left hand had immediately gone from his cheek, covering his right hand on her waist. They were both breathless.

"Fuck… I'm sorry," he said, disgusted that he had hurt her, what was wrong with him.

"I'm not," she said breathlessly.

Looking at him, imploring him with her whole body, to kiss her again.

"I see my patient is awake."

A jovial voice broke the tension and they both turned towards the door.

"Bay, can you give us a minute?" Ethan grimaced and Ava tried to regain some composure, hoping she didn't have that 'just been kissed' look on her face.

How long had he been standing there?

"Sorry buddy, I have my patient's best interests to consider and as she has concussion and possibly a broken rib, I think you and her should not be left alone for a while," he laughed and winked, as Ava felt her cheeks blush.

Ethan stood and stepped back from the bed, looking at Ava in horror.

"Broken rib?" he questioned solemnly.

Ava just returned his look, not knowing what to say or do.

"You need some fresh air Eth…" Bailey said gently. "…and I need to check you over if that's alright?" He tilted his head slightly at the question and Ava nodded in response, the small movement hurting her head.

Completely ignoring Ethan, he held Ava's wrist again, explaining to her that he was checking her heart rate and that it had spiked when he had first seen her unconscious after the attack. At the word attack, Ethan had stalked from the room, to get a strong drink, by God he needed one.

"My name is Bailey," he said still smiling, "you can call me Bay."

She couldn't help but smile back.

"Hello." Ava said simply, not knowing if she should explain what had happened with Collins, or what had literally just happened with Ethan.

She felt flustered and a growing sense of need. If this man hadn't just walked in, she might of… oh, my Christ! She slapped her free hand over her eyes and shook her head, ignoring the pounding headache.

"Hey," said Bailey sitting down on the bed, "everything's going to be alright you know, Collins has been banished and Ethan will look after you."

She dropped her hand and looked into his kind face

"Bay…" She paused "that's what I am afraid of."

Chapter 17

The sound of the wooden fan whirring above her and the gentle hum of the air conditioning unit, meant that Ava knew she was back in her water villa, before she had even opened her eyes. Both her hands felt heavy and as she peaked through her half open eyes, she saw both were being held tightly.

Her left hand was encased in Jez's huge, tanned hand and her right in Kitty's pale, delicate and beautifully manicured hand. Ava smiled as she spoke.

"Good job I have a big bed," she said weakly.

"Oh my god, you're awake!" Kitty was first to speak. "I've been so worried about you."

She had jumped up and was now kneeling on the bed, kissing Ava's hand.

"I'm fine," Ava lied.

"Fine! Ava, you had a nasty fall, I can't believe you both got hurt!" Kitty scolded.

"Okay you two, can you both give me a few minutes with my patient?" Bailey stood at the bottom of the bed, smiling at the people flanking Ava.

Kitty leant forward and kissed her sister gently on her forehead.

"I will wait on the decking," she smiled, but the concern remained etched on her beautiful face.

"Kitty, I'm fine!" Ava said with all the bravado she could muster.

Kitty smiled back, relieved. Ava turned to face Jez for the first time since opening her eyes. His face was serious and she knew he had been watching her like a hawk.

"You and I will discuss this later," he said abruptly and his gaze skipped to Bailey.

"Look after her." This was not a request, but a demand.

Ava opened her mouth to speak, but Jez had lithely jumped up off the bed and was stalking his way out on to the decking, closing the sliding door using more force than necessary.

"I'm sorry, he's not usually so rude." Ava said apologetically.

"They have both been very concerned about you, in fact you had a room full of well-wishers in here and I had to restrict them to only two."

He laughed as he approached the bed.

"I am just going to check your ribs if that's okay with you?"

Ava looked down and realised she was now in her silk pjs, a pair of shorts and vest top in pale orange with flower blossoms on them.

"Um, when did I change?" She was so disorientated and confused, her banging head was not helping.

"Well… firstly, we got you back safely to the island and I scanned your head and x-rayed your ribs to check for breaks. You have a concussion, the swelling has already regressed and so apart from a bad headache for the rest of the day, you should be good. Your ribs on the other hand, are badly bruised. So, you are going to have to take things easy for a few days," he smiled kindly as he pushed and prodded Ava's ribs, causing her to wince and suck in a breath.

"Sorry, but I have to do this," he apologised as he replaced her vest top and the bed cover.

He took her wrist and squeezed tightly between his thumb and finger, presumably checking her heart rate.

Ava stayed quiet until he had finished.

"All good you're doing well," he said smiling.

He sat on the edge of the bed and tilted his head, taking in Ava's expression.

"You look like you have a question?" he asked.

"Several," she replied.

"Shoot," he said, but instantly looked like he regretted his choice of words.

Clearing his throat, he said, "Go ahead," correcting himself.

"How did I get off the boat?" she asked.

"Ethan carried you off, you were unconscious," he said simply.

"Then what?" Ava wanted to fill in the blank spaces in her throbbing head.

"Then we took you to the medical centre, I checked you over thoroughly and you had scans and x-rays. When I was happy that no long-term damage had been done, I thought you would be more comfortable in your own room, so we brought you here," he finished.

"We?" Ava questioned.

"Ethan carried you, I escorted you both," he said simply.

"But Ethan left," she said slowly.

It was as if her heart was breaking in two.

"He had business to attend to," Bailey said trying to change the look of sadness on her lovely face.

"I see." she whispered.

That was it, it was all over. That sensational kiss had quite literally woken up feelings and urges she thought she had lost forever, all that was over. Collins had attacked her and Ethan must obviously be worried about his sister's welfare, quite rightly, as Ava knew things that he didn't. The fact Ethan hadn't waited for her to wake up, that it was Kitty and Jez beside her when she regained consciousness, said it all. He must regret the moment he laid eyes on her and in that respect, he would want this wedding to go ahead, even less than before.

"Oh god..." Ava whispered "...he must hate me."

She spoke to no one in particular and was surprised when Bailey took her hand in his.

"I believe he did not want to leave you alone for one second, but your family arrived and he thought it best to leave you with them," he said frowning.

Ava felt angry now, how could he leave her. She might not have regained consciousness and then where would he be. She felt awful for thinking this and an image of Kitty's worried face came to mind. Christ Kitty would have no blood family left if anything happened to her, how could she be so selfish. How could she be thinking about Ethan, when she should be worrying about her sister?

"Ava?" Bailey spoke quietly. "Ethan left when your family arrived, when I say family...all of them turned up, even Bella." He smiled at this.

"Why wouldn't Bell have come?" Ava was even more confused now.

Bella was part of her little family, why wouldn't she come with the others.

"Well, you see, Bella had an accident too," he said grimly.

"An accident? Oh my god is she okay?" Ava tried to sit up, but the pain in her abdomen kept her horizontal.

"Bella fell between the yacht and the water taxi, she has a possible fracture in her leg. Unfortunately, she has to wear a support boot, to keep it still and secure," he said looking thoughtful. "She is a very lucky lady," he said as an afterthought.

"Lucky?" Ava's voice was shaking.

"Lucky that she has hurt her leg?" Ava was concerned for her lovely friend.

"She went with the others to the bar, she was in quite good spirits. She will be fine… she was just very lucky she wasn't more seriously hurt." He finished with a squeeze of Ava's hand.

"I will leave you to rest now. The pain relief medicine I have given you will start to kick in and you will hopefully have a painless and restful sleep. Your friend said he will stop with you overnight, like he 'usually does'?" he added raising a quizzical brow.

Ava did not respond, it was none of his business who sleeps in her room and if he was trying to dig for dirt on Ethan's behalf, he could kiss her arse. She was upset now, upset that Bella had been hurt, angry that her and Jez's relationship should be the topic of anyone's conversation and completely devastated that whatever had gone on between her and Ethan (*omg that kiss!*) was now over.

"I'm tired," she lied, wanting to be on her own.

The good doctor chose not to continue the conversation and rose swiftly from the edge of the bed.

"Of course, just one last thing…" she looked at him and waited, he looked uncomfortable "ummm… Ethan thought it better that we tell everyone you fell and hurt yourself today, he was worried about his sister and…"

He had the decency to look embarrassed now.

"I understand." Ava interrupted quickly, just wanting him to be gone so she could process the events of today.

"If you need anything at any time, I have left my number with your friend, day or night," he emphasized.

"Thank you." Ava replied softly, he was only being kind and she shouldn't take out her bad mood on him.

He nodded politely before crossing the room and opening the sliding doors. Ava closed her eyes as she listened to the conversation, Kitty full of concern and the good doctor reassuring her and Jez that all was well. Jez muttered a few words and she heard Bailey confirm.

"Yes of course, day or night."

She heard them all step into the room and the doors sliding to a close, a lot gentler than the last time. With the pleasantries over, they said their goodbyes and Bailey left the villa. Ava felt Kitty kiss the top of her head.

"Jez if anything serious had happened to her it would all be my fault, I brought her out here for this wedding," she said sadly.

Ava heard movement and then Kitty tearfully saying thank you to Jez. He must have been hugging her.

"Now come on Missus-to-be, pull yourself together and go get celebrating at the bar with your future husband and all our clan," humour had returned to his voice and Kitty responded to the turn of playfulness.

"Will do……and we will have one for you too," she laughed now, as she wiped the tears away.

"Make it two," he joined in laughing.

After saying goodbye, the front door opened and closed quietly and it was back to the whir of the ceiling fan and the hum of the air con. She heard Jez open the fridge door, but before he had re-joined her on the bed, she had fallen asleep.

Another dreamless slumber, however, this time she knew she was in her water villa and she also knew that when she opened her eyes, Jez would be waiting with a million questions. She was right, the second she opened her eyes, she was rewarded with Jez's handsome face, looking down at her from where he sat up on the bed, keeping watch.

He immediately slid down to lie beside her, turning on his side, his head on the same pillow as hers. He looked tired, stubble now casting a shadow over his dramatic jawline and yet he still managed to look incredibly hot and sexy.

"At last," Jez said quietly. "I thought you were pretending to sleep to get out of talking to me, but I guess that stuff the doc gave you, knocked you out."

Oh, dear he's not happy, thought Ava.

"Well?" he said, now face to face, only inches apart.

Ava smiled, "Hi."

Jez melted immediately.

"Do you have any idea how worried we have all been?" he said seriously, his eyes dark.

"I'm so sorry" she replied.

"Well, I know you are not accident prone, so the idea of you falling down the stairs is ridiculous," he said knowingly, "plus your body is covered in bruises and hand marks…" he stopped and gulped, unable to continue.

"I really am okay," Ava said more confidently than she actually felt. I'm going to be sore for a few days but that's all." She smiled and Jez tried to return it, but couldn't.

Someone had hurt her and he wanted to know who, could it have been Ethan? He had buggered off when they had all clambered in to the room.

"I want the truth as always, so start from the beginning."

And so, she did, beginning with Sofia being upset as they arrived on the super yacht, although she did not explain why, as that was not her secret to divulge. She told him the events as they had happened, all the way through to waking up in the villa. He was shocked that Collins had been the attacker. As she was recounting the events of the day, Ava got to the kiss with Ethan. She thought she could see a faint blush on Jez's cheeks, but she must have imagined it as Jez was never embarrassed about anything, ever. She answered every question including where Collins was now.

"Off the island apparently, I feel so sorry for Sofia… I mean… they've not been married for long," she said sadly.

Jez's hand encompassed Ava's face, as he looked directly into her eyes.

"As long as you're safe Ave, if anything happened to you…" he broke off.

"It's late and I think we have all been through enough today, don't you?" She said smiling again. She didn't want the melancholy of Ethan disappearing, to take over and so she changed the subject completely.

"I'm looking forward to seeing Kit's last dress fitting tomorrow. It is simply stunning and I can't wait to see her in it again," she smiled genuinely excited for the fitting.

"So, we are not going to discuss Ethan and that kiss?" Jez was frowning now and wanted to talk things through.

"He wants to stop the wedding Jez, how could I have kissed someone like that? How can I possibly have feelings for someone who wants to deliberately end my sister's happiness?" she was whispering now.

"Hey," he said soothingly. "This wedding will be going ahead and Kitty and Alfie are going to live happily ever after."

He was so sure of their relationship, he had no doubts that no matter what, Kitty and Alfie belonged together. Ava closed her eyes, wanting to believe him, but her head was throbbing again and she knew that Ethan was a serious threat to Kit and Alfie's future. The strong medication took over and without another word, she drifted off into a dreamless sleep.

Chapter 18

Ava awoke to the smell of fresh coffee and a mouth-watering aroma of fresh baking, that made her stomach rumble. Jez had ordered fresh croissants, seedless raspberry jam and butter. She hadn't heard the door knock or even the hustle and bustle of Abdul bringing the trolley in to the villa. As she opened her eyes and stretched out her body, she felt a bolt of pain from her ribs. She groaned and slowly opened her eyes.

"Morning gorgeous," Jez was busying himself buttering a croissant. "I've ordered your favourite for breakfast," he said smiling.

Ava sat up slowly and adjusted the pillow behind her, to support her body.

"How do you feel?" Jez stopped the spreading and looked at her, trying to judge for himself.

"To be honest my head feels alright, but my ribs are sore," she answered honestly.

"Mmm," Jez answered, as if debating something in his head.

"What?" Ava asked him, but he didn't reply.

"Jez?" she questioned again.

He had now put a thin layer of jam across the croissant and was carefully walking over to the bed where he plopped down, bouncing the mattress slightly and making Ava groan at the movement it caused to her body.

He handed her the delicacy and she felt the warm, buttery pastry in her hand. She took a bite and instantly felt a little better, good old food, never failed.

"Thought that would cheer you up," he said smiling.

"Aren't you having one?" Ava questioned.

"Already had two," he winked, making her laugh, causing her ribs to ache.

"Kit texted earlier, she wants us in her room at ten o'clock. Bell is going to make sure the dress still fits after all the cocktails they were drinking last night," he smiled as Ava visibly brightened.

"I cannot wait to see her in her dress again," Ava was genuinely excited.

"You don't want to talk about yesterday?" Jez asked raising his eyebrows and tilting his head slightly. "It's not every day you get attacked by a psycho," he finished.

"I don't even want to think about it, I just want to enjoy the rest of the pre-wedding celebrations."

She smiled weakly and Jez knew that Ava was never flippant and the ordeal she had been through, must really be playing on her mind.

"Will you be my date tonight?" Jez asked, back to his jovial self.

"Of course," Ava replied, "I have a lovely dress."

Ava smiled back and made the decision to blank out yesterday completely and make the most of the day. The thought of seeing her little sister in her hand made wedding gown, filled Ava with such happiness, everything else paled into insignificance, even Ethan.

"You are going to need a shower and then some make up," Jez's expression changed slightly and Ava was a little taken back that he had suggested makeup.

He of all people, was a stalwart for her being a natural beauty.

"Do I look that bad?" Ava questioned, not really wanting to know the answer.

"Ave," his voice was gentle and he reached out and held her hand before continuing. "My darling angel, you are and always have been, beautiful on the inside and the outside," he paused, looking serious.

"Oh god, I feel a 'but' coming," Ava interrupted him.

"However," he grimaced and Ava looked mortified. "Professor you have bruises that have worsened overnight," he said quietly.

Now it was his turn to look mortified.

"Oh," was all she could manage in a response.

The way he was looking at her made her feel sick, what was that expression pity? Sadness? She couldn't place it. She finished her croissant, the enjoyment gone, as she had to force down the small mouthful she had been chewing.

Deciding she wanted to see the bruises or herself, she made to get off the huge bed.

"Let me help you," Jez exclaimed and put out his hand in support.

She took it gratefully and manoeuvred slowly off the bed. As she stood, she felt a little dizzy and as ever Jez was by her side, arm around her waist in support. As she caught her breath and steadied herself, she felt emboldened to get to the bathroom and see what Jez was talking about, plus she really needed a wee. As she got to the door of the bathroom she turned and gently kissed Jez on the cheek.

"Thank you for everything."

"I feel a 'but' coming?" he said mirroring her words from earlier.

"However," she smiled bravely, "I need to do this on my own, I will be fine." she added at the admonishing look he gave her.

"Fucked up, insecure, neurotic and emotional?" he replied with a grimace and a frown.

This made Ava laugh, although she stopped abruptly as the pain shot through her body.

She smiled weakly and said again, "I really am fine" and with that she opened the door to the bathroom.

On entering the huge suite, she could see it was bathed in the early morning sunlight, that leaked through the wooden blinds, which were slightly ajar. Jez obviously thought she could handle herself, as he made no further comment and stayed on the other side of the door.

She kept her eyes on the floor in front of her until she reached the floor to ceiling mirror. She lifted her gaze slowly. She blinked several times, as she thought she was staring at Edward Munich's 'Scream' portrait. Sunken eyes and a mouth gawping open, eyes wide in shock.

Fuck, I look a mess, she thought. No wonder Ethan left me last night. She closed her eyes and her mouth and shook her head gently, trying to get the notion of Ethan out of her head. She opened her eyes again and tried to be more positive. She looked thin and that was about the only good thing she could think of. She caught sight of her neck. Oh my god.

The bruises where Collins had tried to strangle her, were standing out like a sore thumb. She slowly lifted her vest top and the horrific bruises continued down her left-hand side, where she had been shoved against the wall. She let her vest top go, along with a slow steadying breath. The top of her arms was also bruised and you could literally see the finger marks where she had been grabbed and held. She felt numb. So much for putting it all behind her.

"Text Lou for me please," she called to Jez, "tell her I need her to bring her make up box." Ava finished.

"Yes Professor," came Jez's reply.

Poor man must be wondering what the hell to do with me, Ava thought wistfully. She raised her head and straightened her shoulders, walked slowly over to the colossal shower and switched it on. Within minutes the bathroom had filled with steam and the mirrors had filled with condensation. This was much to Ava's relief, so she could no longer ogle the marks left on her body. She also relieved herself and it dawned on her she hadn't had a wee since yesterday lunchtime and that she must consider herself lucky that she hadn't wet herself. That was an appalling thought. She managed to get undressed and stepped into the shower, where the jets of hot water helped ease her aching body and she felt her muscles relax. She somehow managed to wash her hair and used the huge natural sponge to gently wash her body, enjoying the smell of coconut.

After drying herself off and gently towel drying her hair, Ava donned the soft white robe that hung on the back of the bathroom door. She felt much better after the shower and as she opened the bathroom door and turned to see the spectacular view from her glass wall, she couldn't help but cheer up.

"You look brighter." Jez walked over from where he stood admiring the view, sipping his coffee. He put his arms around her and planted a kiss, softly on her head.

"I am feeling better thank you… did Lou reply?" she asked.

"Yes, she's on her way over, although she's very curious and hungover." he smiled a beautiful, heart melting smile. "So good luck!"

They both smiled now as they stood there hugging each other gently. Both enjoying the closeness. Suddenly, there was a hammering on the door, which jolted them apart. Ava winced as the sharp pain in her ribs, flared at the sudden movement.

They could hear her chuntering before Jez had a chance to open the door.

"For fuck's sake, I'm baking out here!" Lou's dulcet tones came from behind the wooden blockade, as Jez opened the door.

"It's about time Jez, bloody hell it's hot out there," she moaned and then she stopped still, the large Louis Vuitton makeup box gripped tightly in her hand.

She dipped her head and pulled her sunglasses off, whilst taking in Ava's appearance.

"Close your mouth Lou, we are not codfish!" Jez said lightening the mood.

"What the fuck…" Lou trailed off.

"Long story, I'm ok, I just need an expert make up lady to cover me up." Ava smiled.

Lou didn't feel too grand herself, she had big black bags under eyes and looked pasty, considering she had beautiful dark skin. She was also walking strangely, a bit like a cowboy, something both Ava and Jez decided it was best not to discuss. She stood there in her lion king nightie, which barely covered her bottom.

"Hungover?" Jez queried.

Lou turned to face him, moving the attention away from a grateful Ava.

"Slightly," she lied.

"Coffee?" Jez offered.

"Go on then and you can put a brandy in it, I'm feeling rough here you know," she smiled as she said it, which broke the slight tension of seeing Ava so badly bruised.

She turned back to her dear friend.

"So this was no accident then," she said seriously, observing the finger marks on Ava's neck.

"I will fill you in, whilst you work on our girl," Jez intervened and with that Lou set about her artistry in make-up magic.

By the time Ava and Jez knocked the door of the extensive honeymoon villa, no one would ever have known that Ava had been battered the day before. She wore a green wraparound sun dress with three quarter length sleeves, which thankfully covered a lot of the bruises and marks. With Lou's help, the makeup had expertly covered any visible bruises that would still be showing with the dress on.

Ava and Jez had called for a lift on one of the buggy's and were waiting outside the huge honeymoon villa, full of excitement to see the bride-to-be. Kitty came to the door and Ava could see the relief fill her face when she saw her big sister. She flung herself at Ava and squeezed her tightly. Ava screwed up her face in pain, but didn't make a sound, not wanting to worry her on a day that should be full of happiness.

"Hello," Bella's voice came from a huge side room and when Kitty finally let go of Ava, she led her by the hand, into the expansive living area.

It was similar in style to Ava's water villa, however, this garden honeymoon villa was huge and had its own grand swimming pool and private section of beach. It was simply stunning. The massive white leather settees oozed luxury and there was little Bella, looking lost in the middle of one of the three in this room. Her right leg was covered by a sturdy black boot, that rested on a small wooden coffee table. Sketches surrounded her, a pencil was tucked neatly behind her ear and a tape measure draped around her neck. A sight Ava was used to, as

Bella had done hundreds of wedding dress fittings in her boutique back home, only without the boot restricting her.

"How are you?" both Ava and Bella spoke at the same time and everyone laughed.

Ava and Jez went over to Bella and kissed her on the top of her head, the bending over not helping Ava's ribs.

"So, are we ready?" Bella asked, looking at everyone in turn.

Suddenly the room was very serious and the occupants a little apprehensive.

"I am so excited to see you in your dress again," Ava said happily.

"Me too," said Jez, his arm wrapped around Ava's waist, applying no pressure, but there for a support if needed.

She was grateful.

"Kit?" Bella looked at Kitty who looked a little nervous.

"Are you ok?" Ava moved towards her beautiful sister.

She could see that Kitty hadn't had much sleep, as she too had darkened skin under her eyes, plus she looked a little pale.

"Too many cocktails?" Jez laughed, "Don't worry, Lou looks worse than you!"

Kitty smiled looking relieved.

"I'm feeling a bit delicate too," Bella admitted, making them all turn and gawp.

"You were drinking Bell?" Ava asked in shock.

"What can I say… I think I have found my inner drinker, although the 'mornings after' are not fun," Bella replied, pulling a face and they all laughed together.

"Kit has made some coffee, so I'm sure that will help us all wake up," she smiled warmly.

"Lou had a brandy in her coffee this morning," Ava informed them.

"urghhh," Bella made a vomiting gesture and swung her booted leg on to the floor, standing up with unexpected ease, considering her predicament.

"Come on then Mrs Pennington-to-be, let's make sure your dress still fits," again Bella smiled and picking up two crutches, hobbled her way towards the master bedroom.

Kitty didn't follow her and Jez sensed the sisters needed to talk, so made his excuses and went to fetch some coffee. Ava moved in front of Kitty and held her hands.

"You, ok?" she asked concerned.

"Yes of course, just a little bit tired. I was so worried about you Ave," and once again, Kitty lunged forward and hugged Ava tightly.

She was just starting to feel the need to faint, when Kitty let go and stood back, as if gaining some strength from the hug.

"I'm so sorry I worried you Kit, but I'm fine now. Not like poor old Bell and her boot," Ava said trying to change the subject on to someone else.

"I know, poor Bella," Kitty said sadly, "she's actually being quite brave and said the boot doesn't bother her, as long as I was happy that she still be a bridesmaid. Of course, I wouldn't change my mind, I want you all up there with me," Kitty rolled her eyes, something she did as a teenager when Ava tried to advise her. "Right then," Kitty seemed to compose herself and made her way towards the door way.

"Kit," Ava called after her, Kitty turned and smiled at Ava, "Kit if you are having second thoughts or anything is worrying you, you can tell me you know," Ava said earnestly.

Kitty smiled, making her way back to her beloved older sister and kissing her on the cheek, "Thank you, I'm fine," Kitty said smiling, although the smile didn't quite reach her eyes.

Kitty turned and left the room, just as Ava whispered to herself "Fucked up, insecure, neurotic and emotional."

Chapter 19

It had been hours since the dress fitting and Ava couldn't shake the feeling that Kitty was hiding something. The dress had looked stunning, as they knew it would, however, Kitty's initial fittings had been happy and joyous for all in the room. This morning seemed slightly subdued for some reason.

Ava talked her concern over with Jez, who was quick to put forward that everyone involved in the fitting had worries of their own. For example, Bella was recovering from a nasty accident the day before and was nursing a bad leg, in a cumbersome boot.

Kitty was a little upset that Bella had remarked that the dress was now a little snug and had lectured her to calm down on the booze and food tonight, plus, it didn't help that Kitty was hungover and had had a sleepless night worrying about her big sister. He had continued to say that he himself had not had his usual ten hours of beauty sleep and that he too was worried about Kit's big sister. He did wink at her to lighten the guilt she was feeling. He then pointed out that the bride's sister had been through a traumatic experience the day before and she herself was suffering from bruised ribs and concussion.

Ava had mulled this over and realised Jez was right, they were all dealing with things and so she did what she was good at and decided to blank the worries out. She was actually looking forward to this evening's banquet. All the families and guests were meeting in the main function room for an evening of festivities, including a prolific amount of drinking. Jez had checked out the venue during his afternoon stroll and had emerged from his walk with an infectious, happy aura, that had rubbed off on Ava, completely lifting her spirits. He explained there was a huge elegant dance floor, surrounded by the most beautiful, exotic flower displays. He was filling Ava in, whilst sweeping her around the floor of her villa. He wanted to practice his dancing for later, as he had a line of affluent, young women, who wanted to be in his arms (even if just for one dance).

Although the pain killers she had taken had worked wonders with her bruised ribs, Ava was still getting sharp twinges if she turned too quickly, this didn't stop her enjoying every second of dancing in Jez's arms.

"Right then, I'm going to go and get beautified," Jez had finished his dance and was bowing grandly. "I will be back here at seven o'clock on the dot, so you had better be ready for the ball, Cinderella." He stood and kissed Ava on the cheek.

"I will be ready," she promised.

She had already showered again and decided that as it was only four o'clock, she really didn't need three hours to get ready. Lou had promised to come and re-do the bruise makeup around six-thirty, so Ava grabbed a can of Pepsi max and a 'Dildo', Jez still found the renaming of their new favourite chocolate bar hilarious.

She slid gently between the cool covers and after eating her snack, she set her alarm for an hour and a half's time. With that she snuggled down under the soft sheet and with the help of her next dose of pain killers, she soon dozed off.

At seven on the dot, there was a knock on the door. Lou sauntered over with a large glass of white wine in her hand and opened it. Jez was on his knees holding a red rose between his perfect teeth.

"Come in you idiot," Lou scoffed, laughing at his usual antics. He stood and brushed off his knees. He was wearing a black Tom Ford tuxedo, crisp white dress shirt and black silk bow tie. Lou wolf whistled and after taking a large slug of wine she managed, "You are looking very fuckable tonight Jez," making both of them laugh.

"I do my best," he replied gallantly, with a smirk on his face.

"May I say, you look the same Lou," he added.

Lou was wearing a fitted purple body con dress, which came down to her knees. It showed off every curve of her gorgeous body. With her cleavage straining to be contained, in what could only be described as a boulder holder, she was ready for action. Her jet-black hair had been crimped and fell in waves over her shoulders. Jez called in the direction of the bathroom, where he presumed Ava was doing her final touches. The bathroom door opened and his darling girl walked through, looking a vision in red.

Her dress was made of the softest dark red silk. It had three quarter length sleeves, its V-neckline showed off the top of her perfect cleavage to perfection. She had opted for the same colour underwear, consisting of a delicate, but uplifting lace bra and tiny G-string knickers. The skirt flowed, falling just below her mid-calf showing off her smooth, toned, lower legs and ankles. Teamed with a stunning pair of matching dark red high heels, decorated with small diamante flowers on the back of each heel. She looked stunning and Jez stood with his mouth open in admiration.

"Fuck," he whispered.

"You mean fuckable," Lou laughed knocking back what was left in her glass.

Ava was struggling with putting a small diamond earring in to her right ear. They were a present from Jez for her thirtieth birthday, but she only wore them on special occasions, as they had cost a small fortune. Jez moved swiftly to assist her. Her hair was in a loose French plait, held in place by a slim diamante clip. Several blonde tendrils were loose, falling naturally to frame her angelic face. He took the earing out of her hand and deftly placed it securely in her ear, kissing the top of her ear, once it was in place.

"Cinderella will go to the ball," he whispered. "You look incredible," he finished.

"Let's just hope it doesn't rain," Lou cut in, "Ol said we might have a storm in the early hours. If we do, you will have to get a brolly Ave, or those bruises will appear," she said curtly.

Ava put her hand on her neck, a horrified look on her face.

"Lou!" Jez scolded.

"I've told Bell the same thing about her eyebrow," she said affronted.

Jez turned to face Ava and took her hands in his, "It will all be ok, I promise," he said adoringly.

"Who is Ol?" Ava questioned, just catching on that Lou had said a name she didn't know.

"Oliver, the sex on legs, Australian barefoot pilot." Lou answered unashamedly. "Haven't any of you noticed I'm walking funny?" She said pulling a pained face and adjusting her G string knickers.

"And on that note…" Jez interrupted, "…come on then ladies, let's go and get this party started," he rallied and laughing at their private joke, they made their way to the waiting buggy.

On arrival to the vast banquet room, they stood and gaped at the unadulterated opulence laid out before them. The magnificent room opened out onto a huge decked area which led to the lantern-lit panorama of the beach. The sounds of the surf rolling up the sand, could just be heard above the music softly playing.

The room was filled with glittering chandeliers and fairy lights and looked completely enchanting. Beautiful, fresh flowers arranged in round, crystal vases surrounded the room and the scent of them all was amazing. The circular tables seated at least twelve guests at each and were covered in crisp white tablecloths, laden with expensive silver cutlery, an exquisite china service and cut-glass crystal flutes.

Antique candelabras and stunning flower arrangements, sat gracefully in the middle of tables. Small, twinkling lights and candles were flickering around the room, making it look charming and romantic.

Jez squeezed Ava's hand and nodded in the direction of the dance area, which was situated to the left of this vast room. It had been outlined by a hedge of fresh flowers and Ava could see the disco lights and a DJ desk at the edge of one side of the dance floor. For now, a small orchestra was playing in the far-left corner.

The whole place was incredible and Ava's stomach churned with nerves, as she wanted tonight to go well. Lou had already veered off to the right-hand side of the room, where the long cocktail bar stood. Bar staff were already busy executing cocktails and beverages for the congregating wedding guests.

"Drinks," Jez said cheerfully, kissing her hand and heading off in search of a fancy cocktail for them both.

"Wow, you look fantastic," Rachel appeared from nowhere, wearing a Chinese style grey fitted dress, a delicate pale pink bloom, intricately stitched up the left side.

"Rach you look beautiful!" Ava hugged her friend, wincing slightly at the pull on her ribs. "I'm sorry I haven't spent much time with you, but I'm looking forward to tomorrow," she said smiling broadly.

"Me too and don't stress about me, I'm having the most relaxing, wonderful time," Rachel's face twisted as she added "apart from worrying about you and Bell being so accident prone."

Ava would have to tell her the truth at some point, but after the wedding, not now. She wanted tonight to go without any incidents or accidents and for everyone to be happy.

Rachel raised a glass full of a delicious looking red cocktail, with the mandatory expandable silver straw and a heart which had been neatly crafted out of a slice of blood red orange, floating on the top.

"Cheers to a good evening," Rachel smiled and took a huge slug. "Bloody hell this is good, the girls would love this, I need the recipe!" and with that and a nod of her head, she went off to interrogate the bar staff.

Ava stood there, taking in the beautiful setting for this evening's pre wedding banquet, when an elegant looking lady glided into view. She was an older version of Sofia, except she had stunning dark brown eyes. Ava knew immediately that this was Sofia senior, mother of the Pennington children. My god, she could see where they got their magnificent genes from.

"Good evening Miss Hart," she spoke with an elegant American accent, which oozed money.

"Hello," Ava replied simply, a little intimidated by this formidable woman.

There was a pause as Mrs Pennington seemed to be sizing up the woman stood before her. Her eyes narrowed slightly, but no other movement appeared on her perfectly made-up face. It was obvious that she had had work done, good work, but definitely work.

Ava felt a stab of anger thinking of Kitty. Would she be subjected to plastic surgery, just to try and keep up with this lot? Over her dead body. Her expression must have showed her lack of enthusiasm, as Mrs Pennington broke the awkward silence.

"I hope you are well enough to be here Miss Hart."

Ava took this as a challenge and immediately stood up a little taller and straightened her shoulders, her high heels giving her an advantage that she didn't need. Sofia senior was as petite as her mother, although she obviously kept fit, as her long evening gown showed off her slender figure.

"I'm fine, thank you for your concern." Ava replied curtly, "Please excuse me I need a drink" and with that Ava turned on her gorgeous heels and made her way towards the bar.

Oh fuck, she had just offended Ethan's mum. Why did she just think of her as Ethan's mum and not Kitty's mother-in-law? Ava's mind was reeling as she contemplated that question, when she felt a crushing arm lock around her waist. For a few awful seconds, Ava thought Collins had returned. She closed her eyes tightly, wanting to scream out in pain, the colour draining from her face.

"Ahhh Ava, beautiful girl."

She opened her eyes to see Aurora, clinging to her in a huge bear hug.

"Nonna." Ethan's firm voice came from her right-hand side, as he admonished his grandmother in fluent Italian.

It was the sexiest sound Ava had ever heard. She stood and watched him as his eyes flitted between her and his beloved grandmother. He had obviously told her that Ava was in pain, as his feisty grandmother let go and stood back, hands to her mouth and eyes wide in shock.

"Oh, sorry, sorry," she said, genuinely upset that she could have caused Ava any pain.

Ethan was furious, but somehow managed to keep his scary, sexy Italian words to a low level. His grandmother turned to him and said something quickly in Italian, he breathed out and seemed to relax. He stepped forward and kissed her on top of her dark grey curls and she beamed immediately.

"Good boy," she said looking at Ava, but holding Ethan's hand.

Ava realised that the old lady had wonky, yellowing teeth and for some reason she liked her even more. She hadn't fallen for the celebrity lifestyle, of false white veneers.

"I'm ok," Ava said lightly, smiling the best she could, although she still felt a little sick.

Ethan frowned and glared at her. Ava held his intense gaze. His eyes had lost their cool sparkling blue and were now dark and stormy. This only seemed to happen, when he was really mad or really turned on. Sadly, he looked really mad and Ava sighed disappointed it wasn't the latter.

With a few more Italian words he kissed his grandmother's hand and took Ava's. Not saying one word, he started walking towards the open terrace, which sprawled its way on to the stunning beach, pulling her behind him. A few guests stood at the terrace entrance, enjoying their cigarettes and the cool of the air conditioning.

The decking was completely empty and with a shiver of anticipation, Ava realised they were alone. Ethan kept on walking, making their way across the wooden boards. She felt the heat of the evening hit her. The room they had just left, although open, had been cool and comfortable. She felt clammy and overheated, but she wasn't sure if it was the warmth of the Maldivian evening, or the fact Ethan Pennington was in such close proximity.

He guided her to the outer corner of the decking, which was lit only by the dim beach lanterns. They were in the shadows, compared to the rest of the outdoor area. He stopped abruptly and turned, letting go of her hand, quickly raising both hands up to hold her face. Although in the dusky light, she could still distinguish his handsome features, he was so fucking hot.

"Ava," just that one word, her name from his lips, was too much and she couldn't help herself.

She pushed her face forward and their lips touched. As the kiss deepened his hands moved to her shoulders. Their tongues exploring and setting off a fire deep inside them both. Ava had her hands on his chest and she could feel the toned muscles beneath his shirt, his tuxedo jacket was open and she took the opportunity to slide her hands around his chest and wrap her them tightly around him. With this action the kiss became wilder, more animalistic, as their bodies crushed together.

Ethan could feel her amazing body, the toned, yet soft curves. Her breasts felt incredible against his chest, he couldn't remember when, or even if he had ever felt such a natural figure against him.

Ava was lost, kissing him in a frantic, epic whirlwind. She was in the arms of this gorgeous man and all sense of logic and reason for this not to happen, were forgotten. This kiss, this embrace was right, it was meant to be.

Ethan's arms had been wrapped around her shoulders, but satisfied she wasn't going to pull away, his right-hand trailed down her back, along the soft, warm silk, sending tingles down her spine.

At this point, they both wanted more and Ava caught his tongue in between her teeth, gently biting it, sending him over the edge. His hands grabbed her waist and pulled her hard against his groin. Agony and ecstasy hit Ava simultaneously. Feeling his arousal against her body was incredible, but at the same time his grip had tightened and the sharp pain from her ribs, shot through her body, causing her to scream out into his mouth.

Both of their eyes had opened wide in alarm and their exquisite kiss was broken. Ava closed her eyes again, mortified that she had spoilt this moment, the pain slowly subsiding. Ethan's hand was back on her shoulders, holding her in place. Their laboured breathing was slowly returning to normal and she could feel his breath on her face.

"Ava," he spoke gently, his voice pulling her out of her reverie.

"Ethan," she replied, eyes still closed.

She was biting her lip, now embarrassed that she had lost all control whilst kissing this stud of a man.

Surely, he was used to supermodels and rich, fit young women. The thought made her feel queasy again. She felt his hand lift from her shoulder and his finger found her bottom lip.

"Stop biting your lip," he said seriously, remembering him saying that this action made him want to bite it too, she opened her sparkling topaz eyes.

His eyes were still dark with lust and longing and Ava felt a spark of pride, that a man like him should like a girl like her.

"I'm sorry about..." He trailed off as he took a step back, looking down at her rib cage, both hands gripping her shoulders again, not wanting to let go of her.

His face serious, etched with concern. Ava realised that the other wedding guests may have seen them and was even more embarrassed by her own behaviour. She turned her head back to the entrance of the banquet hall. The smokers had gone and the guests had started to take their seats.

"Don't run," he said frowning.

Ava turned back to him and could see the fear in his face.

"I am not running," she said genuinely taken aback with his expression.

He looked scared. She raised her hands which had dropped to her sides and held his face, mirroring his earlier action. She took a step forward and they were once again body to body. She gently kissed his lips and he responded, kissing her back.

Just as the kiss was deepening again, he broke away, "Christ Ava, what are you doing to me?" he growled, the sound reverberating deep down in Ava's stomach. "I don't want to hurt you," he said earnestly.

"You won't," she argued and the look of sheer angelic beauty on her face, made him smile.

He shook his head in wonder and taking in a huge calming breath, he gently kissed the top of her head. She smelt heavenly, like coconut and honey. He looked at her one last time, enjoying the fact she was in heels and was almost the same height as him. She looked seriously sexy and it turned him on even more.

"Are you pouting Miss Hart?" he said playfully, running his finger a longer her full, all-natural lips.

She closed her eyes again and took a few, deep breaths.

"Ave?" Kitty's voice pierced the silence, as she turned in horror.

"Yes, I'm coming," she called back.

"I wish you were," Ethan whispered.

Thank God it was dark and Kitty was a fair way away, hopefully not seeing how close Ava and Ethan actually were and the fact her older sister blushing fiercely.

"Go, I will follow shortly," Ethan said quietly.

Ava turned back to him, oh god, was he that embarrassed to be seen with her. As if reading her mind, he stood back and looked down at his bulging tuxedo trousers.

"Oh," Ava wasn't really sure how to respond, so she kissed his cheek gently and turned, breaking their intimate contact.

She stood up tall, straightening her shoulders and walked towards the banqueting suite with as much dignity and decorum as she could muster.

Ethan watched her stunning figure, as she walked away from him. She looked incredible in that dress, although he wanted nothing more than to see her without it. Completely naked, but maybe still in those heels.

Fuck, he thought, adjusting his trousers. He closed his eyes and replayed the last few minutes in his mind. He had been so angry with his grandmother. He had seen her approach Ava, who was looking simply stunning in a long red, silk dress. His Nonna had hugged Ava tightly and he could see the pain etched on her beautiful face.

Fuck, he could kill Collins, if ever he got his hands on him, God help him. Marching Ava out to the shadows of the decking, he was going to tell her off, to explain she cannot put herself at risk like this and that she should be in her villa resting. However, when he had looked into that angelic face, all reason and control had been lost. He must have been out in the shadows for at least twenty minutes, waiting for his dick to calm down. The things he wanted to do to this English beauty, were flitting through his head, not helping his trouser situation.

When he eventually made it back into the main banquet area, everyone was in their seats. He was annoyed to see that Ava was on a different table to him. She was with that male model, Alfie, Kitty and the rest of her friends. He was stuck on a table with his mother, father, grandparents and Gio. There was one empty seat at his table and he considered telling Ava she would have to sit by him, but he didn't want to cause a scene.

Gio raised an eyebrow, as Ethan angrily took his seat.

"Everything alright?" Gio asked his younger brother, with a smirk.

"Of course," came Ethan's smooth reply.

Gio offered his pristine white napkin to him and as his forehead lined with confusion, Gio pointed to Ethan's mouth, with a broad grin. Ethan wiped his mouth and looked at the napkin, red lipstick marks soiling the clean, white linen. Their mother was watching every move with a look of distaste. Zara and Jennifer had been glaring nastily from the next table and Nonna was sipping her champagne with an ever-knowing smile.

Chapter 20

Alfie had given a small speech, thanking everyone for coming such a long way. Reserving the main speeches for tomorrow's celebrations, he had paid tribute to his beautiful fiancé and her family, who were brave enough to attend his wedding and spend time with the Pennington clan. Most of the guests laughed, except Zara Blackwell and Jennifer La True, who were busy whispering and scheming.

Ethan's mood had lifted with a few glasses of champagne and the thought that once this meal was over, he was going to dance with Ava. He had glanced over during Alfie's speech and admired her beautiful, angelic face, with her beaming smile. She really was the most gorgeous, alluring creature he had ever seen. He was grateful for the long tablecloth, as his groin strained under the material of his fitted trousers, he fidgeted uncomfortably. Gio had pointed out that their sister had asked to be excused. Ethan had tried to speak to her earlier, but she had not answered her door.

"I tried to see her, but she is not talking to anyone." Gio said sadly. "I should have paid more attention to her, instead of focusing on work," he seemed regretful and thoughtful.

"Me too," agreed Ethan simply.

He and his siblings ran the Pennington empire, however, he and Gio bore the brunt of most of the responsibilities. Ethan, Gio and Alfie were brothers who loved each other very much and were close business allies. Due to such hectic schedules, they didn't really socialise together apart from big family events, the last of which was Sofia's wedding and now, for Alfie's up and coming nuptials.

Ethan looked at his older brother's handsome profile, they were so alike in looks. They both worked out daily and looked after their slim, toned bodies. They needed to be physically and mentally fit, as they worked long days and needed stamina to run their multi-billion-dollar business. He was watching his older brother closely, it was not like Gio to look so wistful and melancholy. Maybe the incident with Collins had shook him up too.

Knowing their sisters' husband was a violent bastard, had even broken Ethan's thick skin. There was not much that affected him this way, but now thoughts of his sisters' welfare were paramount in his mind. Ethan's mind dwelled on his sister and he now wondered how her new husband had been treating her since their marriage, literally a few weeks ago. Sofia junior had been a little lax in attending the office, since the huge social event, but her three brothers had put it down to her being in the 'honeymoon period' of her relationship and her wanting to spend time with her new husband.

The thought now hit him that maybe Collins may have been keeping her away on purpose. Keeping her locked up at home. The thought sickened him to his stomach. If it turned out that Collins had been violent with their beloved sister, then he would kill him and he knew Gio would feel the same.

Taking a huge slug of champagne, he wished the desserts would be served quickly, as he was itching to hold Ava in his arms again. He felt a small hand on his shoulder and as he turned his head, his whole body was hoping it was her. He recognised the large emerald ring, belonging to his sister. He stood, pushing his chair back and took her hand in his. She looked tired and drawn, but at least she was here. Ever beautiful, in a long sleeved, green wrap around dress, that finished at her delicate ankles, her dark brown hair expertly tied in a neat bun. Even in great sadness she looked stunning.

"I'm so glad you came," he said honestly and kissed her tenderly on her cheek.

Gio had also stood and moved to the empty space beside him, leaving Sofia to sit between her older brothers. Gio kissed her hand gently.

"Wanna talk?" he said hopefully.

"No, I want a drink," she said helping herself to Gio's champagne.

Her mother looking on disapprovingly. The Pennington's never aired their dirty laundry in public and hitting the booze was not a sensible option or one their parents would ever condone.

Ava was enjoying the banquet, the champagne was flowing and the food was delicious. Kitty seemed a little reserved, but she was getting married tomorrow, so she was bound to be having a few last-minute nerves. Jez was absolutely on form, happy, jovial and as handsome as ever. He was particularly delighted that their whole group was on the same table, with the bride and groom-to-be no less.

"This champagne is gorgeous Alfie, I take it you are going to keep us all well supplied when you become family tomorrow?" Rachel said with a wink.

"Rachel!" Bella admonished.

She was wearing a tight lime green dress, which showed off every curve on her petite body, teamed with one silver beaded sandal. No ridiculous high heels for her, as she was restricted with the large black boot. She had opted for dramatic makeup, including fake eyebrow, thanks to Lou's expertise. She looked nothing like her usual self, which although gorgeous, was completely understated. Tonight, she looked striking. She had a new found confidence and every time she caught Ava's eye, her smile widened, as if sharing a secret joke.

Dan sat by her side, looking devastatingly handsome in his black tuxedo. Why is it men looked even hotter when they wore one. He seemed preoccupied and Ava noticed him occasionally scanning the room. She was a people watcher and was enjoying the celebrations even more so, as she was watching the happiness and joy on her gorgeous, friends faces.

Dan's expression had suddenly changed, just after the main meal had been cleared away. His eyes had widened and his whole face lit up. Ava saw Sofia junior glide past and noticed she had glanced quickly at Dan, her mouth twitching slightly, but not quite making a smile. She had approached the table where her family were seated and Ava watched as she placed her hand on Ethan's shoulder, he immediately stood up, with nothing but love and pride written on his clean cut, handsome face, he had kissed her cheek. Ava wished it was her at his side.

She returned focus to her table, where Alfie, who was also looking magnificent, was entertaining them all with a story of when Kitty had tried to draw him, but he couldn't sit still.

"My god did she yell at me," he beamed at Kitty who was totally mesmerised by him.

He leant in and kissed her passionately, gaining whoops and cries from the rest of the table.

"Put her down Alfie, save yourself for tomorrow night!" Lou blurted out.

Ava blushed at the thought of her little sister having sex, not something she cared to dwell on. Jez squeezed her hand tightly, he had of course been studying her beautiful face.

"Hey angel," he smiled his lop-sided smile. "Dance with me," he said eagerly.

"They haven't even served the dessert," she said in mock outrage.

Not one for formalities, Jez stood dramatically and held his hand out to Ava. She looked up at him and shook her head, "Please sit down, this is a posh dinner you know," she made the mistake of smiling.

He leant over so his nose was almost touching hers.

"Ava Hart, if you don't get up and dance with me right now, I will carry you over to the dance floor myself," he said the smile gone and a serious expression in its place.

The whole table had gone quiet and were watching with delight. Jez really would lift her up and carry her kicking and screaming to the dance floor. Fuck.

Ava turned to little sister, "I'm doing this for you, so this big idiot doesn't embarrass us all in front of your new in-laws," she smiled tightly and stood gracefully from her seat, placing her napkin on to the table.

Kitty clapped her hands together and squealed in delight. Jez was still holding his hand out and Ava accepted it, shaking her head gently. Everyone was watching them. Jez was one of the most good-looking men in the room and the competition for his attention was great. With him, Dan and all of the Pennington men knocking around, the male eye candy was impressive. Ava was definitely the most beautiful woman in the room and all eyes were on them both, as they walked around the bustling tables, making their way to the dance floor. The guests chatter ebbed away, as they looked on at this beautiful couple. Ava wondered briefly if Ethan was watching and with that thought in her mind, thought back to that incredible kiss.

As they reached the dance floor, the members of the orchestra seemed jubilant that guests were actually dancing, somewhat breaking the ice on this mammoth occasion. As Jez took Ava gently in his arms, she was grateful for his unusually soft grip. He was well aware of her bruised ribs and was being very considerate. She kissed him on his cheek and he beamed his full on, playboy, panty-wetting smile.

Ava was sure she heard the sound of women's knickers exploding.

"I needed to talk to you," he said still beaming.

"Couldn't have waited until after the pudding was served?" Ava said raising her eyebrow, beaming back.

"I've met someone special," he said simply.

Ava almost stopped dancing, but somehow managed to keep her feet moving. There was a long pause.

"Ok," she said slowly.

She was intrigued as Jez had had lots of flings over the years, but had never told her he had met anyone special before, so this was obviously important.

"I am in love," he said quietly, watching her every move, his own expression serious.

Ava looked into his hazel eyes, the gold flecks were glinting in the twinkling lights that surrounded them.

"I'm so happy for you," Ava said, feeling a little choked.

Jez almost broke as his face fell and emotions washed over him. He had never felt this happy in his life and he wanted Ava to be the first to know.

"I am so happy for you too," he said his eyes welling with unshed tears.

Ava opened her mouth to speak, but no sound came out. Her feet had now stopped moving of their own volition and they both stood immobilised in the middle of the dance floor. Time seemed to stand still, as they gazed at each other, lost in their own world.

"May I?"

A gruff American voice broke their trance and they both turned to see Ethan Pennington, a thunderous look on his handsome face. He wasn't asking to cut in, he was telling them. Jez smiled politely and just to really piss Ethan off, he kissed Ava lovingly on her cheek. With a polite nod towards Ethan, he disappeared off the dance floor. Ethan stepped forward.

"Dance with me," he growled, again this was not a request.

Although annoyed at the interruption of her conversation, she wanted nothing more than to be his arms again. She smiled and took a deep breath, before she took a step towards him, their bodies now touching. The frown fell from his face as his arms slipped round her gently, they began to dance slowly. She didn't care if everyone in the room was staring at them, which they probably were, she was just happy to be close to him.

He shook his head and grimaced.

"Christ Ava, what you do to me," he grumbled, trying to get a grip on his anger.

She just stared at him, taking in his incredibly striking face. He looked into her eyes, stunning cerulean pools, he could get lost in forever.

She smiled, "I'm just thinking… Blara and La Fou will be losing their minds, watching you dancing with me," her humour was infectious and he smiled back.

Fuck, she wanted to kiss him, wanted to feel his hands exploring her body, wanted to make love to him right here on the dance floor. Ava squeezed her eyes close and slowed her breathing, the best she could.

"Ava?" Ethan's concerned voice penetrated her head and she blinked her eyes open. "Am I hurting you?"

Still dancing he stepped back, looking down at her ribs, worried he was holding her too tightly. She immediately took a step forward, missing the warmth of their bodies touching. Snuggly back against his firm body, she sighed.

"I'm just trying to behave myself," Ava said honestly.

"Behave yourself?" His quizzical brow lifted.

"Do you have any idea how difficult it is not to kiss you… or more, with your whole family watching?" She had closed her eyes again, mortified that she had just said that out loud.

The faint blush on her soft cheeks, was the sweetest, sexiest thing Ethan had ever seen. The honesty in her words struck him and he knew how she was being completely genuine. He had been so jealous when he saw her and that playboy model take to the dance floor. He could feel his temper rising as he watched them dancing together. She had only just been kissing him outside and now she was in this lothario's arms. They had stopped dancing and stood looking deep into each other's eyes and Ethan just flipped.

He had stood abruptly making his whole table judder, as he knocked it with his powerful thighs. He ignored everyone around him and strode purposefully towards the dancefloor. Aware that all eyes would be on him, he tried to remain calm, although all he wanted to do, was rip this 'models' head off. Now here he was here, holding this beautiful woman, who had somehow knocked down his walls and melted his heart.

"…and more?" he questioned, again raising his brow.

Ava opened her eyes and pulled her lips between her teeth mortified that she had just said that.

"Stop that." His expression suddenly serious, his eyes darkening with want, as his finger traced the line of her lips.

"You know what that does to me," he groaned.

Her insides felt like molten liquid as she ached for his touch. Her blush deepened and closing her eyes again, she tried to regain her composure, as she leant her head on his shoulder. He in turn, lent his head on hers, taking in the scent of coconut and honey, that made his groin strain again. They continued dancing slowly, occasionally being joined by other guests, as the dance floor filled with onlookers, taking in the great Ethan Pennington, dancing closely with this English nobody.

"May I have this dance?" Alfie was politely interrupting.

Both Ethan and Ava stopped moving and looked at him and then at each other.

"Pretty please?" Alfie made his puppy dog eyes at them both and they laughed.

Ethan reluctantly stepped back, allowing his little brother to dance with the women who had taken his heart. He was completely smitten. As Ethan stalked off the dancefloor, Alfie took Ava gently in his arms and was now smirking, looking between this beautiful siren in his arms and his older brother.

"SOOO…" he began "…you and Ethan?" he wiggled his eyebrows and laughed good naturedly.

Ava relaxed and laughed with him.

"What can I say, you Pennington's are a handsome lot," she replied playfully. "Look Alfie…" she was serious now. "… I'm not sure what Kit has told you, but this isn't something I usually…" she trailed off. "…I mean it's not like me to…"

She wanted to say fall in love, but surely it wasn't that. She had once vowed that she would never fall in love again, so it can't be that.

"I would love to tease you about it, but I know this is difficult for you." Alfie smiled, sensing her awkwardness.

He knew Ava had lost the love of her life years ago and that having feelings for another man must be hard to navigate. Both he and Kitty had looked at each other in shock as Ethan interrupted Ava and Jez's dance. They had gripped each other's hands tightly, watching the events unfold, Kitty's sister and Alfie's brother. They were in shock, but both utterly delighted. Alfie loved his siblings and Ethan's happiness was paramount. His older brothers always seemed to go for the underfed, American socialites, but neither had ever introduced any woman to the family. The fact Ethan had danced with Ava so closely and the looks they were giving each other, had given Alfie a little hope that his big brother may have finally met a decent woman. The fact that the female concerned was Kitty's sister, was the icing on the cake.

"Just so you know, we are very happy for you," Alfie winked and Ava shot Kitty a quick glance, she was watching them like a hawk, an exuberant expression on her pretty face.

"Really Alfie, I'm not sure what's happening yet, but thank you," Ava replied politely.

"So, I can't tell you how excited I am for the wedding," Ava was grateful he changed the subject.

"Me too," Ava said genuinely happy that her sister was marrying such a lovely man.

They talked easily about the big day tomorrow and at the end of their second dance Ava excused herself. Alfie kissed her gently on her cheek and she made her way back to her table. The little group cheered as she sat down, again blushing as she noted Ethan was watching her every move.

"Alright you lot, calm down," she said good naturedly.

"Fuck me Ave, are you getting your rocks off with a Pennington?" Lou said a little too loudly.

"Louise!" Bella scolded.

"I'm very happy for you lovely girl," Rachel said, a little teary.

"Oh, please don't get upset Rach," Ava pleaded.

"I'm not," Rachel replied as she gulped some more champagne down, trying to quell the happy sobs she wanted to let out.

Ava had been a true friend to her over the years and was always there for her, day or night. She loved her like a sister. In fact, they all did and they just wanted Ava to meet someone and be happy. Rachel loved her husband and children more than life itself and wanted that same joy and happiness for her dear friend.

Bella was also filling up, who would have thought that some of their group would find love on this exotic island. She too felt like crying at the wonder of it all. Lou pointed out that Dan was on the dance floor with Sofia junior and Jez was dancing very closely, with some leggy, big-boobed brunette.

Kitty had moved into Jez's seat and was holding Ava's hand tightly, she was also feeling a little emotional.

As the others chatted amongst themselves, Kitty whispered, "Ave I can't believe it…" her eyes were wide and shining brightly. "… you and Ethan!" she said in awe.

"Look KitKat, I don't know what's happening yet," Ava replied quietly, although deep down she knew she was head over heels in love with him.

Kitty squeezed her hand and smiled, "I really hope it works out, I've always been a little intimidated by him," Kitty said honestly.

Ava frowned, not able to hide her concern.

"Oh, I'm sure he's lovely, I mean, after all he is Alfie's big brother…and he of course is perfect."

She was still smiling and Ava decided not to worry about her sister's feelings towards Ethan at this very moment in time, although she replayed Ethan's words over in her head, when he said he was trying to stop the wedding. She really needed to speak to him about that.

As the evening wore on, the group slowly dispersed one by one. Lou said she had plans and along with a wink and bottle of expensive plonk under her arm, had left the table. Dan had disappeared without saying good night, most unlike him. Jez had been seen leaving the suite with that leggy brunette. Bella had left early, saying she was tired from the long day, shuffling off to her comfy bed, which she looked very keen to get too. Rachel was happily dancing with a small group of teenagers, on the dance floor. She loved dancing with her own children at home and having fun and letting her hair down was just what she needed. Kitty, Alfie and Ava were the only ones left on their table. The loved-up couple were smooching and giggling and Ava decided to let them have some alone time. It must be nearly midnight and she was tired, plus it was the big day tomorrow.

She slipped off her heels, scooped them off the floor and held them in one hand. She stood and kissed Kitty and Alfie goodnight. A little disappointed that Ethan had also disappeared from sight, she took one last look around before making her way towards the opening on to the outdoor decking area. Guests were scattered around, some sat in the cosy wicker chairs, drinking and smoking. Some couples were dancing in the romantic shadows of the lantern lit deck. Ava smiled at the romantic scene, couples slowly moving to the music, although the DJ was playing some great tunes and the dance floor was much more energetic than out here. She stepped on to the cool, soft sand of the beach, deciding on a moonlit walk along the shoreline, back to the villa.

Suddenly someone grabbed her arm tightly and she spun round in fright. Ethan's prominent features were clear, even in the moonlight. He stepped forward and kissed her forcefully. Closing her eyes, she luxuriated in the feel of his body pressing against hers, his firm chest, the hardness of his dick, pushing against her body. The kiss grew more passionate and his hand wrapped gently around her slim waist, the other reaching up into her hair, undoing the diamante clip that secured it. Her long, blonde hair fell instantly down her back, framing her beautiful face. He broke the kiss and looked down at her, her skin ethereal and iridescent in the moon light, just like the first time he had set eyes on her.

"Ava," her name on his lips was all she needed.

She crushed her lips back onto his and they pushed themselves closer than before, Ava's hands moving up and down his shirt clad back, his tuxedo jacket, discarded on his chair, back at the Pennington table. The kiss deepened and Ava felt a longing, a need, for him to be inside her. She knew she wanted him completely and for once in her life she felt no guilt.

Ethan moved his right hand from her hair and gently stroked his fingers down her neck, his touch leaving a burning sensation in its wake. His hand found her full aching breast and he squeezed and manipulated it, making her moan into his mouth, driving him on. He grabbed her face, as he felt all self-control evaporate and their tongues lashed against each other. He groaned as he felt her body push against him, wanting to get even closer.

"Darling is that you?"

A high-pitched American drawl shouted from across the decking. The kiss was broken, but they stood stock still, hoping the shadows would hide them both.

"Ethan darling?" Blara's voice oozed sarcasm.

Realising that they would not be able to evade her, he called back over his shoulder.

"I'm busy," his voice was serious and the words sounded more like a threat.

"Ethan... darling, your mother would like to speak to you," Blara was undaunted.

He was angry now, how dare she interrupt them. He looked into Ava's beautiful face, torn between family duty and the need to explore every inch of this incredible woman's body.

"Ethan?" a classy American voice broke the silence.

Ethan let out an exasperated breath, and rested his forehead on Ava's.

"Mother," he replied with obvious annoyance.

"I need to speak to you son," she called out again, unperturbed by the anger in his voice.

"Sorry," he whispered, reluctantly letting Ava go and turning in the sand, stalking determinedly out of the shadows of the palm trees and over to the decking, where his mother and psycho stalker were waiting.

Without another look back, the three figures disappeared back in to the banqueting suite. Ava stood there in mortified silence for a few minutes. Her whole body was hot and sticky. Where his fingers had touched her delicate skin, felt like he had left a trial of fire. Her breasts ached heavily, longing to be touched again. She realised her knickers were wet, she squashed her legs together to try and ease the want. Her insides squirmed with desire.

The feeling when he stepped away from her had left her bereft. *How could he just leave her in this state?* She didn't know if she felt angry or desolate.

Having regained her decorum and her breathing returning to as normal as her body allowed, she made the long walk along the beach and back to her villa. She finished her evening with a hot, steamy shower and falling into her empty bed alone, she was soon asleep, dreaming of Ethan.

Chapter 21

As she closed the door to Kit's room, she felt a strange and overwhelming sense of peace. It was like all of her stars had finally aligned and life was positive again. She hadn't felt such joy in a very long time. She quickly blanked the bad memories from her mind, as she usually did, when she didn't want to get all emotional. It simply wasn't her style. She felt a glow of happiness that her baby sister was in a good place, with a good man who adored her. They had a long and bright future ahead of them. Although never complacent, she felt positive that her sister's honesty at this crucial time, literally before she was supposed to walk down the aisle, showed great personal growth and in a moment of clarity, Ava realised she was no longer the acting parent or guardian for her little sister. She was a grown woman who was making her own decisions and living her own life.

Ava was hit with another wave of emotion. Her own hopes and dreams had been cruelly snatched from her years before and apart from her work and her 'family' what did she have? She stopped walking and looked down at her feet as if to ask them why she had come to a halt. Inhaling deeply, taking in the gentle, salty sea breeze, she instantly calmed. She was on the most beautiful island in the world, surrounded by family both old and new, all of whom were in a joyous happy wedding day bubble. She again used her blanking mechanism to forget about the 'evil ones, Lou had renamed Blara and La Fou.

As she didn't want her mood to spiral on this special day, she decided to give herself ten minutes to catch her breath. Finding the nearest cushioned wicker chair, nestling under the shade of a white umbrella, she sat down to gather her thoughts. Her KitKat was getting married. Their mum and dad would have been so proud of her.

Kitty had asked Jez to walk her down the aisle, something he was immensely touched about, as he was delighted to play his part. He had told Kitty, during her dress fitting all the dos and don'ts, in regards to married life. His best piece of advice, or so he called it, was to always offer your husband a blow job. They had all found this hilarious, especially Kitty who, whilst laughing, raised both thumbs in the air.

Ava's mind wondered on to Ethan. Last night's encounters still making her body ache for more. She was hoping he would come to her villa last night, when he had finished dealing with his mother and Blara. Sadly, the only late-night caller was Jez. She sighed sadly, her beloved Jez.

She had showered and put on her sexiest night wear, a black lace nightie, that lifted her boobs and showed off her slim body. Showering had washed off the bruise covering makeup, but Ava had just left the small corner lamp on, shedding a delicate, soft glow in the room, hoping that the dim light would hide the marks left on her.

She had laid on her enormous bed, watching the wooden blades of the ceiling fan, spin round and round. Feeling incredibly lonely she soon fell asleep and was having an erotic dream about Ethan, when there had been a knock at her door. She raced to open it, literally wanting to jump on Ethan and make love to him. She tried to hide her disappointment when it was her beloved Jez, devastatingly heart broken.

As she smoothed the soft material of her stunning dress, the movement of her own fingers, reminded her of Ethan's blazing touch. As the minutes passed, she enjoyed flashbacks to last night, making her feel hot and bothered. As she replayed the kisses and the steamy embraces, she stood abruptly, her feet started moving by their own volition, as if her body wanted to be near him. She had to see him. Her stomach flipped over and she allowed thoughts of him to flow through her mind. She had banned them this morning or so she had told herself. Every night since she had met him, he had appeared in her dreams. Vivid dreams where she was being held by him, being kissed by him.

Her mind was whirling with secrets and the memories of those erotic dreams, so it took a moment or two, for the noise to sink in. She had crossed the pool bridge in a daze and had absentmindedly walked along the sand dusted pathway towards the beach where the wedding celebrations were to begin. Suddenly jolted from her own little world, she heard shrieking and shouting coming from the wedding arbour in the distance. As she tried to speed up her walk, she found it was difficult to walk quickly in her high Manolos. When she reached the ceremony area and stood still, her mouth was agape, as she took in the scene before her.

Ahead of her was a long walkway of decking, covered with a huge white satin sail canopy. Underneath the expansive shaded area was the aisle, enclosed by row upon row of white antique style chairs, each one adorned with a teal satin bow. Vast amounts of exotic blooms lined the impressive aisle.

The right-hand side (the groom's side) was completely empty, which struck her as strange, as the wedding was due to take place shortly, surely the guests should be here by now. The bride's side seats were also empty, apart from the front row, where someone was sitting with their head in their hands.

The wedding arbour, which was covered in the most heavenly flowers Ava had ever seen, was full of people. She kicked off her heels and grabbed them, before walking swiftly down the decked aisle. The decking was warm on the balls of her feet, however, thanks to the canopy shade, they didn't burn.

The shouting was escalating and she could see Ethan and Jez having a heated exchange. Sofia and Dan were stood back, not knowing what to do. Bewildered expressions on every face. Rachel was trying to stand in front of Jez and was pushing her hands against Ethan's huge frame, in a futile bid to put some distance between them both. Bella sat on the edge of the decking with her encased leg stretched out in the sand, her arms wrapped around a hysterically crying Lou. Her discarded crutches lay on the floor beside them.

"You thought you would get away with this?" bellowed Ethan into Jez's face.

The ferocity and anger he used stopped Ava in her tracks. She was at the edge of the arbour and both Ethan and Jez had not seen her approach. Rachel was pleading with Ethan.

"You're wrong, this is bullshit," she shouted, losing her temper.

Even amongst this chaotic scene, Ava made a mental note to congratulate Rachel for using a swear word in conversation, something she never did. Lou's crying had gone up a notch and Sofia intervened trying to calm matters.

"Eth please calm down, let's go back to the suite," her smooth, firm voice changed nothing and Ethan leant in towards Jez's face.

"Hope you're both proud of yourselves, I knew there was something going on," he growled, Jez raised both hands and slowly shook his head.

With his strong jaw jutting out defiantly, he said slowly and clearly, "You are so wrong."

Ava knew she had to step in and stop whatever this was and it only took her two steps to be on the wedding arbour decking, which was the centre of the chaos. She stood just to the right of Ethan's huge frame and just as she had stepped onto the arbour, Jez had decided he'd had enough of Ethan's bravado and performed his best sly smirk to date. Upon seeing this, Ethan saw red and quickly drew back his arm as if to punch Jez in the face. As Ava had stepped up behind him unnoticed, combined with the fact the Ethan was incredibly powerful, his elbow had connected with Ava's face with such force, that she was knocked backwards across the alter table. This in turn sent flowers, shells and anything that had been placed on the table, flying in all directions, whilst Ava's body hit the wooden floor with a sickening thud.

Ethan had turned to see what had impacted his elbow, expecting to see Sofia's arm trying to stop him throwing a punch. Instead, he saw a blur of teal chiffon and then the glint of a pair of high-heeled shoes as the sun caught the diamantes on Ava's Manolos, as they fell from her hands.

"Fuck!" he shouted, at no one in particular and leapt forward to where Ava on her side.

Her arm lay across her face, on which a small but deep cut was bleeding profusely. Ethan's face was pale as he leant over and turned her gently on to her back. There was a nasty cut above her right eye and blood was seeping from her nose.

"Fuck," he growled again.

"Ava," Jez whispered as he bent over her, his head inches away from hers.

The others stared gobsmacked and even Lou had stopped her drunken hysterics. Ethan held Ava's hand, he had really hurt her, but she had hurt him. He shook his head to shift that unwanted thought.

"Ava please…" he begged, as he held her limp hand to his chest.

She responded with a murmur and turned her head to the right.

"You're ok Professor," Jez tried to keep the emotion from his voice, but failed miserably.

He stroked back her blonde tresses that had come loose, away from the seeping cut on her head. Ava sucked in a breath as she opened her eyes. Looming over her were Ethan and Jez. Sofia and Dan were also close too, staring at her in shock.

"She needs a doctor," came Rachel's worried voice.

Ava shook her head and tried to sit up, but was stopped instantly by a searing pain in her ribs. Her head started throbbing like someone had hit it with an iron bar. She closed her eyes tightly to see if that helped, but that just made her feel sick, so she opened them again quickly. Slowly, the world stopped spinning enough for her to attempt to sit up again. However, the pain in her torso was excruciating. She was aware of mumbled voices and half conversations around her.

"You've been misinformed," came Jez's sarcastic drawl.

"I know everything." Ethan's American accent was thick with hate.

Ava stared mutely at the two of them, whilst Rachel's arm was around her shoulders offering comfort. Dan was holding Ava's hand. Bella was leaning on the corner of the arbour for support and Lou was gripping her hand tightly. Ava gazed at Lou and very briefly saw a glimpse of something she had only seen once before in her friend, a childlike vulnerability. Within a second it had disappeared and Lou's formidable walls were back. Maybe Ava had dreamed it, maybe she was concussed again.

She leant back on to her elbows in order to push herself up, but felt strong arms wrap around her, lifting her off the floor. Her eyes were closed, then she blinked several times to try and subdue the pain and ease the feeling of nausea.

Ethan was holding her close, she could feel his firm, taut body holding her upright. A feeling she might have enjoyed if it wasn't for the pain that was now emanating from her ribs and her head.

"Ava, I." Ethan shook his head and stepped back.

His arms which had been wrapped around her body, moved upwards so they were gripping each of her shoulders. There was now space between their bodies and Ava shivered as she felt the chill down to her bones.

"She's in shock." Sofia's concerned voice broke in. "I've texted Bailey to come," she finished softly.

Jez gently draped his tuxedo jacket around Ava's shaking shoulders.

"I'm fine." Ava spoke slowly and clearly, as she tried to remove the fog that seemed to have filled her head. "What's happened? Why are you two arguing… this is supposed to be a happy day," and as if suddenly remembering that Kitty was supposed to be getting married right now, she looked around the dishevelled arbour.

"Look at this mess, Kit's going to kill me," she whispered, sorrowfully.

Ava made eye contact with Jez who was on her right-hand side, his arm around her waist holding her up. She dared not look up at Ethan, as she didn't think her emotions were up to it. Jez looked down at his Gucci loafers and had the presence of mind to look a little embarrassed by rowing with the groom's brother, today of all days. Ava looked down at her own perfectly manicured feet, covered in powdery sand and blood. Knowing she had to face Ethan, but trying to think of anything at all she could do to put it off.

"Ava... I know," the gravelly tone of Ethan's voice made her look up at him.

Their eyes locked, however, instead of the endless deep blue pools Ava had seen constantly this week, especially in her dreams, his eyes were dark, almost as if the peaceful clear blue ocean was lost in a storm.

They gazed at each other for what seemed like an eternity, none of the group moved or made a sound, it was as if everyone of them was holding their breath.

"Ethan darling..." the high-pitched, grating shrills came from Ava's left and her heart sunk even lower, as she knew the evil plastic troll had arrived.

Ethan broke eye contact first and turned his head in Blara's direction, he lowered his eyes and took a deep breath.

Chapter 22

Zara practically ran down the aisle, pure hate in her eyes. On the approach to the wedding arbour, she had seen that Ethan was in a clinch with Ava. How could he be holding that English bitch when he should have been holding her? That scheming, hateful woman was just after Ethan's money and she knew it. Why else would she be sniffing around him?

After what she had told Ethan this morning, Zara thought she had put a stop to this. Surely, he wouldn't even want to be in the same room as her, let alone standing under a wedding arbour, with his arms wrapped around her. As she teetered onto the crowded decking, in her precariously high heels, she realised Ava's head and mouth were bleeding and that she looked even paler than usual, grey even.

Inside Zara congratulated herself, as she instantly concluded that Ethan must have hit her, with a well-deserved back hander. That would teach the bitch to come sniffing around where she was not wanted. She couldn't help but sneer that this English bitch had been given what she deserved.

"Ethan, darling," she drawled again, her voice sickly sweet. "We are all waiting for you at the suite. Your brother needs you darling," she finished dramatically.

Zara tilted her head and then switched from a longing look at Ethan's face, to glare at his hands, which were still gripped tightly around Ava's shoulders. Ethan followed her icy stare and as if his palms were burning at the touch of Ava's skin, he let go.

Sensing that Ava could not support her own weight Jez was there in a millisecond, his strong, capable arm already around her waist, instantly supporting her weight and warming her body with the closeness of his. She was still shaking. Ethan's face darkened and with a scowl as he looked down at Ava.

"How could you do this? My family trusted you." Ethan said through gritted teeth.

Ava was at a loss, what the hell was going on, why was he so angry with her.

"I have no idea what you're talking about." Ava felt brave with Jez by her side, even though her body felt like it was shutting down.

She had done nothing to be spoken to like this and she could speak up for herself. Psycho Blara had moved so close to Ethan, there was no daylight between them. She had put her twig-like arm around his broad shoulders. She glared at Ava whilst using her other arm to reach and grab Ethan's hand with her skinny claw.

"Don't do this to yourself darling, come now, your brother and your family need you." Zara implored him, but his eyes didn't leave Ava's.

"You and your sister have taken us all for fools, but I know. We all know what you really wanted," he growled.

Ava looked up into those beautiful, storm-ridden eyes and tried to discover what he was thinking, by looking into his deepest soul. Suddenly, it came to her, how could she have been so stupid. Her sister's secret, she must have told Alfie and the whole family had found out, but how? She had only just left Kitty.

"Ethan, my sister and your brother are old enough to sort out their own issues. I had nothing to do with this." Ava's brain was working overtime, how could Ethan think she knew about this and not tell her little sister to tell the truth.

"Issues," he spat out angrily. "She has been cheating on Alfie and you call it issues."

Ethan looked like he was about to explode, but now it was Ava's turn to be angry. How could he think that?

"You're not serious!" Ava laughed and quickly covered her mouth with her hand, to stop screaming out in pain.

Her ribs were in agony, she knew she must have broken one. Ethan grimaced and clenched his fists. Her mind tried to focus on the conversation in hand and she began to feel a little hysterical at what he had just said. She needed to calm down, this must be some sort of sick joke.

"I don't know what twisted game you have both been playing with my family, with me… but it stops now. Your sister wanted the money and the fame, it's obvious now, but you- I thought you were different," he let out a long breath, his temper had got the better of him.

"My sister loves Alfie and he loves her, this is not about money or fame… they are getting married for Christ's sake!" Ava was trying to remain calm and think rationally.

Had Kitty told Alfie the truth and he had cancelled the wedding? No, surely not. Why was Ethan also throwing insults at her, she had only found out her sister's secret less than half an hour ago.

"They 'were' getting married, but not anymore…she should have kept her legs shut and not slept with her so-called brother." Zara's bitter diatribes lingered in the air between them.

"Brother?" Ava questioned.

She shook her head to try and clear the fog that seemed to be descending again. Maybe she had done some serious damage to her head in the fall, as nothing was making sense.

"Yes, your so-called brother," Blara's troll like head nodded at Jez, whilst spouting her venom.

Jez's mouth gaped open and his eyes widened in shock. He turned to Ava and returned her own blank expression.

"Darling they are all con artists and such poor actors," trilled Blara, her twisted mouth only millimetres away from Ethan's face.

She was laying down the poison and Ethan was lapping it up.

Jez then spoke clearly and forcefully.

"I have not been sleeping with Kitty, she 'is' like a sister to me, you fuck wit," he retorted.

"Oh, you're such a playboy Jeremy," Blara spewed and actually had the nerve to pout, assumingly to be seductive, although it looked like she was sucking a lemon covered with salt.

'Jeremy,' Ava had to stop herself from bursting into hysterical laughter, only the newspapers and media called him Jeremy. "I bet you are in it with them for the money." Blara's words were vicious and wounding.

Just as Jez went to speak, it suddenly dawned on Ava, that this evil witch was accusing Jez of sleeping with Kitty and this is why the wedding wasn't going ahead.

"You are out of your tiny plastic mind," Ava spoke quietly but concisely, her gaze directed fully at this pernicious troll "…and you believe this?" she turned her aching head and looked up at Ethan's face.

His features were rigid and his face looked like it had turned to stone.

"You believe this," she whispered again.

Her eyes implored him to see the truth, to say it was a terrible mistake, a hideous misunderstanding, but he didn't speak. He returned her gaze and for a torturous moment, it was just the two of them. Everyone and everything had faded around them, yet even after all this, after this terrible allegation, her mutinous body was responding to his closeness, to his anger.

She wanted to slap him and kiss him at the same time. Her stomach flipped at the thought of kissing him, longing for her lips to touch his. She wanted to kiss away his anger, tell him he was a fool. She was lost at sea and he stood there, right in front of her. He could save her, or she could save him?

"You are so wrong Ethan." Jez's, now calm and soothing, voice brought Ava back to the present.

She broke eye contact with Ethan and looked awkwardly between Blara bitch face and Jez.

"You don't owe anyone an explanation Jez, if that's how little they think of us, then maybe this is for the best." She tried to remain calm, but inside she was screaming like a banshee, this can't really be happening.

"Ethan darling, let's go." Blara sneered again, the smirk on her face obvious, "Alfie needs you."

The bitch's features contorted as if to relay empathy, but instead the expression made her face look gaunt and witch-like.

"Your sister I understand..." Ethan gained Ava's attention again "...she wanted the celebrity lifestyle, the parties, the fame, the money. I've seen it all before, but you?"

Jez opened his mouth to speak. Ava could see the hurt in his eyes. She squeezed his side to silence him.

"Don't," she said quietly, as she looked at him. "Please don't."

Her plea worked and he closed his mouth.

"Was this a plot?" Ethan continued, "Come here to paradise and get me to like you, to trust you and the whole time you lie to my face?"

As the words escaped his mouth, Jez jerked forward as if to attack Ethan and it took what little strength Ava had left, to hold him back, although it was probably the look, she gave him. Her eyes pleading with him not to make matters worse. Ava had turned and was now facing Jez, whose serious expression belied the anger bubbling underneath.

"Oh, Ethan darling," came bitch face's drawl, "let's go, she's not worth it, they are not worth it."

Ava couldn't bear to turn around and face Ethan again. *How could he believe this plastic troll and her little apprentice?* They had obviously been lying through their perfectly aligned veneers.

"She was so obviously after your money and has no doubt played other men before you, do not lower yourself to her standards by talking to her about it," Blara fawned.

"Done it before?" Lou had now awoken from her subdued state and had pushed past Sofia and Dan to stand at Ava's and Jez's side.

Ava still had her back to Ethan and was currently focusing on the ornate buttons of Jez's shirt to stop herself from passing out.

"Ava has a history of seducing men for money and it seems like her little sister has followed in her footsteps." Blara trilled.

"You what!" Lou screamed.

"It's true," said Ethan simply, agreeing with the poisonous troll.

"You have been hoodwinked by psycho Barbie and her evil friend." Lou was fuming and aimed her words at Ethan. "Ava is the loveliest, kindest sweetheart, I have ever met… yet you stand here on her little sister's wedding day and accuse her of trying to get your money? You're delusional!" Lou's voice was so high pitched, that if she hadn't been standing next to her, with her full chest heaving up and down, Ava wouldn't have recognised it.

"Well, we all know her history," hissed bitch face, "The things she's done for dollars."

Ava spun round to face Zara full on, grabbing Jez's arm to support her as her head continued spinning after her body came to a standstill.

"Huh… I can see I have touched a nerve. Well, I can't believe that you're actually standing here in front of us, instead of being locked up. Ethan will not be your next victim." She hissed vehemently.

Ava felt the blood drain from her face and the skin on her cheeks began to tingle. She would not give them the satisfaction of bursting into tears or passing out, although she was fighting her body not to do either.

"Eth, surely you cannot believe any of this rubbish?" Sofia's gentle voice interjected from Ava's left-hand side, as she placed her arm around Ava's shoulder.

This kind act of compassion was almost her undoing, however, Ava held it together, determined not to look like she had done anything she should be ashamed of, because quite frankly, she hadn't.

Ava glanced around the faces that surrounded her. Jez looked uncertain of what to say or do next. Lou, for the second time today, stood silent, her mouth open and eyes filled with tears. Rachel and Bella with arms tightly gripping each other, with Rachel leaning heavily on the wooden, flower covered post for support.

They had stood quietly taking in the conversation, not wanting anyone upset or hurt on this special day. Hating the confrontation and willing everyone to make up and hoping the wedding would still take place.

Dan was at Sofia's side, his hand in her free hand, looking devastated. Ava knew her friends well and the looks on their faces spoke a thousand words. They loved her and she loved them. She shouldn't have to and wouldn't try to, justify her actions to anyone.

"This is really what you think about me?" Ava whispered looking directly at Ethan.

His solemn face said it all. She shook her head gently in defeat, blood still oozing down her face.

"Enough," she said firmly, "…that's enough."

She broke eye contact with Ethan and looked at her little family, standing around her in the middle of this awful situation. If this is how little Ethan thought of her, Kitty and her loved ones, then he wasn't worth it. Plastic bitch face obviously had his ear and she and her poisonous sidekick had done their work well. Twisting conversations, making snipes and generally ruining Ava and her family's reputation at every opportunity.

Ava turned to Sofia, who had tears rolling down her beautiful cheeks. Her sad eyes begging Ava to say something, argue with him, tell him he's mistaken, do something. Ava had nothing left. She leant forward and gently kissed Sofia's cheek. Dan had a look of empathy on his kind face and in turn leant forward and holding Ava's face in both hands, kissed her softly on her forehead. Ava bit the inside of her lower lip to prevent a flourish of tears descending.

Keep it together, she told herself, *don't give up now.*

Dan put his arm around Sofia's shoulder and as her sobbing increased, led her away from the drama. Blara, bitch face, tried once again to get Ethan's attention and get him away from Ava for good.

"Ethan darling, your family are waiting, they need you."

Her trilling voice hadn't lost the coldness of before and all attention was now on Ethan. He looked at her and then back at Ava.

"You have nothing to say to me?" he asked, his voice was as cold and heartless as Blara's.

"You deserve each other." Ava's voice was stronger and braver than she felt. "Just go."

Blara jumped in quickly, "You heard her darling, let's go."

She practically turned Ethan on his heels and grabbed his arm to tug him away. He held his gaze with Ava and finally as neither spoke, he shook his head and turned away. He followed his sister and Dan down the aisle, with bitch face clinging on to his arm.

"Nobody say a word," Ava's voice was back to a whisper. "Please," her voice almost breaking, she let go of Jez's arm, which had kept her upright all this time.

She carefully stepped over the debris of broken shells and wilting flowers, that had been scattered from the alter table. Slowly reaching the back edge of the arbour, as gracefully as she could manage, with pain ripping through her ribs and head, she sat down on the wooden floor.

Her Manolo's were already imbedded in the sand, where they had been flung from her hands after she had been hit. She slowly sank her feet into the warm, soft, powdery sand and closing her eyes, she shut the world out.

Chapter 23

"Ava?"

Ava thought she recognised the voice that was penetrating her thoughts; she had been daydreaming in the warm sunshine and didn't want to open her eyes. She was snuggled up on the day bed, on her expansive terrace. The ocean softly lapped the wooden struts beneath the water villa, along with the occasional splash of a fish changing direction.

She was relaxed and happy, as strong, protective hands wrapped around her. She could smell him, intoxicating and sexy. His aftershave was her newest, most favourite smell. It was Ethan. Her senses were on over drive and as he gently kissed her neck, she moaned in ecstasy.

"Ava?"

She frowned, as the voice was not Ethan, yet it was him holding her and kissing her.

"Ava!"

The voice was louder and Ava opened her eyes wide in shock. She blinked several times as she took in her surroundings. Bailey knelt before her, holding her face in his hands. Rogers stood at his side. leaning over her, both with concern etched on their faces.

She wasn't in her villa, she was on the beach, on the edge of the wedding arbour. As the events from earlier dawned on her, a gut-wrenching sadness consumed her, as if her whole world had gone dark. The pain in her side and head was still there, although as she had sat still for a while, it was now more a dull ache.

"Ava?" Bailey spoke her name again and she blinked several times.

He was assessing her, presumably for concussion.

"Kitty?" Ava whispered, her voice sounded strange even to her.

"I have checked on her and she is okay." Bailey said.

Ava frowned, the small movement increasing the ache in her head.

"She is definitely not okay and I need to see her." Ava spoke slowly, as if having problems forming each word.

"I need to check you over first." Bailey grimaced. "You have a cut on your head I need to dress and I want to make sure your ribs are intact," he said kindly.

Ava started to argue and Rogers spoke up.

"We will take you to the medical centre."

This sounded like an order. Ava shook head gently, but immediately regretted it. She put her hand to her forehead, to try help dim the pain, however, it didn't subdue. She took in the blood on her hands and up her arm and realised she must look a mess. She didn't want Kitty to be any more upset than she was already.

Letting out a steadying breath, she spoke quietly but firmly, "I need a shower and change of clothes."

Bailey sighed, "We will take you to your room and I will check you over, then you can get showered, changed and go and see Kitty," he said, just as firmly.

Ava realised there was no point arguing. As she tried to push herself up off the decking, she realised her strength had been zapped and both Bailey and Rogers gently supported her under her arms, to help pull her up.

As she stood the pain in her side became worse and she knew she had definitely broken at least one rib. She turned to look at her little family, however, they had all gone from where they had been seated and Ava could only see members of the Pennington's security team, milling around the area.

With a heavy heart Ava realised that her little family had deserted her, even Jez. Maybe they thought she was guilty. Maybe they thought she had led Ethan a merry dance and that she was only after his money? She wasn't thinking straight and was actually glad that Bailey and Rogers were supporting her, on either side.

They somehow made it to the buggy and Ava had to swallow back a lump in her throat, as she took in the exotic, wedding flowers, adorning the front of the vehicle.

Within a few minutes the buggy had trundled its way towards the water villas and the brave driver had driven on to the jetty itself. The boards only just accommodating the width of the buggy, causing the driver to mutter Maldivian expletives as he followed the curve of the walkway.

At last, the cool of the air con hit Ava's body and as she lay on the bed as instructed by the good doctor and she felt her body relax a little. She didn't speak as Bailey checked her thoroughly and decided to close her eyes again, to try and block out the events of the day. She was trying to re-live the daydream on the day bed, but no such luck.

As soon as Bailey put pressure on her ribcage, her eyes shot open in pain. Bailey turned to Rogers, who was standing back, at the side of the room. They exchanged a look that Ava witnessed.

"What is it?" Ava asked, directing her question at Bailey.

He turned to look at her.

"Ava, you have three broken ribs and possibly fractured more," his expression serious.

Rogers stepped forward as if to speak, but said nothing.

"She needs to rest." Bailey was speaking to Rogers.

"Yes sir." Rogers replied.

"I need a shower." Ava spoke with determination.

She was hot and sticky, even in the coolness of her room. The dried blood was everywhere. She sighed heavily, at the thought of her beautiful dress, which was now in tatters. With great effort, she sat up and moved to the edge of the bed, aware that her every move was being scrutinised.

"Your ribs will need support. I will have to bandage them," Bailey spoke softly now.

Ava nodded gently in response and carefully stood. She grasped the bed post for support and took a deep breath, which caused pain down her left and right side. Rogers quickly moved to her side and offered his hand. She glared at him, as she remembered who paid his wages.

"Why are you here?" Ava didn't want pity and she certainly didn't want Rogers running back to Ethan and telling him what a state she was in.

He tilted his head slightly, as he contemplated his response.

"Mr Pennington asked me to get you medical help and support you in any way I can," he said simply and with concern.

"Which Mr Pennington?" she asked already knowing the answer.

"Ethan ma'am," he answered.

She bit the inside of her lip, as his name had become more painful to hear.

"Get out," she said forcefully, glaring at him.

He didn't move. His mouth opened as if to argue, but then he must have realised it would be futile and closed it quickly. He nodded at her and then

Bailey, before making his way out of the villa, the front door gently closing behind him.

"I'm going to take a shower," she said just as forcefully to Bailey. "Alone," she finished, to make it clear she need some space.

After a struggle to take off her ragged, blood-stained dress and underwear, Ava closed her eyes as the jets of hot water blasted her battered body. Even the coconut luxuries didn't help lift her mood. The wedding was not going to happen. Kitty must be devastated. She needed to get to her, as soon as she was dressed.

Those plastic bitch trolls had got the Pennington's exactly where they wanted them. It made her blood boil thinking about them. She squeezed her eyes shut and tried to get Ethan out of her thoughts. She couldn't deal with him right now, she had to put Kitty first.

After drying off and avoiding looking at herself in the mirrors, Ava donned the fluffy white robe and felt she was ready to face the world. Bailey stared, wide eyed, as she walked into the room.

"What now?" she said exasperated.

After a long pause he turned away to fumble with his medical bag.

"Your bruises," he said simply.

She realised she had washed off the body make up, which Lou had expertly applied earlier that day. She must look a right sight. She went to the clothes drawers and pulled out knickers, a bra, a long-sleeved white shirt and a pair of shorts. Returning into the bathroom, she somehow managed to put on her underwear, without crying out in pain. She then made her way back to the huge bed, where Bailey wrapped tight bandages around her aching sides. He also gave her an injection for the pain, after confirming that it would not make her drowsy.

She needed to have her wits about her. He helped her put her shorts and shirt on, which she was grateful for. She bundled her wet hair into a loose bun, on top of her head. Her ribs pulling painfully as she raised her arms. They left the villa together, however, Ava had asked that she see Kitty on her own.

Having made their way to the massive honeymoon beach villa, via the ever-reliant buggy, they parted ways. Ava knocked on the door and waited. The sky was darkening as the sun was starting to lower in the brilliant blue sky. It was still very hot and with the extra layers of bandages wrapped around her torso, Ava had become quickly over heated. She hammered on the door, but no response.

"Professor?"

The sound made her jump and spin round, once again her head continued spinning after her body came to a halt.

"Anju," she breathed out, relieved to see a friendly face.

She saw his face contort as he took in her appearance.

"You are hurt ma'am?" he said worriedly, as he walked up to her and took her hand in his. "Can I help?"

He looked so concerned that she just wanted to sit on the doorstep and burst into tears. However, she somehow managed to stay composed.

"I'm looking for my sister," she said simply.

"Ahh Miss Kitty," he smiled, but his face quickly returned to the worried expression. "I have just seen her ma'am, heading towards the private dining area," he pointed in the direction to which he was referring. "I believe she was trying to find her fiancé," he smiled, all teeth showing.

This was encouraging news and Ava smiled back. Maybe they were going to sort things out, tell each other the truth, thank God for that.

"I believe the Pennington family are dining there this evening and that all other guests are dining at the main entertainment area," he said, with his flourishing bow.

The smile dropped from Ava's face and she put her hand against the door for support.

"Fuck," she said out loud and then quickly apologised to Anju for the bad language. "I am so sorry, it's been a very long day, Anju…can you get me to the private dining room fast?" she asked, knowing that if it were within his power, he would move heaven and earth to ensure his guest's happiness.

"Of course, ma'am," he said extending his hand out towards her.

"Thank you, Anju, you really are a star," she replied as she took his hand and followed him down the lush, foliage edged pathway.

Chapter 24

Anju had driven his buggy like Ayrton Senna and Ava was grateful for his speed. Her stomach churned as they sped towards what she knew would be a final showdown with the Pennington dynasty. She couldn't bear to think of Kitty facing them all alone. Ava was prepared to stand up to them all and tell them what arseholes they were for trusting in the low life scum of both Blara and La Fou.

The physical pain was nothing, compared to the hurt she felt. Most of the Pennington family didn't trust her or her sister and that her sister's future happiness had been ruined, was devastatingly sad. Surely, they could see that Kit was totally smitten with Alfie and vice versa. There were so many secrets within their family, no wonder they were all so fucked up.

The buggy screeched to a halt, with Ava gripping tightly onto the handrail. Her other arm around her aching waist, trying to protect it.

"I can come with you ma'am?" Anju said his face full of concern.

"Thank you, that is very kind of you, but it's not necessary." She gently kissed his cheek, truly grateful for having someone on her side.

She was in the expansive marble lobby, which was immaculately clean and well presented. Wicker seats, with green cushions, were neatly placed at the front of the reception area, alongside a cocktail bar. It was empty, apart from staff, busily sweeping and milling around. The guests must all be at the main restaurant, gossiping about her and her sister. The thought was depressing.

As she slowly made her way across the vast lobby, she could see Pennington security and bodyguards, posted at the multiple doors to the private dining suite. Rogers was talking quietly to a huge man, who also looked like ex-military. They both looked up as she approached and she could see their faces change, as they took in her appearance.

"Miss Hart." Rogers spoke first.

"I'm looking for my sister," she said bravely, although she was holding her hands together as they were now shaking.

"She has just gone in," he said, standing to one side and gesturing with his right hand, through the doorway and into the elegant dining room.

"Thank you," she said quietly and slowly walked through the door.

The room was magnificent. A long banquet table took its place in the middle of the ornately painted room. Flowers seemed to grow out of every surface possible, the smell of which was amazing. Most of the gilded chairs around the table were occupied and Ava could see all of the main members of the Pennington family were present. The table itself was laden with beautiful displays of food, artfully and creatively presented and of course, more stunning flowers. The back drop was the impressive dusk sky, as the room opened up onto a wooden terrace, with sparkling lights around the edge, a smaller version of last night's banqueting suite. A four-piece orchestra sat to the right, softly playing classical music.

Ava saw Ethan first, to the right of the table, Blara was talking conspiringly in his ear. Then she heard Kitty.

"Why not?" She was demanding, obviously upset.

Ava took a step closer into the room, although no one had noticed her arrival.

"I think everyone should calm down," came Blake's commanding voice,

"Maybe now is not the time Katrina," he said smoothly. "Now is the time, I need to speak to my fiancé," Kitty's strong, commanding voice brought the soft music to a halt.

Ava felt a rush of pride at the way her little sister was addressing this dynasty of a family. She heard a trill of laughter and felt instantly nauseas, as La Fou took the attention off her little sister.

"You've broken his heart and he doesn't want you anymore!" La Fou's spite-filled voice carried across the room.

"You need to shut the fuck up!" Kitty retorted.

"Please mind your language dear" came Sofia senior's eloquent voice, "maybe now really isn't the time for this," she finished.

Ava couldn't decide if Sofia senior was being kind or condescending.

"I just want to talk to Alfie." Kitty said taking a deep breath and trying to stay calm.

"He doesn't want anything to do with you, don't you understand?" Blara piped up, her head turning away from Ethan, tilting with a pitying look in Kitty's direction.

At this Ava boldly walked forward, her sister needed her. Ethan saw Ava approach and stood so quickly, that he knocked the table, causing the expensive china and crystal to shudder.

"What the fuck…" He shouted, glaring at Ava.

All eyes including Kitty's, were now on Ava. She walked up to her sister, completely ignoring Ethan and grabbed her hand, giving her instant support and power.

"Ava…" Kitty took in Ava's appearance and moved her hand to gently touch Ava's bruised face. A white plaster now covering the butterfly stitches, securing the nasty gash on her forehead.

Ava turned away from her and the sweet gesture, to face the table of glaring would be in-laws. Directly in front of Ava sat Sofia junior, her body turned on her chair. Her hands covered her mouth in shock at Ava's battered and bruised appearance, her eyes wide and bewildered. Ava focused on Alfie, across the table, who had also stood up, mouth open, but not knowing what to say.

"You should be resting." Ethan growled from the right.

Again Ava ignored him, she had nothing to say to him. La Fou was seated next to Alfie and had now also risen from her chair, in her skin-tight, shocking pink body stocking of a dress, which left nothing to the imagination. Her fake breasts resembled watermelons, pulling the material tightly, causing it to strain at the seams. Her makeup matched the bright neon fabric and she looked horrendous.

If it wasn't for the seriousness of this situation, Ava would have laughed. La Fou put her hand across Alfie's chest territorially, as she looked adoringly into his face. Ava felt Kit's hand tighten its grip in hers.

"She only wanted you for your money Alfie baby, just ignore her," La Fou spoke in a sickly-sweet voice, as if addressing a small child. Kitty was stunned into silence, so Ava stepped in.

"Kit loves you Alfie," she spoke with more bravery than she felt.

These Penningtons were scary.

"She wouldn't even sign the pre-nup," La Fou screeched, turning to glare at Ava, through dilated, red eyes, her false sweetness slipping.

She looked slightly deranged, as if she had been snorting drugs.

180

"Alfie?" Ava kept her focus on him. He didn't speak. "Alfie, either you tell them or I will." Ava spoke with a ferocity she didn't know she had and Alfie actually gulped, taken aback.

"I don't think we need to drag that up now," said Blake, evenly.

He too had stood and for all of his stature and worldly knowledge, he was finding this exchange uncomfortable. Kitty pulled on Ava's hand and looked at her sister pleadingly.

"It doesn't matter..." she said quietly, "...he has made his choice."

Ava turned to Alfie again.

"Alfie, I mean it, tell them."

Ava was so angry with him, how dare he make her sister out to be a money-grabber. La Fou started to speak again and Alfie put his hand up to silence her and then shook his head.

"Okay, okay," he paused. "Kit did sign the prenuptial agreement," he said looking directly at Kitty.

Audible gasps came from the group, as the family finally heard the truth.

"She signed it when I first presented it to her," he said to no one in particular, his eyes not leaving Kitty's.

"You told us she hadn't signed it Alfie, why would you make us think bad of her?" Giovanni spoke up.

As the oldest brother, he immediately felt guilty, at his role, in this wedding day, ending, as it did. "Christ, I told you she was after your money when you told me she refused to sign it, why would you say that?" he was incredulous and had joined the Pennington men who were now standing.

"I wanted to see what you all really thought of her, only two people said marry her despite not having a prenup," and he turned and looked fondly at his Nonna and Nonno, who were following every word in silenced shock.

"Yes but, but she also cheated on you Alfie." La Fou's shrill tones broke the silence.

"She did not cheat on you Alfie." Ava said firmly, how many more accusations were going to be thrown at her beloved sister.

"Of course she cheated on you, Alfie" piped up Blara bitch face, "Thank God her guilty conscience kicked in, before she finally trapped you," she spat out each word.

"Trapped?" Kitty repeated.

"That's why you asked to see me this morning Kit and I couldn't face it. I couldn't face hearing you say those words, knowing you didn't love me…" his voice trailed off sadly and his eyes welled up.

Kitty just stood there, mouth open, gripping Ava's hand tightly.

"Kit," Ava said gently. "Tell him." She prompted.

Kitty turned to face Ava, her expression blank.

"He doesn't love me Ave, he doesn't love me," she said sadly.

Ava let go of her hand and held onto the top of Kitty's arms, resisting the urge to shake some sense into her.

"Tell him," she said firmly.

"Tell me what?" Alfie interjected.

"Oh, darling it's all an act, ignore them both." La Fou had both arms around Alfie now and was clinging to him protectively.

"Tell me what?" he shouted.

There was a long pause.

"Oh god… oh god, are you ill?" he whispered, his face draining of colour.

"Kit," Ava spoke quietly now and held Kitty's face as she spoke. "You need to talk, just the two of you… forget about us lot and go and talk to each other."

She was so gentle and endearing, that Kitty knew she made sense and slowly nodded her head, a single tear rolling down her cheek.

"She cheated on you!" La Fou screamed in Alfie's face and with her hands clenched tightly into fists, she started beating his chest.

Gio stepped forward and grabbed her arms, pulling her back, security at his side immediately, but he shook his head, he had this.

"She cheated on you with her own brother."

It was Blara's turn now, a strange high-pitched tone to her voice. Her eyes were wide and dilated as well and Ava could see she was obviously as high as a kite.

Blara stood and faced Ethan, standing uncomfortably close, "…and you know they have both been sleeping with their so-called brother."

The evil bitch was actually enjoying herself as she watched Ethan's reaction. He winced as she spat out each word.

"Jeremy has been at it with both of them," she spun her web and it looked like he believed what this lying bitch was saying, as the frown on his face deepened.

"Excuse me, may I have a chance to defend myself?" Jez swaggered in, still wearing his tux trousers, the top two buttons of his shirt undone, his bow tie had disappeared.

His hair was more ruffled than usual and Ava knew this was from running his hand through it, something he did when he was agitated. His stubble shadowed his strong jaw and he looked drop dead gorgeous. He sauntered up to Ava, grabbed her hand and kissed it gently, pausing slightly as he took in the now apparent bruises on her face and body. He chose not to comment, but the indent of his brows showed Ava he wasn't happy and she would be in for a lecture at some point.

"Don't deny it!" La Fou screamed wildly, tears running down her plastic features.

Still screeching and shrill, she was desperate to keep Alfie all for herself. Gio tightened his vice like grip, as she struggled to get free.

"I saw you, last night." Ethan's strong voice drew the group's attention. "I wanted to see you... I needed to speak to you..." He trailed off as he glared at Ava, but she couldn't bear to look at him.

She was concentrating on Sofia's jewelled hairclip, that was expertly clipped into her dark brown locks, directly in front of her.

"You were together at the door to your villa, holding each other..." His voice started to break.

"I told you they have both been sleeping with him Alfie," La Fou blurted through the wild sobbing, she was desperate now.

"If I may say something?" Jez ignored the hysterics and when Ava looked up at him, she was a little shocked to see he was actually smirking.

He briefly looked at her and winked.

"He tried to sleep with me but I had to fight him off," La Fou shouted, saying anything to get Alfie's attention, but he was focused solely on Kitty, who was avoiding eye contact with him.

"It was the same with me, I had to physically beat him off. The only reason I didn't tell you before this, Ethan, is because I didn't want to ruin the wedding for you." Blara's manic voice betrayed her panic, as her expressionless face could show no emotion.

Ethan glared at Jez, he was still smirking and Ethan wanted to wipe it off his smarmy face.

"I have an announcement to make," Jez seemed to be enjoying this.

Ava didn't know what to think or say.

"I'm gay," he said, his smirk now a timid smile.

"Jez please." Ava shook her head appalled. "You don't have to do this," she said pleading with him.

"My beautiful angel, its time." He turned to face his gobsmacked audience. "I came here for my little sister's wedding and ended up falling in love for the first time in my life."

No one spoke a word or moved an inch, completely enraptured with him.

"For the first time in my life, I told someone I loved them and I thought they loved me… I was wrong, they didn't love me enough." He finished sadly, although he felt like an unbelievable weight had been lifted.

Ava felt even worse than she did before. Her best friend had just had to out himself, because the Penningtons didn't believe what she and Kitty said. She was so angry with them all for making him do this, *how could they*. She looked directly at Ethan.

"How could you?" The disgust in her voice was apparent and Ethan felt her words like a slap in the face.

"It's the truth" Jez said simply.

"Jez?" Kitty was in shock, how could she not know this.

"He's lying," shouted Blara, "Ethan he's lying, I told you he tried it on with me and I had to fight him off."

She too was now clinging onto her man's chest tightly, pulling at his shirt.

Ethan looked directly at Jez, "Why should I believe you?" he asked.

"He's lying!" Blara screamed, completely losing the plot, so much so that some of the Pennington security team had manoeuvred themselves closer to her, in readiness to move her away from the precious Pennington men and their closest family.

"You will just have to trust me," Jez said, now serious. "I told a relative stranger that I was in love with him and he told me he could never love me, so it was over before it began. I was heartbroken…" he said honestly, "so I went to my beautiful friend for support," he finished and turned back to Ava, looking at her adoringly.

"I would like to say something." Giovanni's strong, domineering voice now commanded everyone's attention.

With a nod to the security team, he handed Jennifer over to them, so he could continue. Ava suddenly realised what was about to happen. Looking horrified she raised both hands to try and stop Gio continuing.

"It's okay… really, please don't," Ava pleaded.

At this he smiled and addressed Jez.

"She really is the sweetest angel I have ever met," Jez nodded in agreement, his mouth set in a grim line. "I know Jeremy is telling the truth."

He waited making sure everyone was quiet and the attention was all on him.

"I know because I am the man he has fallen in love with." He smiled broadly at Jez, who stood stock still, his eyes wide in shock.

There was stunned silence, you could have heard a pin drop.

"I told him I could never really love him and that I could not see him again, as my family…my business… basically my life, would be over if anyone found out about us. I broke his heart and mine too." He continued, even Blara and La Fou had stopped their balling. "I didn't sleep last night, however, unlike Jez I had no one I could confide in." He again glanced adoringly at Ava. "No-one I could trust, no one to love me for who I really am, until now."

He took a deep steadying breath and focused again on Jez. "I put the Pennington name before my happiness and I was wrong. I am completely in love with you and I am sorry for breaking your heart last night," he said earnestly. "I promise to spend the rest of my life trying to make it up to you, if you will let me?" he breathed out and smiled broadly.

"Bravo," shouted Nonna, clapping her hands and rising to her feet, closely followed by her husband, wiping tears from his eyes and talking fluently in Italian.

"What the fuck!"

Everyone turned to look to the back of the room, where Lou, Dan, Rachel and Bella had now convened. Lou had shouted out and was now beaming, the rest of them were in shock.

"What the fuck!" Lou said loudly again, this time laughing heartily.

Jez turned to smile at his little family, then turned back to the Penningtons.

"Ava is the only person I have ever fully trusted and she has kept my secret for all of these years, risking her own reputation and happiness to look after me." He winked at Ethan.

"You know they are lying Ethan," Blara's demonic voice was rising again, loud enough for all to hear. "She killed off her fiancé for money and she would have done the same to you!"

The poison spewed from her trout-pout lips like larva from a volcano. Ava gasped and looked at Ethan, who was still speechless.

"What?" She whispered in disbelief.

Everyone had frozen like statues, as all eyes flicked between Ethan and Ava. He didn't answer her, he had no idea what to say. She felt as if she had been punched in her broken ribs and took a step back. At that moment Blara started screaming and shouting at Ethan, lashing out with her bony hands and feet. La Fou tried to copy her, but she was now in the capable hands of one of the security team.

The rest of the security surged forward to intervene. Chaos then ensued. Blara managed to kick a heavy gilded chair into the table, scattering china, glass and flowers everywhere. Members of the security team rushed to assist, pinning her down. Giovanni's Nonna and Nonno made a determined route around the large table to get to him and hug him tightly. His own parents stood in shock, mouths hanging open, but not speaking. Lou had also made her way round the long table and had pushed some of the security men out of the way and was now wrestling with La Fou.

Dan was holding a sobbing Sofia junior, tightly in his arms. Rachel was hugging Jez, tears streaming down her face. Alfie had literally jumped over the table and was now passionately kissing Kitty, who was also crying. Whilst all this was going on, Bella had been huddled against Rogers, who was directing his team, via his discreet headset, his strong arms wrapped around her protectively.

Ensuring that each Pennington was protected and not in any danger, he proceeded to order his team to get the two psychotic Barbie dolls out of the room and on to the first sea plane or boat they could find.

Bella had buried her face in his chest, upon hearing all the screaming, shouting and crying, she dared not turn around. Rogers however, had just seen a pale-looking Ava leaving quietly through a side door. He squeezed Bella even tighter and whispered in her ear not to move, as he sat her down on the nearest ornate chair, in the corner of the room. After ensuring his beautiful Bella was safe, Rogers made his way to the side door. As he opened it, he saw Ava disappear into the lady's bathroom, on the other side of the expansive lobby area.

As the screaming and commotion escalated, he turned to assess the mayhem behind him, not knowing that someone else had just observed Ava's movements.

Chapter 25

Ava somehow managed to navigate her way across the huge expanse of the immaculate, marbled reception area, where a handful of staff were busy tidying and arranging vases of stunning exotic flowers. She kept her head down, arms wrapped around her beaten body, trying to swallow back the bile that was rising in her throat. Kit's heart was broken. Alfie had cancelled the wedding. Jez had just outed himself as gay, trying to save her from the lies that had been spread. On top of which Giovanni had also come out in order to help her too. She slammed her hand across her mouth, to prevent her from vomiting on the meticulously clean, shiny floors.

She sped up her pace and was relieved when she reached the heavy, carved wooden door. Pushing it open, she finally made it into the spacious, air conditioned, ladies toilets. She ran to the end sink, observing the four toilet doors were all ajar and to her relief, therefore unoccupied. She flicked the modern looking tap upwards and the waterfall spout delivered a cool, stream of water.

Ava's head was pounding and her abdomen felt as if an immense pressure was squeezing it tight. Amongst all of this physical pain, her broken heart was causing the most injury. Kitty, Jez, Giovanni… all of them had tried to help her and had been hurt in the process. The secrets and lies that were spinning round Ava's head made her feel like she was going to vomit or pass out. She hung her head over the sink and splashed the cold water on to her clammy face, in a feeble attempt to stop her whole world collapsing.

As she shakily lifted her head, eyes squeezed tightly closed, she fumbled to the right of the sink, her hand finding the pile of soft white hand towels. She picked one up and gently dabbed her face dry. With her eyes still closed, she felt the hairs on the back of her neck rise. Her stomach turned over, as she smelt the stench of stale whisky and cigars. Fuck. Her eyes flicked open wide in terror, as Collins' scruffy image stood behind her in the mirror. It was too late to react, as he threw her against the tiled wall to his right. She hit the wall with such force, that some of the tiles actually cracked.

The impact on Ava's already broken body was devastating. Excruciating pain erupted in her head and torso and once again warm, sticky liquid oozed, from the reopened cut on her forehead. Ava's body slumped to the floor, she had no strength to fight, no resolve to hit back. She felt his hand grab her around the throat, as he dragged her back to a standing position, her back pressed firmly against the cool tiles. He carried on lifting her until her feet were no longer touching the floor and she found herself fighting not to lose consciousness.

"You fucking whore!" He shouted in her face. "Your boyfriend has ruined my life, so now I'm taking what's his."

With that he let go of her throat, smacking her hard across the face again with his right hand, forcing her body to hit the sink area with a sickening crack. Ava then fell backwards and landed on the hard marble floor with a sickening thud. She turned onto her stomach and pushed herself shakily up onto her knees, in a last desperate attempt to escape this lunatic. Blood was pouring from her nose, mouth and temple. She felt so dizzy, that she genuinely believed the room was spinning around her.

"Going somewhere?" His manic voice sprung out of nowhere and she felt a solid object press firmly against her forehead.

Her eyes were closed, and for a millisecond, she had no idea what was happening. She heard a click and instantly knew he had a gun against her forehead. In that moment, images flickered through her mind, Kitty's smiling, pretty face. Jez, serious and beautiful, as he scrutinized her every move. Lou holding a glass of wine, Dan by her side laughing. Rachel and her family all cuddled up on their huge settee. Bella, at her sewing machine, pencil behind her ear, concentrating on her latest, exquisite creation. Finally, Ethan. He was looking down at her, eyes like the darkest storm, angry with her, upset with her. Then nothing.

Rogers had turned to ensure the mayhem in the private dining area was under control. Zara's psychotic screaming drawing everyone's attention. Still kicking out and raging with fury, as she was literally lifted and carried from the room by two members of his team. Jenifer was under control now, she had given up on the lashing out and was now ugly sobbing on Gary, a muscle bound, six foot five inches of pure power and also a member of the Pennington security team. She was receiving no sympathy whatsoever, as she was guided firmly out of the room. He was relieved to see Mr and Mrs Pennington embracing their eldest son and in those few seconds of observations, something made him turn back to the reception area, where he just caught the back of a male figure entering the ladies' toilets.

He didn't recognise the man, but instinctively knew something was wrong and turned to the group behind him.

"Mr Pennington," he shouted loudly.

Several of the male members of the family turned and frowned, realising his mistake he shouted again.

"Ethan."

Drawing his gun, he shouted one more word before running across the vast open reception area, "Ava!"

Ethan's face did not hide the panic he felt as he let go of his sister, who had made her way round the table, along with Dan, to hug her big brother. Ethan's mind raced as he pushed past security and flew out of the side door. He just caught sight of Rogers bursting through a door, the other side of vast lobby. He ran full pelt, his heart thumping in his chest. Jez was close behind him, with the Pennington brothers following.

Without warning an ear-splitting bang echoed around them. Ethan and Jez continued running, but the others stopped in their tracks. Ethan got to the door first and ripped it open. As he burst in, he stopped dead in his tracks, taking in the horrific scene before him. Jez ran into him and the worried look on his face turned to disbelief, as he turned to see the horrendous site. Ava lay on her side, on the floor, her arm over her face, she was covered in blood. Rogers was leaning over her, using his finger to try and find a pulse. A scruffy looking Collins lay crumpled at her side, dark overgrown stubble covered his chin, making him look older than his years. He was dressed in dirty trousers and a tatty shirt and baseball cap askew on his blood covered head. Rogers was talking into his comms system, issuing more orders and confirming there was a fatality.

"No!" Ethan shouted, dropping to his knees besides Ava's lifeless body, gently moving her arm so he could see her face.

"Ava," he whispered hoarsely, his heart breaking.

Jez fell at her side and placed a hand on her pale, blood-stained cheek.

"My darling angel," he said unable to hold back the tears.

Rogers looked up, his face serious.

"She certainly is a fighter" he said, his mouth turning up slightly at the corners.

"She's alive?" Ethan questioned.

His heart felt like it had stopped beating.

"Yes, but her pulse is weak." Rogers replied.

He then used his hidden comms system to order Bailey to the scene, explaining urgent medical attention was required. Ethan and Jez looked at each other in relief. Rogers turned to his side and took a gun out of Collins clenched hand. As he uncocked the weapon to make it safe, he spoke quickly and efficiently in to his comms, demanding urgent medical attention again and ordering all security teams to stay with their wards.

Ethan gently lifted Ava's limp body and cradled her, a glimmer of hope now that he knew she was breathing.

"Stay with me baby," he whispered, his own eyes welling with tears.

Chapter 26

In the dimly lit room, dotted lights in reds, blues and greens, flicked on and off, highlighting the space age looking equipment, which hummed quietly at the back of the hospital bed. It had been five traumatic days since the incident that had rocked their lives and put all petty worries and disagreements in to perspective.

The might of the great Pennington dynasty had meant that a speedy and well organised exit from the Maldives, had gone as smoothly as anyone could have hoped for. Their private jets (of course they had a fleet of them), had ferried the immediate family and security teams back to New York with surprisingly little effort.

Ethan and Jez had refused to leave Ava's side, as Bailey had no choice but to put her in to an induced coma. The swelling in her brain and the damage done to the rest of her body had left her extremely vulnerable. She had more broken and fractured ribs to add to her collection, as well as fluid in her lungs, contusions to her head and body and in general, she was in pretty bad shape.

However, she was a fighter and Bailey had been more than optimistic that she would pull through. He had spoken to Ethan about her treatment and although the medical centre on the island was more than adequate, he would be happier if she could be treated at his exclusive medical facility back home, which had all the bells and whistles that vast wealth could afford.

An unconscious Ava, would be accompanied by Bailey, Ethan, Jez, Gio, Kitty and Alfie. A handful of their security detail, including Rogers, joined them for their journey and having left the idyllic island, the exhausted, sombre group flew straight to La Guardia airport, in New York City. They were greeted with a private ambulance, which took Ava's stretchered, broken body, plus Bailey, Ethan and Jez, straight to All Saints Private Medical facility.

A fleet of black Land Rover Discovery's followed in convoy, with a weepy Kitty, a solemn Alfie and Gio and their original security detail. A fresh new team of security also escorted the ambulance, ensuring a safe and speedy journey to the swanky medical centre.

Ava was taken to the most expensive suite, where she would undergo every test and scan necessary. That was five days ago and apart from Ethan and Jez, who had refused to leave her side, the extended family had taken it in turns to sit with her. Ethan held her small pale hand in his, occasionally lifting it to his lips to kiss it gently. Both he and Jez had only left her side to use the toilet, shower and change clothes. There was a large en-suite bathroom attached to the room, plus comfortable lounge area. Both men would only use the washroom, safe in the knowledge that the other would inform them immediately should there be any change.

Ava felt really strange. She thought she heard Jez's voice penetrating the darkness. She must have been asleep as images of Jez's face and body swirled around her head.

"We met at school," he said his voice choked with emotion.

He was upset and all Ava wanted to do was comfort him and confront whoever upset him.

His voice echoed through her head again, "I told her that night and instead of laughing at me or being horrified, she simply held my hand and I knew she was a guardian angel sent to save me," he said, his voice gravelly and full of awe.

"She really is the most beautiful angel, both on the inside and the outside." An American voice that sounded familiar had responded, but Ava couldn't put a face to it.

"I can't lose her," Jez was back and she heard what she thought were soft sobbing noises.

Oh no, someone was crying, she needed to help them. She tried to open her eyes, but they didn't respond. She tried to reach out her hand in the direction of Jez's voice, but nothing. It was really odd and surreal.

"She is going nowhere," a strong voice came from her right and it felt as if Ava's whole body tingled in response, Ethan.

She willed her eyes to open, they obviously needed her, someone was hurt and they needed her support. Fuck, was it Kitty? She hadn't heard her voice and she was upset last time she saw her. Slowly her mind replayed clips of the aftermath, of what should have been Kitty and Alfie's wedding day. Like a weird YouTube video, she skipped from one to another.

Kitty, please be ok. I'm right here, Ava heard her own voice in her head, however, her lips remained still.

She now had the image of Collins standing behind her, his repulsive reflection glaring at her. She tried to move, but her body was as heavy as lead. The image skipped to her lying on the cold marble floor and being dragged up by her throat. She could feel the barrel of the gun digging into her forehead. An explosive bang, then back to the darkness and nothing.

Sometime later, Ava heard Kitty's voice. She had thought Kitty was hurt or in some sort of danger. Again the images appeared of her little sister standing in her wedding dress, looking like the most beautiful bride Ava had ever seen. Bella's stunning creation was exquisite and of course it fitted Kitty perfectly. Her little sister was getting married and the joy of that moment and picture in her head, made Ava so happy. As Kitty turned her head towards Ava, she could see tears rolling down her sister's soft pink cheek.

"Hey sis, wake up will you, I need to ask you something," Kitty's voice broke through the fog.

She needs me. Ava's head started spinning, *why am I asleep? I need to wake up.*

Ava was willing her eyes open, but again nothing. It was so frustrating. The darkness descended again and silence.

"I've been a complete idiot." Ethan's commanding American drawl broke the silence.

Ava wasn't sure if it had been minutes or hours since she had heard Kitty's voice and was annoyed at herself for not getting things straight in her head. If she was asleep, this was the most irritating dream ever. Somebody mumbled something, but she couldn't make it out.

"I should have told her how I felt, I should have never have left her side," his voice broke.

Ethan. Ava's mind felt as if it were on overdrive, her heart thumping at full speed. *Was Ethan talking about Blara, fuck no.* She told herself off for using bad language. *Surely... surely, he could see that she was a lying, manipulative bitch, her and that La Fou.* Pressing pause on the images of the two skanky women in their tight crocheted dresses, with their teeny tiny bikinis bursting through the gaps, made Ava feel a bit better.

Maybe it wasn't Blara Ethan was talking about, what if? What if? The image of the tanned evil waifs disappeared and again she felt the cold metal of the gun's barrel pressed firmly against her forehead, followed by an earth-shattering bang. Darkness again.

At last, she managed to open her eyes and saw that she was on the luxurious day bed, in the comfort of her water villa. Her laptop open at her side. She was wrapped in one of the large beach towels and felt so cosy, but no wonder she felt so bloody hot. The sun was high in the sky and she had no idea what time it was. She idly stretched, kicking off the warm towel. Her entire body was aching, she must have been working and had fallen asleep.

Suddenly, she sat bolt upright on the squishy bed, eyes open wide. She lifted her hand to the middle of her forehead, well, she definitely hadn't been shot. She felt her stomach, below her breast bone and there was no pain, so she couldn't have broken her ribs. Her mind raced, as the sound of ocean ebbed and flowed beneath the decking, it actually relaxed her.

Had she dreamed it all? Fuck! Once again, she scolded herself for her choice language. Her mind raced with the images she was remembering, had none of it happened? Here she was, lying here on her sunbed, dozing the day away, having the most horrible nightmare. Jez had always told her she had a vivid imagination, especially after he read one of her many novels.

She was used to having bad nightmares; however, this had been the worse one yet. To have a dream where she had lost everything, her loved ones had lost everything. Maybe Jez was right. Maybe all the romcoms and dramas she wrote so easily, had finally taken their toll and her imagination had just ran riot.

With these thoughts spinning around her already fuzzy head, she jumped up, the large towel falling to the scorching hot wooden floor. Kitty is still getting married, no one had had to expose their secrets in order to help her. All was well with the world. She let out a deep, reassuring breath and stretched her arms up in the air. She found her silver flip-flops by her feet and slipped them on, as she didn't want to scald her feet on the baking-hot decking.

She made her way down the four wooden steps and onto the lower decking, where the two unused sunbeds sat looking ridiculously inviting. Henry the Heron was perched on the end of one.

"Hello Henry," she said cheerfully, happy to see him.

She felt liberated and a swell of joy overtook the panic and terror her nightmare had evoked. Briefly, it crossed her mind about how she could ever face Mr Collins again. In her nightmare, he had been an evil villain.

She sighed as a large splash to her right drew her attention. She saw a shadow swimming under water and for the first time in years she didn't feel apprehensive or frightened.

The silhouette grew bigger as it approached her villa and with another slosh of water, the pulchritudinous Ethan appeared. He had scared the little fish who had been peacefully feeding, they darted off in all directions. Ava's rapid heartbeat and serious hot flush, belied the torturous feeling that made her insides squirm in longing.

He was so bloody gorgeous. His wet face and torso were a sight to behold and the billion-dollar, panty-wetting smile on his beautiful face, made her squeeze the tops of her legs together.

"Join me," he called up to her.

She smiled shyly, secretly delighted that she was wearing her favourite red bikini. Ava walked purposefully to the edge of the decking. Slipping off her flip-flops and wincing as the scorching wood came into contact with the flats of her feet. She wondered if she should try and act seductively, but instantly realised she wouldn't have a clue where to start.

She was just about to jump in when Ethan raised his hand from the water and wagged his finger at her, "No clothes allowed," his face suddenly serious, eyes darkening with desire.

She thought her insides would implode with longing, as she wanted him to kiss her so badly. Without another thought, she leapt from the deck and landed with a loud splash into the cooling tranquil waters below. As her head reappeared above the surface, she moved both hands to her face, wiping the salty droplets away from her eyes and smoothing her hair back. Her feet gently kicking below her, keeping her afloat. She looked over to where Ethan had been, but he had disappeared. She bit her bottom lip in anticipation, waiting for him to appear in a splash and kiss her. She swung her head round and saw his dark silhouette a few meters away. She laughed out loud, before diving down into the crystal-clear waters. The hazy shadow was still moving towards her, although it seemed to be moving in slow motion. She smiled underwater, the salty-sea stinging her open eyes, making her blink. With each blink, the shadow drew closer. Just as she was questioning why he was taking so long, she blinked again. This time the shadow had turned into an enormous, open-mouthed shark with rows upon rows of blood-stained teeth, literally within touching distance.

Ava screamed into the water, choking down the cold ocean into her exhausted lungs.

"Ethan!"

Ethan and Jez had watched Ava for hours, scrutinizing her closely as Bailey had removed most of the tubes and pipes that had been helping her breath and let her organs rest and recover. It had been four hours since this had been done and Bailey had left them in the capable hands of nurse Gorman, as he continued his rounds. The formidable, no-nonsense nurse, kept constant watch, noting down blood pressure readings and checking all was as it should be.

Suddenly, Ava's whole body jerked, a muffled scream coming from behind her mask. The nurse rushed to her side and lifted the plastic, oxygen mask, pressing the call button simultaneously. Ethan gripped onto Ava's hand tightly, willing her to open her eyes. Jez stood and moved to the end of the bed, allowing the nurse full access to help Ava.

"Ethan." Ava screamed out, more clearly this time.

Ethan stood and leant in closely to Ava's face, "I'm right here," his voice was thick with emotion as Ava shouted out again, but this time she screamed, "Shark!"

Her eyes flew open, her body bolted upright, drawing in a harsh breath. She clasped her arms around her waist in anguish, as the pain hit. Her body slumped backwards onto the bed. Nurse Gorman's soothing words of comfort, were the first things Ava heard, as her eyes were screwed shut in pain.

"You're doing great my love, just keep taking long, deep breaths, like this…"

The kind nurse then proceeded to take slow, deep breaths, encouraging Ava to copy her, which she did. Ava felt her body relax a little, but the pain in her ribs and waist was excruciating. She was clammy and shaking, the images of the shark still fresh in her mind.

"Christ Ava," Ethan clung to her pale, shaking hand with both of his.

Her eyes flicked open and as they adjusted to the light, she saw Ethan's impressive features, his huge blue eyes full of concern. He was right in front of her.

"Hey," he said, for once in his life he had no other words to express the emotion and relief, pulsing around his body.

Bailey burst into the room, nurse Gorman, instantly reeling off stats and observations to update him. The handsome doctor grinned as he loomed over

Ava, checking her responses, pushing an emotive Ethan to the side. With a small silver torch, he checked her reactions and asked her if she knew where she was.

Ava wrinkled her nose and looked around the strange room. It was whiter than white and almost clinical looking. Huge bouquets of beautiful flowers were dotted around and sunlight streamed through the blinds from the large window on her left. She scanned past the pretty nurse, who was checking her blood pressure the old-fashioned way, holding Ava's wrist tightly and concentrating on her silver fob watch. Behind nurse Gorman, stood her Jez. Although he was grinning broadly, there were tears streaming down his handsome face.

"Hello Professor," he sniffed out.

She looked confused and as she scanned round the rest of the space, her eyes landed back on Ethan. Bailey had moved to the side again, pressing buttons on the high-tech machines. Ethan had returned to his prime position and was gently stroking Ava's forehead, thanking God for her finally waking up.

"Did it hurt you?" Ava asked in a gruff voice, her throat dry and scratched from the tubes that had been keeping her alive.

Her eyes frantically searching his body for any obvious injuries.

"Me…hurt?" He shook his head in confusion. "No baby, I'm fine… you're the one who was hurt," he grimaced and blinked, as he remembered the events of the last week.

"Me?" she questioned, "Where did it bite?" she asked.

Ethan and Jez exchanged confused looks.

"Bite?" Bailey interjected, moving to the foot of the bed, holding an iPad, with all of the medical data in relating to Ava. "Ava, do you know where you are?" Bailey repeated his question clearly, pausing his tapping fingers on the screen.

Ava was going to say the Maldives, but her brain seemed so muddled that on reflection, she wasn't really sure where she was.

"Due to your injuries, we brought you here, to my medical centre in New York," he said solemnly, concentrating on Ava's face, watching for any small response.

"My injuries?" Ava questioned, "So I was bitten?" She screwed her eyes shut, her nose wrinkled again as she tried to move her hands and feet, to see what was missing.

She couldn't feel anything, her whole body felt like a lead weight and her limbs were numb. She had no idea if she had lost an arm or leg. She felt as sick as a dog at the thought of it.

"Ava!" Ethan's hands encompassed her face.

He was in sheer panic at the thought of her losing consciousness again. She opened her eyes and looked into Ethan's, trying to read his thoughts.

"Ave, are you talking about a shark bite?" Jez leant over the bed and Ethan stood back, leaving Ava's cheeks feel cold without the comfort of his touch.

She took in Jez's chiselled, serious features and nodded slowly.

"Angel, there was no shark, you were having a bad dream," he said slowly watching her reaction, she was so confused, poor girl.

"No shark?" Ava repeated his words, "…a bad dream?"

Jez smiled tightly.

"Yep, we really need to get some therapy for that you know."

Letting that knowledge sink in, Ava had a flashback to Collins and the gun. She moved her left hand to her forehead, touching it gingerly, surprised not to find a huge hole. Jez laughed out loud, as he grabbed her hand back and moved his face close to hers. His classic Ultraviolet aftershave scent filling her nostrils.

"You haven't been shot either," his smile fell from his lips as he continued, "that bastard Collins beat you up," he said grinding his teeth, a look of pure hate flashing across his beautiful face.

He kissed her forehead softly and looked over to Ethan.

"I will leave you two alone for a bit, but I will be right outside the door, so no hanky-panky." he winked, his expression changing and eyes full of light and love.

His best friend was alive and he was so incredibly relieved and happy. Gio was waiting for him in the next room and he couldn't wait to tell him. After some time, Bailey was happy with Ava's progress and observations. He had administered pain relief medication, which had started working instantly. It was bloody good stuff and Ava must remember to get the name of it. Bailey relayed a list of injuries and how they were being treated. Nurse Gorman had adjusted the electric bed, so that Ava was in more of a sitting position. She had sipped some orange juice, which had tasted better than any drink she had ever tasted in her life and it had helped ease her sore throat.

Although still feeling dizzy and every part of her aching, she was a little unsure of what to say to Ethan. He had sat back, on the white, leather guest-chair, staying out of Bailey and nurse Gorman's way, whilst they worked.

He slowly tapped his finger to his mouth, in agitation, desperate to be alone with her. When Bailey was finally happy with everything, he advised that he would leave them both in peace for a while, asking the nurse to leave with him. A withering look towards her boss, showed her irritation, as nurse Gorman didn't want to leave her ward. It was not good practice. However, the ultimate professional that she was and the fact she had worked with him for many years, she followed him from the room without saying a word. Although he would owe her a bottle of rum for this.

Ava's stomach flipped over as nerves got the better of her. Ethan sat in the chair at the edge of the large room, his face now in his hands. She didn't know what to do or say. She wanted to jump out of bed and run to him, console him. With determination, she whipped the crisp, white sheet off her legs and in one lumbersome move, managed to swing both legs over the side of the metal bed. Pushing herself up, she somehow managed to stand. It took an enormous amount of effort and the drip that was still attached to her left arm, pulled at the strain.

"What the fuck!" Ethan's growl made her insides squirm.

In a split-second his arms were around her, his face so close to hers, filling her senses with his aftershave. She wasn't sure if it was her injuries that were making her feel so dizzy, or the fact that he was holding her. She looked up into his handsome, serious face and raised her hand awkwardly to palm his cheek. The canula in her arm was now pulling too and made her wince.

"Christ Ava… what are you trying to do to me."

He looked down tenderly at her pale, drawn face, covered in cuts and bruises. Any glimpse of her honey, sun-tanned skin had faded. She smiled and his heart completely melted, as she raised her mouth to his and kissed him softly on the lips. Her arms wrapped around his body and his arms tightened around hers, as they both inhaled and tried to even their breathing.

"Hello," she looked up at him, glad he was supporting her, as her legs felt like lead weights and were not up to the job at present.

"Hey baby," he replied, finally smiling. "I've missed you," he said, his eyes growing dark again, her whole body tensed in response. "Don't EVER leave me again," his eyes softened and they embraced, both silent and lost in each other's arms.

After what seemed like an eternity, Ethan reluctantly broke away, taking in Ava's tired expression.

"Come on, l need to get you back into bed," he smiled warmly.

It was Ava's turn to look serious and she flumped down on the bed, ignoring the pain in her ribs and head. Ethan gently lifted her legs on to the mattress.

"Finally, he wants to get me into bed." Ava mumbled, as her heavy eyelids gave in to their fight against the complete exhaustion and medication.

She drifted off to the sound of Ethan's hearty laugh still echoing around her head.

Chapter 27

After another five days of being under the excellent care and technical ability of the All-Saints facility, Bailey finally agreed to discharge a stir-crazed Ava. The last week had been so frustrating for her, being told constantly to rest. Every day was full of scans, blood tests and prodding and poking of her sore, battered body. She wanted to be up and about. She missed working on her iMac and really wanted to go home. Ava did enjoy seeing her family and using this time to catch up.

Kitty had been completely overwhelmed, when she had seen Ava finally awake. The first to enter the room when Bailey and Nurse Gorman had left it. She had cried and laughed simultaneously, all the while being supported by Alfie, who had stroked her back lovingly. Ethan had refused to leave Ava's side, so had sat holding her hand. Once Ava had awoken Kitty had regaled her with the events of what would have been her wedding day. Blara and La Fou had apparently been escorted to a waiting speed boat, which had taken them, plus a small security team, to Male airport. They had been forced to purchase their own tickets back to the USA and as they had arrived so close before departure, there were only economy seats left on the plane. Disgusted that they were having to travel cattle class, they spent the long flights back to America, squabbling about who was to blame for this mess, both rebuking each other. They had lost the advantage and wealth of the Pennington connection and soon the word would spread about their behaviour and their elite, fame seeking, celebrity lifestyle, would be over.

Kitty suddenly hesitated and looked at Ethan as she went quiet. Ava was waiting patiently to hear everything her little sister had to say and suddenly realised that Ethan was unaware of Kit's secret.

"You can trust him KitKat," Ava said softly, squeezing Kitty's hand in encouragement.

Ethan sat up straight and gripped Ava's other hand tightly, his face suddenly serious. The thought 'what the fuck now' going through his mind. Kitty and Alfie exchanged looks and nodded at each other in silent agreement.

"Christ what is it?" Ethan's voice was full of concern, surely there couldn't possibly be any more drama.

Alfie cleared his throat and with his arm wrapped around Kitty's shoulders, he began, "Eth, we have decided to rename you," he said with a serious expression.

Ava twigged as to how this conversation would go, but Ethan looked confused.

"What are you talking about?" he replied gruffly.

"We would like to rename you..." Kitty paused and took a deep breath, "...Uncle Ethan," she finished.

They both sat there grinning like Cheshire cats, as they let the news sink in. Ava bit her lip, delighted that Kit had obviously told Alfie and that they looked as happy as pigs in...

"Uncle Ethan?" Ethan repeated slowly.

Looking at Ava, his eyes darkened. She let her lip slip back from under her teeth, as her insides clenched deliciously. Wow.

"You knew about this?" he questioned, his face still dark.

Before Ava could respond, Kitty mistook his look as anger and interrupted, "I told her the morning of the wedding."

She spoke quietly now, as if waiting for Ethan to shout at her. "Alfie and I had a dodgy meal in the city, a few weeks before we flew out for the wedding and we were both as sick as dogs," she looked lovingly at Alfie, his expression now that of deep concern. "With all the wedding preparations, I didn't realise that it had affected the pill. I took it every day, but obviously if you're sick, it might not work and I had no idea." She trailed off and Ethan looked uncomfortable. "I started being sick a few days before flying and I was in complete denial. I know I should have spoken to Alfie as soon as I thought I might be pregnant, but I was scared. You already hated me," she said looking up at Ethan, from under long dark lashes.

He at least had the decency to look a little guilty.

"I pretended to everyone that I was out partying, to cover how ill I felt and ended up buying a pregnancy test at the airport, which confirmed I was expecting," the awe in her voice made Ava squeeze Ethan's hand tightly.

Alfie then took over.

"I had no idea, I just thought she was stressed with the wedding planning and having to put up with us lot."

The brothers exchanged a knowing look, as he was referring to the daunting prospect of coping with the whole Pennington clan.

"I told Ava, literally half an hour before the wedding and of course she didn't shout at me or judge in any way, she just hugged me and told me everything would be alright." Kitty looked adoringly at her sister, as Ethan stroked back a loose strand of Ava's hair, tucking it gently behind her ear.

The trail of his finger, leaving her skin on fire and making her blush. She really needed to calm herself down, this was ridiculous.

"She told me I had to speak to Alfie, as no marriage should start with a secret. So, I called him and asked him to come to the suite," her voice was quiet now and she looked sad.

"Of course, I thought she wanted to finish with me, so I didn't go," Alfie shook his head, trying to block out his actions on that day. "…to my complete and everlasting shame, I listened to Zara and Jennifer, who were of course saying all sorts. I was so insecure, I'm ashamed that I actually believed them," he finished shaking his head gently.

Ethan made them all jump as he suddenly stood, letting go of Ava's hand. He walked around the bed and Alfie rose to face him. Ethan put his hands on his brother's shoulders, his face serious.

"All I can say is," there was an uncomfortable pause as they all waited for Ethan to explode with rage. "Congratulations." His face lit up into that incredible megawatt smile and he embraced his little brother.

Alfie laughed in relieved shock and hugged his brother back tightly, both unwilling to admit they had tears in their eyes. Kitty was sobbing quietly as Ethan released Alfie and gently pulled her up by her shoulders, to embrace her too. She clung on to him and the tears of joy flowed. Ava managed to keep it together, delighted that Alfie knew the truth and that her sister could still be happy with the man she loved.

"Come on KitKat," Alfie laughed now as he patted Ethan on the back, "Eth doesn't do emotions." He said as he took over the hug with his beautiful fiancé.

Ethan made his way back around the bed to sit in his chair, grabbing Ava's hand and kissing it, the smile not leaving his face. He was going to be an uncle, that was incredible news.

Kitty had finally calmed down and after they had all retaken their seats she said pleadingly, "Please don't tell anyone else, you're the only ones who know, apart from Bailey."

Alfie interrupted, "He checked her over, to make sure she was safe to fly here," his voice full of pride for his fiancé.

"It's still early days..." Kitty added nervously.

"It will all be ok Kit, you just need to look after yourself," Alfie said sincerely. "Don't worry, I'm looking after you too." he said it with such love and adoration, it made them all smile.

Ava was shattered and tried to politely stifle a yawn, "Ava needs to rest now," Ethan's serious tone meant it wasn't up for discussion.

Ava frowned at him and his head tilted, trying to work out what she was thinking.

"Of course, we don't want to wear you out!" Kitty said smiling, she stood and kissed Ava's forehead. "Love you," she said softly.

"Love you," Ava said smiling.

"Love you too," Alfie joined in, making everyone smile.

He bent over and kissed Ava's cheek gently. Ethan stood and walked them to the door, again hugging them both.

"Love you too," Kitty said to Ethan, squeezing him tightly, taking him aback. By the time he had walked back to his chair, Ava was fast asleep.

"I thought she was supposed to be awake." Lou's strong voice broke through blackness.

Ava opened one eye and both Lou and Rachel cheered.

"Your noisy lot." Ava smiled as she opened both eyes.

Ethan was still at her side, his fingers rubbing her hand softly.

"It is so good to see you awake," Rachel said relieved.

Ava smiled.

"You've missed loads Ave," Lou said not being able to hide the excitement in her voice.

"Oh no, there has to be a man involved," Ava laughed softly and stopped abruptly, as pain shot through her body.

Ethan's hand tightened around hers and his expression darkened.

"Of course," said Lou brightly, ignoring the interruption.

"This is all we've had Ave." Rachel pulled a face, and chuckled at Lou's expense. "Before she bores you, I need to tell you something," a frown now on her pretty face. "I wanted you to know that I'm going to look for a flight back home Hun," Rachel said sadly. "I'm really missing Cary and the girls and the dogs," she said, not forgetting her gorgeous pups.

"Oh Rach of course, I'm so sorry I've kept you away from them for so long." Ave was mortified that her friend was missing her family and that it was all her fault.

"Honestly Ave, I have had a brilliant time." Rachel paused thoughtfully. "Obviously, not this part," she waved at the bed and around the room "...and obviously not the wedding part, umm... non wedding part," she stuttered awkwardly with a frown on her face. "But the Penningtons have been amazing and have shown us all the sites of New York," she smiled at Ethan and her face lit up in excitement, "and we are staying in the most fantastic hotel suites."

She was so animated, Ava couldn't help but smile.

"Cary would love it here and the girls would be in seventh heaven with the shopping."

Ava was glad her friends were being looked after and she turned to Ethan.

"Thank you," she said simply and his heart melted, as it seemed to be doing a lot lately around this woman.

"Please don't thank me, it's down to me that you are here," he said looking thoughtful.

"Hey," Ava spoke a little sterner than she had meant to. "You're looking after my family, so just accept the thank you." She said, putting an end to it.

He grinned, "Yes Professor," she smiled at the endearment.

Ava turned back to her friends.

"Rach I'm sorry you have to go, but I totally understand, you must be missing your lot," Ava smiled thinking of the organised chaos of Rachel's home, full of noise, laughter and lots of love.

"Please leave it with me Rachel..." Ethan spoke up, "...I will organise the flight." He smiled politely.

"Oh no, Ethan, really you've done enough, I couldn't ask you to do that," she said mortified.

"You're not asking me, I'm telling you, I will organise it," he smiled his sexy, knicker exploding smile and both Rachel and Lou beamed back at him, completely under his spell.

Ava rolled her eyes.

"Thank you," Rachel said in awe.

There was a pause and Lou started again.

"Well, on to my news. His name is Gary…" she began excitedly as Rachel groaned.

Lou ignored her and carried on regardless. "…He is six foot six and built like a brick shit house…" she said beaming "…and you ought to see the size of his…"

"Okay, okay," Ethan stood and raised his free hand in defeat. "I get it, this is women's talk," he said grimacing as he leant over to kiss Ava's hand. "I need to make some calls. I will be right outside that door," he said nodding towards the door to the suite.

Smiling at Lou and Rachel, he left the room, all three women admiring his profile as Lou continued to fill Ava in on Gary and their sexual antics, as Rachel sat rolling her eyes and making vomiting gestures. Ava had enjoyed the light hearted conversation and her mood had lifted even more thinking of Ethan's all-American playboy smile. *Wow.*

Bella and Rogers arrived about fifteen minutes into Lou's quite detailed exploits. Rogers feeling a little uncomfortable as he quickly realised that the 'Gary', Lou was raving about, was part of his security team. Bella being a little primmer than the others, had asked Lou to change the subject, pointing out that they didn't want to hear intimate details about her and her new man. Lou pouted like a spoilt child and folded her arms across her glorious bosom, in protest.

Soon after, Rachel politely made their excuses and she and Lou left Ava with her new set of company, all exchanging huge smiles and hugs. Bella looked a little apprehensive, as she adjusted her leg, still encased in the large black boot.

"Hello you," she said when she finally looked directly at Ava.

"Hello Bell and Mr Rogers," Ava grinned, realising she didn't know his first name.

"Peter," Bella said as she turned and gazed at the hunk to her right.

Finally, her Italian bombshell of a friend, had met someone she liked. Ava knew they were seeing each other, the Stanford university baseball cap had given them away.

"My eye brow is coming on nicely," Bella began, wiggling her newly growing brow.

"That's good, what about your leg?" Ava questioned.

"Oh that, that's no problem, in fact Bailey said the boot might be coming off tomorrow and I cannot wait." Bella's eyes were wide and her face full of excitement, Ava wasn't sure what her friend was trying to tell her, but smiled anyway.

"How are you feeling?" Rogers asked.

He really was a good-looking guy. He must work out a lot, his muscle-bound body was taut and firm. Lucky Bella.

"I'm very tired and achy, but I'm doing ok, thank you," Ava replied "…this painkiller medication is amazing." Ava said beaming and the atmosphere grew lighter.

"Mr Rogers… I mean Peter," she corrected herself quickly, "Thank you for looking after Ethan and everyone else." Ava said, suddenly serious.

Peter smiled politely. "It is my pleasure ma'am," he said genuinely proud of his role in the security of the Pennington's.

Ethan was his main ward and he had protected him for years. Rogers had built his career within this family after an exemplary stint in the military. With dedication and hard work, he was now head of security for Pennington industries.

"He looked after you too," Bella interjected proudly, holding Peter's hand.

"Me?" Ava was confused, the tiredness and medication making her head feel a little foggy.

"Bella," Rogers admonished gently, "not now," he said firmly, his face suddenly serious.

Bella looked like a naughty school girl who had just been told off by the headmaster. "…but if you hadn't had shot Collins," she tried to continue.

"Bella," he said shaking his head incredulously, she finally got the message when she turned to see Ava's pale face, her mouth opened in shock.

"You shot Collins?" Ava whispered, her eyes set intently on Roger's face.

He grimaced and shifted uncomfortably in his seat.

"You didn't know?" Bella was shocked at this fact.

The penny had dropped as she realised why Peter had tried to stop her conversation.

"You shot him?" Ava asked again, the vision of Collins abhorrent face filling her head.

"Yes, ma'am I shot him," he said seriously.

Ava's mouth opened and closed again.

"I'm sorry but I'm really tired," she said genuinely exhausted, but wanting to think over this new piece of information.

"Ave, I'm sorry, I thought Ethan would have told you," Bella trailed off as she turned to look at Peter.

He stood and offered Bella his hand, "We should go, Ava is tired," he was not taking no for an answer and Bella realised she had put her big black booted foot, well and truly, in it.

Ava had closed her eyes, not wanting to talk anymore, this new information completely messing with her head. Collins had been shot; Rogers had saved her life. *Fuck.*

Taking Peter's hand, Bella had stood and exchanged bewildered looks between him and Ava. They had left quietly, not saying another word, as Ava looked as if she was asleep. When they had walked into the expansive private lounge area, everyone's attention was on them, as they had only been in with Ava for a few minutes.

Ethan was in the middle of a call and froze as he took in Rogers's serious expression.

"What happened," he couldn't hide the panic in his voice.

"She fell asleep." Bella said in a small voice.

Ethan Pennington completely intimidated her. He glanced at Rogers who nodded in agreement.

"Okay, thanks," he said not being able to shake the serious expressions on their faces.

Lou and Rachel had been chatting to Kitty, Alfie, Jez and Gio.

"We are going back to the hotel for lunch, if anyone would care to join us?" Rachel asked the group.

"We will come," Kitty said brightly, "I'm starving," she said, happy in the knowledge her sister was on the mend.

Bella looked at Peter who nodded in agreement. It was his day off and he didn't want to leave Bella's side, in fact he had a whole romantic evening planned.

"I want to spend some time with Ave," Jez said genuinely looking forward to seeing his buddy.

"We will stay here," agreed Gio, looking happily at Jez.

As the group said their goodbyes, Jez and Gio made their way into the medical suite, where Ava lay peacefully. Her bruised, fragile body covered up to her chest, by a pristine white sheet. All the monitors had been detached and switched off, so the room was silent. Jez kissed Ava's forehead and gently took her hand, as he and Gio settled into the chairs, alongside the bed.

"You can stop pretending angel," Jez said seriously, "it's just us... me and Gio," he finished.

Gio raised a perfect eyebrow in confusion, the poor girl was asleep. Ava opened her beautiful blue eyes.

"There you are," Jez smiled, "how's it going Professor?"

Ava's mouth opened as she wanted to tell him about the fact that Collins had been shot, but realised he would already know this, so she closed it again. She closed her eyes again and Jez squeezed her hand.

"Sweetheart?" he questioned.

"I'm ok Jez, it's just a little overwhelming," Ava opened her eyes again.

Blocking out her conversation with Rogers, she focused on Jez.

"You look happy," she said smiling.

"I am," Jez's face lit up. "We are," he corrected and exchanged a loving look at Gio.

My god they were a handsome pair. Both incredibly suave and gorgeous, Ava was so delighted for them both.

"How has everyone taken the news?" Ava asked carefully.

"Well, our little family are in shock, but I think they are very happy for me." Jez smiled broadly.

"My family are all in shock too, although amazingly, they have dealt with it quite well. Apparently, my Nonna and Nonno have known for years... I had no idea!" he laughed, looking incredulous.

"They can't stop hugging me." Jez said still beaming.

Jez lifted his right arm and put it around Gio's shoulder, a look of immense love and joy on both of their faces. Ava couldn't help but smile. Her foggy head was making it difficult to concentrate on much, but seeing Jez so happy was heart-warming.

Jez was telling her about Gio's suite at their hotel and was just raving about the luxurious Jacuzzi, when he realised that Ava was fighting to keep her eyes open.

"Don't stop," she whispered, her breathing steady and slow as her body started to relax.

Having Jez here by her side was a real tonic, she felt safe. He smiled his lop sided, sexy smile, but Ava had already succumbed to the mix of utter exhaustion and powerful painkillers, Jez's voice in her dreams, as she drifted off into a light sleep. Jez and Gio were talking, still discussing Gio's suite and their favourite aspects of it, when Ethan walked in.

"Sorry, I was just catching up on some work calls," he said apologetically, as his eyes focused on Ava's beautiful, bruised face.

"You're in love with her," Jez was serious as he watched Ethan's expression soften.

"Yes," he said simply.

"Christ Eth!" Gio was taken back. "It's about time," he said, happy that his brother was finally in love with someone and that she happened to be the most incredible woman he had ever met.

"I could say the same about you Gio," Ethan replied grinning.

They had had a heart to heart about being honest and how moving forward, they would be brothers first and business partners second. They had somehow lost their closeness over the years. There were a lot of conversations over the next few days, but Ethan had not discussed his feelings with Ava and vice versa, although he sat by her side and held and kissed her hand, he had not made any other move on her, or spoken to her about how he felt.

They had discussed the Pennington family and business in great detail and found that they were completely at ease in each other's company. As the days had worn on, Ava's strength had returned and Ethan was delighted to see her improve. She was able to walk to and from the bathroom, with no support and was managing to eat small meals. Bailey had agreed to a discharge her, as long as she promised not to travel for another two weeks at least. Ethan had quickly offered her a suite at his hotel, where the rest of her family were staying.

Ava had reluctantly agreed, hoping that she could return home to England as soon as she was fit enough. Although never leaving her side and constantly kissing her hand, Ethan still hadn't discussed 'them' or those kisses they had had in the Maldives. Maybe he was regretting it, now he was back on his home turf and his over protectiveness, was just some misplaced guilt at what Collins had done.

That was a name that had not been mentioned since Bella and Rogers visit. Collins. Ava didn't want to think about him either, so they talked about Ethan's business ventures and their families, including the forthcoming baby, that was a secret that they were keeping from the others.

Today Ava was leaving the medical centre and had managed to shower and dress with the support of the fantastic Nurse Gorman. The hard-working nurse had become more of a friend to Ava over the last week and she was a little sad whilst giving her a gentle hug, goodbye. Bailey had insisted on Ava using a wheelchair to travel down to the private basement car park. Ava felt like a fraud being wheeled to the awaiting car.

Ethan let out a sigh of relief when they were both settled in the back of the shiny, black limo, with Rogers and his driver up front. He had secured the seatbelt gently around Ava's waist and settled into his own seat, grabbing her hand tightly.

"Can't wait to get you home," he said, his voice thick with emotion.

She turned and stared, her mouth agape.

"I meant to get you into bed…" he tried to correct himself, only to make it worse.

Ava stifled a giggle. He shook his head, now laughing.

"Christ Ava, what you do to me."

The words took her back to their last kiss, the night before Kitty's wedding day. She turned away and stared out of the tinted windows, as the car drove smoothly out of the underground parking level and out onto the busy streets of New York City. Ethan pressed the button to raise the dark glass of the privacy screen. She ignored the action, as they both felt the tension rising.

As she gazed out at the hustle and bustle of life going on outside the vehicle, she suddenly felt anxious. The last thing she remembered before waking at the medical centre, was Collins. Her heart was beating fast in her chest and her eyes were wide with alarm. *What if he's out there, what if he's following them?*

She felt sick.

"Ava?"

She was scanning the crowds for Collin's evil face. She felt a movement at her side, making her jump. Ethan had moved across the seating and undone her belt. He pulled her shaking body, roughly on to his lap. She winced in pain as he wrapped his arms around her tightly.

"Ava," he spoke quietly, as she snuggled against his chest.

"I was looking for him," she whispered.

"Who?" His voice was full of concern as he stroked her back.

"Collins," she said, her whole body still shaking.

He froze and let out a long breath.

"He's dead," he said simply.

She held her breath and tried to process this information.

"Christ Ava," his alarmed tone making her raise her head to gain eye contact.

Her stunning blue eyes welled with unshed tears. It was her turn to let out a long slow steadying breath and a single fat tear rolled down her cheek. He kissed it away gently.

"You're safe Ava," he said firmly.

She had twisted awkwardly and \now sat on his lap, her legs kneeling on either side of his firm thighs. She was looking down at him, holding his handsome face in both her hands. More tears were rolling down her face and falling on his navy polo shirt. She looked angelic and his heart broke at the sight of her crying.

"You're safe," he repeated.

She covered her eyes with her hands. Collins was dead. She was safe. With one arm wrapped tightly around her waist, the other lifted and pulled her hands away from her face, replacing his hand on her soft, wet cheek.

"Ava," his voice raw with emotion.

That was it. She pushed her head forward and kissed him with passion. He couldn't hold back any longer and returned her kiss with the same force and hunger. They were lost, their tongues lashing against each other's, trying to get as close as they possibly could. When the kiss finally broke, it had left them both breathless. His hand was still entwined in her hair as they touched foreheads, trying to regain some composure.

Ethan shifted slightly in his seat; his eyes closed tightly. She could feel the hardness of his passion, underneath her. She winced at the slight movement, which made her ribs ache. She wanted to carry on the kiss, to touch him all over. She wanted more. Letting out another long breath he opened his eyes and looked at her longingly.

"I don't want to hurt you."

He was serious, his eyes dark whirlpools of lust, which made her ache for him even more. He was torn, his whole body wanting her, but he knew she was fragile and didn't want to cause her any pain.

"Please," she whispered.

The tears still rolling down her cheeks. He grabbed her face and kissed her again, this time slowly, lovingly and holding back his passion, much to her annoyance. The kiss was beautiful, but she ached for more. She had moved to his side, the feeling of him hard and erect beneath her and not touching her, proving to be too much.

She snuggled into his body, his strong arms wrapped round her, as they both calmed their breathing down.

"I don't want to hurt you Ava," he repeated. "Do you have any idea how hard it's been for me? The number of times I wanted to jump in to the hospital bed with you?" he grumbled and Ava realised he had been keeping his distance on purpose, her mood lifting considerably at this news.

She squeezed her arm around him. "...as for Collins, I didn't want you to worry about anything." he said now serious again.

"Tell me now," she said resting her head on his chest.

"Rogers shot him once, it was fatal." He paused, Ava didn't respond, so he continued. "He had been working with Zara and Jennifer, trying to poison the family against each other." He took a deep breath. "Collins saw me, as his target, he was under the impression I had the main control over the Pennington business. He was wrong, we all share the responsibilities and have the same say. He was getting the wrong information from those poisonous bitches," he paused, taking another slow soothing breath. "They set up a meeting with Sofia, when she was feeling lonely and vulnerable, pushing her to date him. It wasn't until he got that ring on her finger, that she saw his true colours," he shook his head regretfully. "He passed all the security background checks, I never particularly liked him, but my sister was in love and I wanted her to be happy," he kissed the top of Ava's head, absentmindedly. "He lied to her, he lied to us all," his tone was icy now, "...he had hidden his true self well, making out he was a decent businessman, with a property development company, he also had a hand in politics...of course he lied about it all."

At this point Ava sat up, the discomfort showing on her face, she really needed to lie down, but it wasn't very practical in the limo, as she would have liked Ethan to lie on top of her!

Fuck she really needed a cold shower.

"Ethan," her soft voice broke his thoughts and he turned to face her, taking in the sparkle that seemed to make her eyes glimmer, *God she was beautiful.*

"Is Sofia, okay?" she asked carefully.

He smiled.

"Actually, she is." Ava frowned, small wrinkles forming on her bruised forehead.

He didn't know any other woman in his circle of family and friends, that could show the emotions on their faces. Apart from Kitty. The thought made him happy. This was because most of the women he knew had, had surgical procedures, in the disillusioned belief it made them look younger. Instead, it made them all look the same, plastic and slightly alarmed.

He gently brushed her cheek with his thumb, causing her breath to hitch.

"Christ Ava," he said laughing and shaking his head.

She bit her lip, his thumb immediately stroked over her mouth and she released it. Her whole body felt as if it were on fire, her insides were swirling like molten lava.

"Excuse me sir," Roger's voice echoed onto the compartment. "We are just entering the car park," he informed them, over the intercom.

Ethan's eyes were dark and dangerous and Ava thought that she would actually come, just by looking at him.

"We are here," he said seriously.

Ava reluctantly turned to look out of the tinted windows to see they were in another underground car park. She blew air out of her pouting mouth, trying to recover her senses. The car had come to a stop and Rogers was now out of the front seat and talking into his comms system. The impeccably dressed chauffeur opened the door for them to alight.

Ava stretched her back as she stood, sending pain ripping down her abdomen. She froze, trying to breathe slowly through the pain. She felt strong arms wrap around her body and her feet leave the floor, as Ethan lifted her easily into his strong arms. She rested her head on his shoulder, suddenly tired from the short journey.

"Surprise," she jolted awake and realised she was still in Ethan's arms, but they were now in a large bright room, a wall of windows surrounding them, allowing a magnificent view of the city below.

"I think you can put her down now." Lou's loud voice penetrated the chatter.

As he carefully let her down, Ava turned to see the beautiful, smiling faces of all of her family and some of Ethan's family too. Jez was the first to hug her and kiss her cheek. Ethan's arm stayed firmly around her waist, he was not letting her go and she loved that feeling of safety. Gio was next, welcoming her to one of many 'Pennington suites' with a huge smile. Bella was next. Still boot clad, the Italian pocket rocket looked stunning in navy bodycon dress, her face beaming. Rachel came up and hugged her too, moving on to Ethan.

She kissed his cheek and said quietly, "How can I ever thank you?"

Ava watched this interaction in slight confusion, until she heard Cary's cockney accent on the other side of the room, where some of the group had settled by the extensive bar, enjoying their cocktails. Ava gasped and Ethan spun her round to face him, his face full of concern.

"You flew Cary out," she said, her face full of wonder.

He shook his head, relieved she wasn't in pain, and smiled, "Of course," he said simply.

Rachel stood watching them, Ava turned her head to look at her beautiful friend.

"He flew the girls out too, but they are exploring our suite as they haven't long arrived," she said excitedly.

"Wow," Ava was genuinely touched at how sweet that was.

"Wanna drink Ave?" Lou shouted from the bar, Ava shook her head, still smiling.

"Ahhh come on Ave, have a cocktail, they're lovely they are." Cary's ever present cockney accent filled the room and made Ava's smile even bigger.

Dan was now at her side and she realised he hadn't been to the hospital to see her. In all that had been going on, she hadn't asked anyone how he was. They hugged each other, Ethan standing back a little, but still holding onto her hand. He gratefully accepted a large JD and ice from Gio.

"I'm sorry I haven't been to see you, but I've been looking after Sofia," he said, exchanging an awkward look with both Ethan and Gio, he turned back to focus on Ava.

"How is she?" Ava's voice was full of concern.

"I'm doing really well, thank you," the elegant American accent making them all turn.

There was Sofia, looking stunning in a cream suit. Dan stepped back, grinning as she hugged Ava tightly, making her wince and earning a frown from Ethan. She looked happy and relaxed and when Ava saw Dan step forward and put his arm leisurely around Sofia's waist, Ava knew why. They smiled sweetly at each other, causing Ethan's hand to tighten around Ava's.

"Can we talk to you, in private," Sofia gestured towards a door to the left of a huge seating area.

"She's just arrived and she needs to rest," Ethan admonished her.

"Please, its important," she countered standing her ground with her brother.

The Penningtons were truly fierce and Ava reminded herself never to get between them in a fight. Ethan nodded reluctantly and the four of them made their way to the door, behind which was a large conference room. It was decked out in a long oak table, with at least twenty chairs neatly arranged along it.

Ethan was not impressed and wanted Ava to get some rest. It had been a long day and she was still recovering from the brutal attack. As they sat down at the table, Ethan took the seat next to Ava's, never letting go of her hand. Sofia and Dan mirrored the action opposite them.

"I've just thought, where's Kitty and Alfie?" She looked at Ethan with panic and he smiled explaining they were having a romantic day together.

More than happy with that response, she relaxed again and turned back to Sofia and Dan.

"So..." Sofia began, looking like she was trying to find the right words. "So, I need to tell you the truth and I wanted Ava to be here to make sure you don't go mad." She grimaced as she focused on her brother.

Ethan's whole body tensed and his grip on Ava's hand tightened.

"What's going on?" Ethan said gruffly.

Surely, they had all had enough drama and surprises for one week.

"When I met Brody, I thought I was in love. He was kind, attentive and well... I was lonely." She was looking directly at her brother and Dan was keeping his eyes on the emerald ring on her left hand, which he was twisting round and round, out of nervous energy.

Her wedding ring was now missing.

"Zara and Jennifer said they both knew him and I fell for the dream," she said sadly. "I just wanted to be happy."

Ava's stomach was turning and her head felt full of cotton wool.

"Up until our wedding, I thought everything was going well, although looking back now, there were signs," she gazed out of the huge expanse of glass.

"Sofia?" Ethan questioned, where was this all going.

She took a deep breath. "On my wedding night, he showed his true colours... he was manipulative and violent."

Dan scowled as he continued to focus on her dainty hand in his. Ethan froze, a look of horror on his face.

"Violent?" He repeated angrily.

"Yes… he wanted me to bear him a child. He wanted the Collins name to succeed the Pennington's name and over the last few months he has made my life completely miserable and unbearable." She made eye contact with her brother again and Ava could feel his pulse quicken. "I really wanted a baby, it's all Zara and Jennifer talked to me about. Brody was controlling them too. He did tell me recently that he had slept with both of them and that I wasn't as good in bed as them. Charming information to be given by my husband, eh?" Her voice sounding slightly odd now, Ava just held on to Ethan's hand tightly. "Before we flew out to the Maldives, I thought I might be pregnant and I made the mistake of telling Zara. I thought she was a friend, I didn't have anyone else to talk too, until you." She turned her eyes to Ava. "You were my guardian angel. A shining light in a life of darkness." She said admiringly and Dan also looked up at Ava and smiled thankfully.

"What's Ava got to do with this?" Ethan asked annoyed that his sister was sad and had no one to listen or talk too.

"You see Ethan I was pregnant…" she said sadly, Dan placed a comforting arm around her shoulders.

"Pregnant!" Ethan's voice was harsher than he had meant it to be and he noticed Ava flinched.

"Briefly," Sofia responded sadly. "…but Brody didn't know…I was going to tell him."

Her drawn face, now looked gaunt and demoralised as she went on. "I decided to tell him before we travelled, but the night before, he was drunk when he eventually got home. He had been with Zara…I really thought if I told him, he would love me properly and stop sleeping around. My head was so mixed up." She closed her eyes tightly, remembering that horrific night. "Before I could speak, he had hit me and this time he didn't stop. I was so scared. Worried for me, for my baby and for letting down the family name." She paused as her eyes filled with tears. "Madre and papa would never forgive me for letting the mighty Penningtons down." She paused again and looked directly at Ethan. "He hated all of my family, but especially you Eth, he would rave about how you had everything and how he was better than you." She shook her head. "Anyway, he beat me so badly I began bleeding, I knew I had lost the baby." She looked at Ava and saw the tear running down her pale cheek. "Ava I am so sorry, this was all my fault." She said regretfully.

"When I saw Ethan and the way he was behaving around you, the way he looked at you, I knew he was totally besotted." She smiled weakly, as a faint pink blush showed on Ava's cheeks. "We had been on the island a day and Brody told me he had spent the night with Zara and Jennifer, it was the early hours of the morning and he was drunk," she paused not being able to make eye contact, staring down at hers and Dan's hands entwined. "He started on about Ethan not having a woman, when the great Brody Collins could have any he wanted. He said that he was better in bed then you and that's why you weren't with anyone... and that's when I told him..." she choked back the emotion and continued.

"I told him you were seeing Kitty's sister and that you were both happy and in love with each other." She looked up at Ava, tears now falling from her beautiful hazel eyes, "I am so sorry Ava, he went ballistic and well you know the rest." She finished sadly.

Ava stood unsteadily and walked over to her as Sofia stood to face her. The two, stunning woman, simply hugged each other. Sofia now sobbing, letting all of the grief and heartache escape. Ethan had moved towards them, still in shock. He spoke quietly.

"Why didn't you tell me, I could have helped, protected you," his voice trailed off.

Ava and Sofia parted and she embraced her brother.

"I couldn't talk to anyone... I was so sad and grief stricken at losing my baby."

She was still crying and her words came between sobs. She pushed back a little from him and looked at Ava.

"If it wasn't for Ava on that boat trip..." she shook her head and spun round to cling on to Dan.

"You saved her Ave," Dan choked out, as silent tears rolled down his handsome face.

Ethan looked at Ava's beautiful, angelic face.

"She was going to kill herself?" he whispered, disbelieving his own words. Dan nodded.

"I met her after she had spoken to Ava and she told me about Collins, I swear to god if I'd have seen him on that boat, I would have killed him myself," he said angrily.

"Please don't." Sofia cried desperately, "I'm sorry I didn't tell you, I'd blabbed to him about you both." She raised her head from Dan's chest and looked between Ethan and Ava, "I'm so desperately sorry, forgive me?" she cried.

Ava reached out and cupped Sofia's tear-stained face.

"There is nothing to forgive," she said simply, dropping her hand and turning to Ethan. "They need some alone time and I'm a bit tired," she said wearily, taking his huge, tanned hand in hers.

Ethan leant over and kissed the top of his sister's head.

"Look after her Dan," he said genuinely grateful that Sofia had someone she could confide in.

He decided to leave by another door, avoiding the rowdy chatter coming from the bar area of the suite. He held Ava's hand tightly as he led her through a reception hall and out of the suite.

The security team were dotted around the corridors and Ava recognised Gary, raising her free hand to wave. He smiled and waved back and then remembered some of Lou's more detailed descriptions of Gary's body and she dropped her hand quickly, blushing. Luckily, Ethan was determined to get to his destination and had not witnessed this interaction.

Halfway down a luxurious corridor, he stopped, pressing a button for the lift. They stood not speaking or looking at each other, just gripping each other's hands. The lift doors pinged into action and as they opened, Ava followed Ethan as he stepped in and placed his hand flat on a digital scanner to the left of the usual floor buttons. As the doors pinged closed, she was just going to comment on the posh 'mission impossible' style gadget he had just used to move the lift, when he spun quickly and pushed her against the mirrored wall.

She felt a sharp pain in her ribs, as his lips crushed against hers with such ferocity, she felt her whole-body tingle in response. She kissed him back with the same force and passion, that seemed to fuel his furore. With one hand holding her waist firmly against his ever-hardening dick, the other hand twisting in her hair, deliciously pulling her deeper into this passionate kiss. He broke away briefly to stare into her cerulean blue eyes.

"Christ Professor, what you do to me." He groaned, as she tilted her head to meet his lips again, never wanting the kiss to end, never wanting to be out of his arms. A gentle ping told them they had arrived at the required floor and their attention turned to the opening doors.

"I need to get you into bed," he said his eyes darkening.

Ava sighed, "I'm not tired," she countered, pouting.

"Neither am I," he said, winking, as he grabbed her hand and led her out of the lift and into his private suite.

The End